SHORTS
4

Shorts
4

The Macallan/
Scotland on Sunday
Short Story Collection

Edited by Michel Faber

Polygon

Polygon
An imprint of Edinburgh University Press Ltd
22 George Square, Edinburgh

Typeset in Galliard by Hewer Text Ltd, Edinburgh,
and printed and bound in Great Britain by
Creative Print and Design, Ebbw Vale, Wales

A CIP record for this book is
available from the British Library

ISBN 0 7486 6319 3 (paperback)

The Publisher acknowledges subsidy from

towards the publication of this volume.

CONTENTS

Contents

FOREWORD

The cliché that fiction is truer than truth is, in these days of media overload, truer than ever. Consider how many millions of words were flushed through the newspapers on the subject of Princess Diana's death. Surely everything worth saying was said? No, it wasn't, for here in this volume of *Shorts* we have David Fernandes's 'Brick', 2,812 words of fiction that express what none of that journalism could. That's what stories are for. Each day, your head gets flooded with information and opinion, almost all of which evaporates from your brain by the following week. Yet a good story stays with you for life.

How is it achieved, this magic? In an endless variety of ways. Teachers of creative writing often insist that a short story ought to illuminate a single event with a minimum of characters. It's a sound principle, especially for beginners, and it underpins most of the greatest short stories ever written. But not *all*, and what a relief it is when someone accepts the challenge of elucidating an entire social and political structure, and conjuring up a whole town, in just under 3,000 words. This is what Jonathan Falla achieves in 'A Storm Gathering', and more besides.

Scotland was always a far grittier place than the tartan McDisneyland of tourist myth, but the success of Irvine

Welsh's *Trainspotting* has made harsh urban settings a favourite choice of this year's Macallan entrants. In among all the deluded folk who think that a mishmash of chips, alcohol, vomit and dialectical oaths will somehow transmute itself into a story, a few gifted writers have shown genuine promise. George Kobilnyk's 'Tragic Kingdom' is packed with wickedly visceral images and has energy to spare. Jas Sherry's 'Terminus' drives us into a moral twilight in which girls take disturbing risks in their yearning for an alternative to 'the creeps at the Youthie'. Ross Wilson's 'The Rules of Perspective', while not flinching from the ugliness of its social context or the distance dividing its lovers, celebrates the ability of good-hearted people to generate affectionate fun.

'Hell-bent' turns its lens on Scotland's past, a time when the Forth Road Bridge was newly built and girls wore suspenders, but instead of presenting us with a sepia-tinted, sentimental reminiscence, Anne Bree addresses us in a tone that would have been forbidden then, and strikes a blow for the resilience of female sexuality. Lydia Robb's 'Mooncalf' is a vivid glimpse into a past age, too, and although it leaves the old order intact, its nostalgia is tempered with sharp characterisation and wild humour.

Humour was scarce in this year's Macallan entries, making George Anderson's 'Tumshie McFadgen's Bid for Ultimate Bliss' a welcome blast of daftness. The hilarity of Ella Henderson's 'Vesuvius' bubbles deeper below the surface, and is only one facet of a sharply observed tale of social divisions and family dynamics. Jonathan Falla's feverish 'Bad Behaviour Sailors' negotiates queer tension, a splendidly comic climax and a subtly wicked coda.

Pathos, too, can move in many mysterious ways. At its most unabashed, as in Fiona J. Thackeray's 'Mango', it tugs at your heartstrings however immune you think you are, while Richard Louden's 'Three Candles' lifts the soiled sheet of old age's indignities, and puts us in the place of those who refuse to weep anymore. But 'A Matter of Taste', Vale Nordmann's tale of fettered lives freed perhaps just a little too late, achieves just as much emotional power with its wry, unmelodramatic tone. In a mere 1,680 words, Nordmann conjures up two memorable characters, loveable against the odds, sketched with close-to-the-bone humour and sad wisdom. The pathos in Simon Smith's 'Woman with Biro' is more carefully hidden, as befits a tale of an elderly artist holding himself together for a retrospective of his work, while Anne Callaly's sardonic 'Wee Fishes' deftly fuses tragedy with song.

Science Fiction scenarios are a common resort of writers less interested in character and atmosphere than in the self-conscious flagwaving of an Awfully Big Idea, but Alastair Chisholm's eerie 'Closing Time' wisely builds suspense by keeping its supernatural element shut outside its beleaguered pub. Michael Russell's 'Round-trip Spaceship' uses SF clichés for its own disturbing purposes, exploring the outer limits of dimly glimpsed inhumanity. Elsewhere, the traditional Boy's Own Adventure tale gets a vivid Maori makeover, in Janette Munneke's 'Christmas at Waipanoni Falls'.

Few literary experiences are more irritating than spending a lot of furrow-browed concentration on a wilfully difficult story that gives nothing back. Plenty such contrivances were submitted to the Macallan, but a sublime exception was Barbara Clarke's 'Ain't Misbehavin', by far the most unusual piece here. Its fevered evocation of superstition, abuse and human resilience in the deep, deep South of Negro spirituals makes challenging reading, but our reward is to gaze into an achingly sensuous and vivid world. Like the blues songs whose spirit infuses the prose, it blurs the line between brutal reality and the divine. Another story from the edge is Simon Stephenson's 'Jackson's Hotel', which takes us to the darkness waiting below society's safety net. Douglas Noble's 'The Girl Who

Died In Her Sleep' slows down the rate of perception to such an extraordinary degree that it risks maddening some readers, but I was enchanted by its unforced eroticism and its highly distinctive way with dialogue.

The literary revenges that can be wreaked on a bad marriage are numberless, and there are some particularly juicy ones here. Sue Rullière's 'Drying the Man Out' gently squeezes a bucketful of fun out of its victim, while Kate Percival's 'Tell Me a Story' argues its case for spousal pruning without mercy but with a peculiar lyricism. Elsewhere, the death of a relationship is chronicled less neatly, more wistfully: in Morven Crumlish's 'You See Patterns When You Close Your Eyes', a woman slips loose from a man she barely realises she no longer loves. 'The Incomprehensible Mortality of Karen Mack' by Sophie Cooke scalpels open not just a mummifying marriage, but the freeze-dried society in which it exists. The protagonist of Alan Bissett's 'Clear Thunder', too numbed by loss to complain about the sterility of her life, makes a chillingly timid inventory of what she sees – and it hits us like a cry of rage. From almost identical raw materials, Esther McLeod's 'New Shoes' fashions a very different tale of sexual claustrophobia. 'Striking Out', by Isabel Walter, reveals to us that saddest of things: a girl at the very start of her sex life, already yearning for rituals of cleansing and recovery. But blood is sourer than water and perhaps the worst relationship in this anthology is not between lovers but between the viperous sisters in J. C. Robertson's 'Relax'.

Suffusing many of the Macallan entries this year, especially from the more accomplished writers, was a profound disappointment with life as it disintegrates at the edges. Maybe this is inevitable right now. The twentieth century promised us limitless consumer freedom, access to everything, emancipation from so-called Victorian values – in short, evolutionary perfection. Yet we have entered the twenty-first century no happier than before – still dissatisfied, envious, inhibited, overworked, undervalued, yearning for self-esteem and a love that will last. For the writer of fiction, one valid response to this frustration is to document it, to expose it and lay it bare. Another response – all too rare in the stories I saw – is to generate wonder, magic and grace within our own private world, the world which can be anything we imagine. Still another response – again, surprisingly rare – is to seek out inspiring places and people on this vast and exotic planet and, by celebrating these, remind ourselves that there's more out there than the polystyrene tray of half-eaten chips in the gutter. If there is one message I have for future Macallan entrants, it's this: keep your eyes open for alternative realities. That's what the best of the stories in this book have done, and they have exciting things to tell us.

A Matter of Taste

Vale Nordmann

My mother. In a jar. In a bag.

The jar's about the size of the largest supermarket coffee ones, slightly more squat. Opaque plastic. What shade, exactly? Placenta brown? Old-blood red? Yes, that's it – menstrual blood on the last day of a period.

It was handed to me in the pleasing velvet bag. An imperial purple sac, with a drawstring like a cervix.

I unscrew the lid and look at her. Lumpy grey dust. She only half fills it.

Who am I? I am a woman with wild, unmanageable hair. Faded and forty-nine. Divorced. I had parents who lived apart; parents who were a pain. *May* was the name they gave me. May I? May you? May we? Maybe, maybe, maybe. The trouble with me is *maybe* never became *yes*.

I am back in Edinburgh for the funeral of my mother, and I am wandering. The cremation was yesterday – late afternoon, early December. It snowed all day – the wet, slushy sort that nobody likes, the sort that chills you to your bones.

Today it is just grey. I leave Melville Drive and cross the Meadows by Jawbone Walk. It occurs to me that now my mother is dead, I have no reason to ever come back to Edinburgh.

I live in London; my father lives in Bristol. The eternal triangle. I've spent my life visiting first one, then the other. Visiting, and playing their games: investigator for my mother; keeper of secrets for my father.

'How was your father looking, May? What's his new flat like? Has he got lots of friends?'

'May, don't go telling your mother you saw me with Hilda from the canteen, there's a good girl.'

It was my mother that left my father, although she made it clear enough that it was his fault, what with his late nights and other women. She left him, but the trouble was, she couldn't let go.

Without even realising, I've walked down Bristo Place and George IV Bridge. I'm standing and looking over into the Grassmarket. This walking has tired me out, I'm getting a bus from here.

Those two phone boxes at the end of the Grassmarket – the old solid red ones – that's where she used to send me. We moved there when she left my father in Bristol and came home to Edinburgh. We got a little flat up Wardrop's Court, but we couldn't afford a phone, not at first. The unwritten rule was that I could phone my father any time, and reverse the charges, because I was his daughter. If my mother wanted to phone him, she had to have *a reason*.

She would work up little ploys. 'May, why don't you go down and phone Dad? Tell him I'm off work sick, and see what he says?' Then I would be the one feeling sick – a heavy dullness in my stomach – but I would nod and carry out my consignment. It never made any difference: he wasn't interested.

He came up for her funeral, though. Why? Guilty, I suppose. Like me. She drove me mad, going on about my father all those years. I let it show. She wanted me to help them get back together again. What could I do? I moved away, that's what I did. To London.

My father's still here. He stayed on last night, a B & B in Newington Road. It was too late to make that journey back to Bristol. He's coming to my mother's place in an hour or so. I said I'd give him lunch there before he gets his train. Later, I'll clear out her flat. It's one of those little sheltered housing places. It won't take long.

I see myself reflected in a window. Washed out. I am drained and I want to be strong. My mother used to give me cod-liver oil and Virol to build me up. Food was her answer to everything. She thought she could hold onto my father with stews and dumplings, but he wanted plump young blondes. I've grown apart from him. I've grown apart from myself. I'm in pieces. I want to be whole, but I don't know how to put myself together again.

I need to do something special. Something that will change my life. My father, he's all right. He's learnt how to make his own stews.

I'm sorry now that I wasn't better to my mother. She gave me the job of getting my father and her back together again; I ran away from it, and now she's dead. She's in a plastic jar in a velvet bag in a Safeway carrier, and as I walk she's bump-bump-bumping against my side.

She was a great one for making soup. To listen to her, you'd think soup was a magic potion. My father liked it, so that spurred her on: grating kidneys, boiling oxtails, chopping onions. Lentil soup, potato soup, brown onion soup. Of course she'd complain about it: *all that peeling, chopping, sieving, grating – and never a word of thanks. He just comes in, sits down, and spoons it in.* How many times, I wonder, did she grate her knuckles along with the carrots – add a scraping of her skin, a drop or two of her blood?

I reach her flat, let myself in, dump my bags on her tidy kitchen work surface. Her little fridge-freezer is full of home-made soup in Tupperware boxes. After thirty-five years she was still stocking up, waiting for my father to come to his senses and come back to her. Well, he's coming now.

Before I went to collect her from the undertaker's, I took out a substantial portion of scotch broth, made with neck of mutton – *all the goodness of the meat and the bones in it*, I can hear her saying it.

I set my mother's small table. Tomorrow it's being collected by people from the Christian charity shop, along with almost everything else. There's not much I want here. I'll give the other soups to the warden – she can do what she likes with them. We were always told not to waste things. *Finish your soup. Don't leave your soup – it'll make you big and strong.* Once I saw dozens of tiny flies in a bowl of spring vegetable, and downright refused. My mother was indignant. The others didn't believe me, couldn't see the flies. I'm the only one in our family who's never needed glasses.

Here's my father, creeping up the path like a bent little tortoise. His days of pulling the birds are over, that's for sure. Perhaps I should have defrosted the chicken noodle instead.

'Hello, May. All right, are you, girl?' He takes off his cap and I help him stagger out of his overcoat. I notice it needs a clean, but that's his affair.

He looks around, twisting that short little neck of his. 'Nice place your mother got for herself here.'

'Irene knew how to make the best of what she had.'

I always call my mother by her name when I speak to him. I

suppose it's to remind him that she's his wife, not just my mother. It doesn't do any good, not with the thickness of his skin. We never talk that much anyway. He eases himself into a chair.

'My joints are aching.'

Mine, too, I think bitterly, although I say nothing. The trouble with having parents is that you don't get to be old yourself, not until they've popped off. Every bone in my body aches today, but there's no point in saying.

'I've got some nice soup for you. From Irene's freezer. Scotch broth.'

'I'll enjoy that.'

I go into the kitchen. The soup is still in the box, next to the Safeway's carrier bag. The hands that chopped these onions and carrots are now, in powder form, in the screwtop jar. Tupperware and brown plastic, they sit next to each other on the work surface, almost touching.

Without even thinking about it, I tip the soup into a saucepan, unscrew the jar, add a heaped tablespoonful of my mother, and stir her in.

'I've eaten already,' I tell my father as I put the bowl in front of him.

'You sure?' It is difficult for him to control his eagerness. 'Good drop of soup, this.'

He takes a second helping, finishes the lot.

The sun is coming out. I put the rest of my mother back in my bag and take my father to Waverley station. After I have seen him onto his train, I take the bus down to the botanic gardens. There I leave a portion of my mother among the azaleas and rhododendrons. Irene liked the botanics on a sunny afternoon.

Another bus to the bottom of the Royal Mile. In the dusk I walk through Queen's Park and take a little path up Salisbury

Crags. Making sure I stand with the wind behind me, I let some more of my mother be taken away. Irene was born nearby; as a teenager she'd come here with her books, to get a bit of peace.

It is dark now. I sit on top of the bus to Queensferry, looking out of the window. As I get off, I wrap my scarf round my head and mouth. The wind is cold, but the sea is waiting: moving, dark and exciting. Feeling better than I've done in years, I unscrew the lid of my mother's plastic womb for the last time. I tip what's left of her into the Firth of Forth, and then throw the jar in after her. Irene always said she'd like to travel more.

With empty hands and a light, light heart, I turn and walk back to the bus stop. I have a sudden impulse to buy a ticket to Morocco and some henna for my hair.

Irene, goodnight. Irene, goodnight. Goodnight, Irene, goodnight, Irene, I'll see you in my dreams . . .

But not too often, Mother, all right?

Brick

David R. Fernandes

Kevin's mum was acting up when I got round to his. We'd gone up to his room to play a few games but she shouted for us to come down for breakfast, telling Kevin to get dressed. *She's been like this for a while now*, he said, shrugging as we went down the stairs. *One minute she's flapping and then she's crying*. The television was on in the living room and when we got to the kitchen she said I could stay if I wanted, but her and Kevin were going to watch the procession. *It's going to be live*, she said, *all the way from London, so you can stay if you keep quiet*, handing out bowls for the cornflakes. She was still wearing her nightie and I could see the top part of her breasts. The start of her slopes. Her face was all red. Flustered. I looked away, then glanced at Kevin, but he just shrugged and reached for the box of cereal. I whispered to him, *Where's your dad?* He cupped his fingers and rocked an imaginary pint in front of his mouth, but his mum turned round and caught him. She started off on one, *Think it's funny, eh? Eh? Think I'm funny? You're as bad as he is, laughing at me behind my back*, and then she stormed off, slamming all the doors behind her.

We sat in front of the television. Kevin's mum was on the sofa, while me and Kevin were on the floor in front of her. She'd said that she'd wanted to dress in black, to *be all respectful*, but the only thing she had that was black was a low-cut top and that would've looked *a bit tarty*. She was dressed in her work uniform, a long black skirt and a white shirt with Superdrug embroidered on the breast pocket. *I'm going into work later anyway, so it doesn't matter*, she muttered to herself. We sat in silence, watching the screen where these red wreaths hung from tall black railings, swinging out over what looked like a sea of shivering flowers. Their plastic wraps were blowing about in the wind, and as the camera zoomed in to show us the fluttering cards which had been left on the covers, you could see these scrappy signatures dancing across the screen. People had gathered outside the gates, waiting with their heads hung low. They stood still, barely moving, their hands held together in front of them. All we heard was the sound of swaying trees. I could see tourists wandering through the crowd, taking photographs of each other.

I said that we could go there and nick all the flowers for a laugh, when I saw the reflection of Kevin's mum glaring at me through the black coat of one of the mourners. I shut up. Lowered my head. Heard Kevin snickering beside me. Elbowed him. He punched me back and then his mum started up again, knocking over her ashtray. All the cigarette butts were spilt over the floor. She went quiet. She'd spent the whole morning cleaning up the room.

The doorbell rang. Kevin got up and ran out into the corridor. I got on my knees and started gathering up the mess on the carpet with my fingers. I heard Sarah's voice, *Are you watching it? Have you got it on?* And then she walked in and saw Kevin's mum crying on the sofa. Sarah lived a few doors down. She used to drop round on Kevin all the time and he liked to think he was going out with her. I remember him telling me that he'd got her naked in his room. He'd pointed to his bed as if the crumpled duvet was proof that she'd been there.

Are you all right, Linda? she asked. Kevin's mum stood up and started hugging her. Sarah hugged her back. *I know, it's really sad isn't it? I've been watching it all morning. I still can't believe it.*

Kevin kicked me as I knelt over the ash. We giggled. I turned on him and smeared some of the grey flakes on his face.

I was thinking about going down to the motorway, seeing the procession go past. Is it all right if Kevin comes with me? I don't want to go alone.

Kevin's mum patted her on the back, sobbing on her shoulder, *Of course, I wouldn't mind going myself but . . .*, and then she went off upstairs, telling Sarah to follow her.

Me and Kevin looked at each other, muffling our laughter. Kevin had his tongue stuck out, grabbing his crotch. *She wants some*, he said, *she can't stay away*. We could hear them talking upstairs. I pushed Kevin onto the sofa and jumped on top of him, *It's 'cos she knows I'm here*, I shouted, *that's why she's come round, I had her a few times before I came round to yours*. Kevin had his hand over my face, trying to push me off him, but I'd got my knee on his chest.

Make sure they bring you back. I don't want you wandering around there on your own, his mum said, coming back downstairs. Kevin had stopped moving. He was looking at the television, watching this hearse pull out from some gates and drive along a big wide street. People were throwing flowers at the hearse, but some had fallen short and were getting crushed under the wheels.

We got the bus to the motorway and wandered up near the footbridge. You could barely hear the traffic from behind the tall metal barriers. It sounded like being near a river. We were early, so we went off to a housing estate that was being built nearby. The site was all bare and empty, just loads of brick pallets and iron wiring scattered across the mud. In the distance there was a stretch of flowers and Sarah started running towards it, shouting about getting some for the hearse. Me and Kevin followed after her, jostling and pushing each other as we ran. Sarah picked a few, matching the colours, while the two of us just started pulling everything out, weeds an' all, trying to outdo each other until I cut my finger on a thorn.

I jumped back, waving my hand around as Kevin laughed and Sarah came over to me. *You all right? Let's have a look*, and she reached for my finger. It was smeared with blood, all of it coming from a little prick in the skin. She leaned in and kissed it before Kevin shoved me back, *What's all that? You big pussy.* He was sort of smiling, sort of looking at me funny, sort of hurt. Sarah giggled, *Come on. We've got enough*, and she grabbed Kevin's hand, pulling him along with her. I picked up the flowers I'd dropped and tried to catch them up, hoping that Sarah would look back at me.

We passed the stiles and walked out over the motorway, listening as the hum of the traffic suddenly rose up and washed over us. I was dazzled by the flickering motion of cars between the steel struts of the railing, like I was floating across the lanes. There were already other people there, holding bunches of flowers, cards, bits of long ribbon. Everyone looked stony faced and grey. Sarah had come over all solemn and even Kevin had stopped smiling. We just sort of stood there and watched the traffic slowly die. A few minutes passed. Then a murmur went out along the bridge. *Anytime now. Almost here.* Everyone rushed to one side, staring off into the silent distance.

I saw Sarah reach for Kevin's hand. Watched as she pushed her way to the front of the railings. Someone was standing in front of me and even on my toes I couldn't see anything. Then I felt a hand in mine. Felt it gently press my fingers. We heard a helicopter. A dull flutter in the sky. Sarah pulled me towards her, so I wormed in closer, nestling up beside her.

Nobody said anything as the convoy drew towards us. There was a police car ahead and behind it, a few motorcycles on each side, but in the middle the hearse lumbered in the cloudy afternoon, laden with colour. It was as if the thing was crawling towards us like a fat lizard. *Get ready*, Sarah whispered, but I couldn't tell if she was whispering to me or Kevin. We were entranced by the hearse, by the way the flowers just seemed to be spilling out all over it, and suddenly all I cared about was making sure that my flowers landed on it, that I hit the target. I pushed out the flowers over the rail and waited, listening to the helicopter come closer over us, watching the dark figures sitting still in the gloom of the hearse, the coffin behind them. Somebody behind me reckoned it was empty, *It's all for show*, they said. But nobody answered back. I turned to Sarah and she was looking at me, her eyes were pale, sort of watery. She touched my shoulder, acting like an adult. *It's so sad, isn't it? It's so beautiful*, she said.

I nodded my head. Kept my face straight. Over her shoulder I could see Kevin leaning over the rail, his hands poised to drop the flowers, taking aim. He looked at me, his eyes laughing.

Some people were already throwing their flowers, arcing them over the crowd and onto the lane in front of the approaching hearse. But me and Kevin waited, mouths open, competing. I think Sarah said something like rest in peace but all I was looking at was the box rail on the hearse and the flowers that lay inside its frame.

Now, Kevin whispered as he let his handful drop down. I waited. Sarah had let hers go as well. She was holding onto Kevin's other hand, her eyes closed. I hung on for a second, watching his flowers fall like a shower, bouncing off the bonnet, off the windscreen. I let mine go and watched as they missed the rail and fell on the empty tarmac behind the hearse, lost in the drizzle of the other forgotten flowers. Kevin was hugging Sarah. She had her head on his chest, her arms round his neck, but he was looking at me, winking.

We watched the convoy disappear off round the bend, and then everyone started walking away. The motorway was empty. Without any traffic it was eerily quiet, as if everyone in the world had died. We weren't really saying anything, but I could see that Kevin had one up on me. I shrugged it off, acting as if I didn't really care, like I was all cut up about seeing the coffin. I just started rambling, talking about how sad it all was, about how my mum had been crying and all the time I was watching Sarah, waiting to see if she was noticing me. Kevin just started laughing again, taking the piss, making out that I was a spaz for missing the car. He kept on doing this until Sarah came over and hugged me too, and then he went quiet again.

We went back and wandered around the building site, looking to see if there was anything we could do to pass the time. None of us wanted to go home yet and we didn't have enough money to get to the shopping centre, so we just sat around on these concrete pallets and smoked a few cigarettes, sharing out a can between us while me and Kevin threw stones and shingle at each other. The traffic had started up again and the passing cars sounded like rushing water. I turned round and saw Kevin and Sarah start to kiss. He had his hand on her thigh but she had placed her hand over his to stop him from moving it any further up. I sucked on my cigarette and started throwing the shingle over the other side of the lot towards the empty Portakabins, listening to it bounce off the plastic roofs, trying to get the aim right.

Sarah called me over, patted the bare concrete beside her for me to sit down. Kevin was taking a sip from the can, lying back on the pallet with his legs splayed out. I sat down. Sarah put her arm around me. *Do you still feel sad?* she said to me, and then Kevin started muttering, getting up abruptly to throw shingle at the Portakabins. Sarah leaned in close. *It's all right* she said. *She's in a better place*, and I just shrugged in response, waiting to see if she'd do anything. She came closer and I put my hand on her leg. She smiled. Kissed me on the cheek. I reached up to her breast, nuzzled it with my fingers. She giggled, *You shouldn't.* I went for her mouth, covered it with my lips, but I didn't know what to do. I could hear the shingle scattering off the Portakabins. *What are you doing?* she whispered. I shrugged, leaning back, trying to be all relaxed. *I didn't know you were both going out*, I said. She laughed, shaking her head, *We're not.*

I heard Kevin picking up more shingle from the ground. I knew he was looking at us, but I made out like he wasn't there. *How about it, then?* I asked her. She moved in closer, closed her eyes, put her lips to mine and I opened my mouth. I could feel the saliva in my mouth welling up. She pulled back. *You're supposed to close your eyes; it's better that way.* She leaned in again and I closed my eyes and in the darkness I felt her tongue push into my mouth. It felt sticky, all wet and tasting of nicotine. I fought back with my own tongue, pushing it into her mouth, running it against the emptiness, rooting through the dark. And it all seemed sort of sad, like nothing was happening, like I was growing up, feeling her breath against my face, her arm round my neck until she turned round and reached for the can.

I got up, shrugged myself off, looking about me like I couldn't be bothered. Kevin had his back to me. He was messing round with a pallet of bricks, trying to pull off the plastic cords that they were wrapped in. I walked over and started helping him, neither of us saying a word to each other. Sarah finished off the cola. She was getting bored with us, stubbing out the last cigarette in the can before throwing it away. She got up. Said she was leaving, *Are you coming then?* But Kevin didn't answer her. He was prising out one of the bricks, dragging it out of its prison. She looked at me, tucking her hands into her puffa, waiting for me to join her. But I kept on looking over at the brick.

I watched her turn the last corner. She didn't look back at us. I think she was all hurt that we weren't coming with her. I looked at Kevin but he just shrugged. *So what?* he said. *It's not like we have to.* He made out like he didn't care, like he didn't have time. Fair enough, I thought, and we carried on throwing the bricks around, listening to them thump the mud, listening to them crack in mid-air as we threw them at each other. But after a while we got bored.

We went back up along the footbridge and watched the traffic go by. Life was back to normal. Just hundreds of dreary cars going past, all of them looking the same. We went back to the same place and looked over the rails at the on-coming cars, waiting for something big like a lorry to go past. Neither of us said anything. We just stood there looking at the cars, looking at each other, goading each other on, until in the distance a lorry came into view and as it passed underneath we let the bricks we each had hidden in our jackets drop down.

They fell faster than the flowers did.

Kevin's puckered the tarmac before the cab of the lorry, but we didn't see if mine hit it.

All we heard was this huge crack, like a gun being fired, and then we started running, dashing beneath the barrier stiles as the squeal of brakes and the sound of something turning over and churning the tarmac echoed behind us, and we were laughing as we ran, racing each other, pushing each other around until we ran out of breath and stopped laughing, until we were just running.

Tragic Kingdom

George Kobilnyk

On George Street, clinging to the nearest passerby. I bite his fat sandal-clad ankles, tastes of leather and salt. He spits German damnations, discrediting my Jack Russell act. I attempt to munch on a discarded crisp poke, then I sniff a dogshit (no one o mine) to bring myself to my senses. Ignoring my energised pager, I choose to sort hair and lips in the mirror of a urine-stained photo-booth. My eyes look as if they've changed colour.

I swagger into a restaurant that looks like a church from the outside. Inside it's cool, expensive and hushed. Shin Azumi chairs, tables made of sandstone and heavy metal, wan lighting, sepia-coloured walls.

Someone nearby is wearing L'eau D'issey Pour Homme. I pick, pick, pick at the congealing tar and feathers on the eggshell dinner plate. This guinea-fowl steak with goat's cheese and artichokes curdles self-analysis.

I have very bad posture, so sick of wearing my heart on my sleeve, gonny stick it right back inside my ribcage. My third vodka n coke tastes like shit, cheap syrupy cola, not the real thing. Modern life is useless, go home! Another vodka. Libraries gave us power then vodka came and made us free. Before I put this bleeding heart back in place, I'll let it drip on my hands, over my cuffs, stick to my hair.

Gonny wash that man (and woman) right out of my hair . . .

I was always being offered a thick ear for my cheek. She would fold to her neurosis and strike out; he would limp off to the shed. I could never understand or accept that as a child my opinion mattered not. The two of them made plans and big decisions over my head as if I was invisible. Still, I would question their choice of holiday resort, TV viewing or dolloped Sunday dinner.

She would display a rage and offer me the thickened appendage. I would try to sneak off to my room before she lashed out so as to avoid the inevitable playground torment from having an ear the size of a casserole dish.

Alice Shand wore a big wig to school. She always sat out of gym and netball. We never found out why she was bald or respected her infirmity. She was the freak that we ganged up on and mocked for being different. We had Sasha shoes and Aladdin Sane haircuts; she had neither.

The day that her wig was pulled clean off was the same day that I bought sweets from the corner shop and was given new money as my change. Wee lighter coins that Miss Bruce had described as decimalisation on the squeaky blackboard.

Linda Rennie yanked off the mop of yellow swarf. It had an elasticated edge like a cover for a toilet-seat lid. Alice's head was hairless, smooth and white like the cue ball in snooker.

She kicked and screamed. We laughed, as the poor sod became the piggy-in-the-middle, and the five of us chucked the fur ball to one another high over her outstretched arms. When the wig settled into my clutches I almost returned it to her, but I wasn't strong enough to be kind. I hoped she would read the growing sympathy in my eyes as she yelled like a bairn with a shitty nappy.

Miss Bruce stopped the cruel game with two loud blasts on the metal whistle that she used for netball practice. Mr Morrison, the headmaster, tonged us three times each. He was a short, strong man with a grey Mexican moustache and an orange shirt and tie to match.

They knew all about it when I got home from school, even though back then we never owned a phone. This time my ear stung, went scarlet, feeling twice as thick. The whack from her taut hand turned on the tears and snotters.

Later on that night, I could smell food being cooked in the kitchen. I was to stay in my room and miss out on tea as part of my punishment. I have now traced my problems with food back to these starvation punishments.

The throbbing ear I could cut off the side of my face to relieve the pain it brought to my ignoble head. I could bury the amputation beside his cowslips and azaleas, deep in the dark muck with the worms and bugs. He respected the soil. A respect gained working hundreds of feet below the surface cutting coal from Fife's fossilised bowels. His thriving vegetable patch formed mental pictures of a heaped plate of meat and two veg. Images that teased as I noticed that the table was only set for two. A place for her and her cold selfish eyes, another for him with his eyes lined with coal stoor making them look wild and Glam Rockish.

He would touch her backside with his huge, leathery hands as she dished up the food making the front of his trousers bulge. She laughed like a demented actress whilst my bed of nails pricked my conscience for not returning the cruel, NHS, hirsute bandage.

She had good days. Spears of light that punctured her black narcissus. Chemical rushes of light-headedness resulting in amusing forgetfulness. We often stepped out to catch a bus to the pictures or the swimming pool, forty-five minutes before he was due to arrive home off the early day shift, hungry for his dinner. Not a dish washed, not a tattie peeled. He sulked in his chair for the rest of the evening after wolfing down his two-hours-late mince and tatties, fighting back indigestion and criticism.

Our last true connection was when we were attached by the umbilical cord. Her drunken, violent behaviour towards me could never be described as anything other than evil and irreparable. That agaric tube wasn't carefully snipped; it was abruptly severed by the swipe of cold steel, clean and final. She would be as sweet as honey to strangers and workmen, concealing the sting in her shapely tail for domestic wars.

I was blamed for the second kitchen fire because it took place during the school holidays. Her fag had been balanced on the Formica bunker, as she pulled giant rollers from her fine hair.

I interrupted her, asking for money for sweets from the van. As she searched for coins in her purse, her fag dropped into the pile of ironing that sprung out of the over-stuffed laundry basket. Her frilly nightie ignited like the Olympic torch, turning the yellow kitchen black and brittle. Her guilt in prosecuting an innocent would surface from time to time in contrasting degrees of generosity. I accepted the toffee and toys along with the blame. It was my fire now.

I stayed over at Jane Campbell's house during the first fire, which had been caused by an unattended chip pan and an over-attended shampoo and set.

Fags were left to burn all over the house. On top of the cistern, on worktops, windowsills and along the edge of furniture. These teetering tinder-sticks were to become my dallying introduction to tobacco. Her discarded B&H found new energy between my soft, tomboy lips. I inhaled after my fourth draw, I could blow smoke-rings after my fourth fag. My passive smoking had become passionate. I was a natural, in touch with tar and danger like a boy chimney sweep.

One time she caught me sucking on her misplaced property. I froze, she smiled and said, 'Nice smoke-ring. If you're old enough to smoke, you're old enough for other things.' I gulped on reek and fear, trying to make sense of her cryptic comment. As she passed me she patted me on the tum. My skin tingled from her adult touch and my brain hurt like a snowball hit to the head.

He and I had one flimsy connection. Football. We were Raith Rovers fans. United in our hatred of Dunfermline Athletic, Relegation and Referees. I would watch the trains roll by during the dull games at Stark's Park. The clanking carriages often displaying more grace than the so-called ball players on show on the rutted pitch. Our team's defeats were slim, our defenders needed to slim. Jim Baxter was nothing more than a fading memory for him to gauge the performances of lesser-gifted players during his half-time and full-time analysis.

Our visits to Kirkcaldy stopped dead after he had it out with Bert. Bert was his oldest friend. He would take us to the games in his rusty Viva. One Saturday morning Bert was caught with his hand up her skirt as she posed over the ironing board.

He had been setting the fire with kindling and screwed-up pages of newspaper with his back turned to them and had glimpsed the telling hand in the reflection of the dead eye of the television.

He told her to go upstairs, then he hit Bert with the companion set from the fireplace. Bert met the unusual weapon full in the dish and folded like a Burntisland deckchair. Bert staggered out to his car with chirping cartoon birds flying in circles round his head. He hesitated at the driver's side door; he couldn't get into the locked vehicle.

Inside, the fire had been lit, I fished Bert's car keys off the top of a shiny lump of coal as grey ribbons of smoke floated up the lum. I returned the keys to him and asked if he would still take me to the game. He drove off without reply, one hand holding the wheel, the other holding his sticky face.

When I went back into the house, I could hear them from their bedroom going at the sex.

Her headaches were frequent and intense. When one came she barricaded herself in her room and screamed at the walls and furniture. She uninhibitedly scorched the ether with yells and profanities brought on by an illness that seemed part migraine, part Tourette's syndrome.

She could wrap him around her painted index with a sway of hips or a flutter of false eyelashes. Her work at glamour drove his stoic frame crazy. All her domestic shortcomings were overlooked for frantic bursts of noisy, any-time-of-the-day sex.

He mended all the family shoes in his shed. Neighbours would knock on the front door and hand over their worn-out working shoes and Sunday best. He built the heels and toes back into shape with strips of rubber, dressing the raw material on his wonderful spinning buffers and sculptured lasts. This cherished sideline had been his apprenticeship as a young man. The Fife pits had gnarled his hands but hadn't robbed him of his fine touch with knives and files.

I sat in the corner of the shed and watched him work. When he opened the lid on the big tin of glue, it would make me wheeze and feel light-headed. Sitting it out for as long as I could before floating off to the garden for air.

Occasionally, he let me help perform the more menial tasks, shining up the regenerated footwear and placing each pair in a new brown paper bag then printing the client's name and charge for repair in biro on the crisp packaging.

As my body continued to grow and change, his eyes and hands started to wander. One time I foamed at the mouth, I was about twelve. I had been inhaling the glue in the shed. My head buzzed like a fridge as his fingers groped inside my clothes. Black spots appeared before my eyes, thin creamy foam coated my mouth, its taste made me vomit down my front.

He stopped the assault, telling me to go inside and get cleaned up. He made me promise not to tell anyone.

He bought me a wee dug to keep me quiet and happy. One afternoon I fed it some lavender oil to see what would happen. It ran around the house and foamed at the mouth. After it had bitten my thumb, he near strangled the life out of its scrawny neck. He told me he took the creature to the woods at Blairadam. He wouldn't say whether he killed the mutt or set it free. Sometimes in dreams that wee dug becomes the beast of Blairadam. He bites at my legs, but he's no match for my steak knife. I slice him up like a Chuck Jones dog into a platter of sirloin, then pick my teeth with his bones . . .

Now I'm as near to Fife as I've been in the past eighteen years. Resting in Edinburgh, wondering if I should take an Aids test.

I sip on another Absolut, smiling at handsome strangers, plotting my return. I know I'll go home someday soon, with vodka and malice in my veins.

Packing dark thoughts and a knife in my panties.

I've got this far on my looks and my wits. I've been told that I'm beautiful, selfish, complex, cold, misanthropic and barking mad. I know that I'm a dog. Incidentally, I once wore a studded dog collar to a punk-rock gig here in Edinburgh. The band was called the Pop Group. I pogoed to their best song, 'We Are All Prostitutes', in my *Unknown Pleasures* T-shirt, school skirt, black opaque tights (ripped) and oxblood DMs. I had never set foot in Edinburgh until I was sixteen. As a child, if I asked them to take me to the shops or the zoo or to the castle, she killed off the idea stone dead. She would babble on about her fears of crossing deep, moving water, telling me Edinburgh was full of poofs and hoors.

For a spell back then, I believed as she stated that all women in the capital wore fur coats and nay knickers. Now I'm a short-stay resident, all leather coat and charm-me-out-of-my-knickers. Wearing Gucci for pleasure, but it's no holiday when a boyfriend checks his credit card statement. Then I run like a whippet. Fleecing men is the only fun in town. I'm running out of tarmac and patience, now there is only a bridge between us. A span of nuts and bolts that leads to the tragic kingdom.

Another blurry day is slipping through my fingers. The ambiance of this room soothes the canine pant in my throat. Recent dreams of revenge are exhilarating, unprepared and without regret. Revenge will set me free. Revenge will take the bark out of my bite. They'll know I'm on my way, there will be no element of surprise. He will most likely be in the shed easing his arthritis with heady glue and roll-ups. She'll be in front of the mirror teasing her stupid hair, hanging onto a kingsize, her eyes glassy from the Enva Cream.

Most days my wits are sharp and my aim is ruthless. I can balance an ex-boyfriend and a current boyfriend on their credit limits along with the rising wave of rage that threatens to overwhelm. A perfect balance, weights and measures in sync like an abstract mobile. Other days are bad and ugly. I trip over words and stilettos, fall out of strange beds in cheap hotels. I suffer Caligula-like hangovers and imagine the hounds of hell are at my heels and my thrusting blade is made of chocolate. Heaven and hell experienced on the streets of London, Amsterdam, Magaluf, Dublin, Edinburgh and Lochgelly.

Living with intermitting bouts of self-punishment and self-preservation. Often biting on the hands that feed me. Sinking my teeth into fingers, forearms, necks, ankles and ears. The ear is a particular favourite for my chainsaw smile. An attack can leave the victim crawling on the carpet shouting for Jesus Christ!

I remember she once whacked me on the side of the face with a tin of hairspray and said that I had ears like open taxi doors. Another time while nuzzling the side of my head with his fuzzy chin he said I had ears like wee vanilla orchids.

I have no stomach for food. Another plate of expensive gloop gone cold on me. My mind is bruised. Thoughts have been sucked into the blackness at the eye of a storm. It's my storm, like it was my fire. A good storm clears the air. Home is where the heart is . . . broken. The heart is useless, go home.

The Incomprehensible Mortality of Karen Mack

Sophie Cooke

Karen's husband came home. She heard him treading towards the room where she worked. He came in and kissed the hair on her head.

'Hello,' he said.

'Hi there,' she answered. David nodded, left the room and sat on a faraway sofa, shaking out sheets of newspaper.

Karen sat back in the chair. Her hands were spread flat on the table, her finger pads like ivy suckers on a wall. The backs of her hands were finely lined with a pattern of tiny interlocking kites. They couldn't fly away, the kites in her skin. She held up one hand and examined it closely. She should have worn gloves when she was younger. The hand dropped and she stared at nothing.

'Hi,' said Karen, entering the drawing room.

Her husband often wondered where her body had come from. He smiled. 'Hey, gorgeous.' Karen sometimes thought David looked like a stranger. She would forget that he was a separate entity from herself, and then, when she remembered, she couldn't think who he was. He was not a part of her now, as he sat on the sofa with the top button of his shirt undone.

'Joe and Mairi are coming round at seven,' she said.

'Oh, so they are.'

Karen sat down next to him.

'How's work going?' he asked her while he read.

'Good,' said Karen. She never asked him back.

She stretched out her leg and looked at her shoe.

'Joe's brother's coming, too,' she told him. 'He's bringing his girlfriend, they're down from Inverness.'

'Oh right. Leslie.'

'They're staying with Joe and Mairi. He's an artist.'

'Oh yes. You should get on.'

'Yeah.'

She rotated her foot.

'Do you like these shoes?' she asked, pointing the red-satin slipper's pointed toe to and fro. 'I think they're sexy.'

'Yes,' he said, 'yes, they are.' He carried on reading. 'Very sexy.'

They sat for a few minutes, him reading the pages and her swivelling her ankle. 'I'm going to get ready,' she said.

She took off all her clothes and stood in the big white enamel bath. Mirrored tiles covered the walls in a slab of reflection broken only by the little white lines of grouting between them. The white grid checkered her body, plotting her out on graph paper like an archaeological dig. C6, left breast, aged thirty-five, no breast feeding but still sagging a little. D12, stomach, wrinkled from sun.

There had been photos of her and a friend in Gran Canaria, long ago. They both had perms and were posing like models in their bikinis. The other girl was called Jackie. Their hair was wet and the curls were plastered round their faces. They were sixteen. So young, she thought, and the bit of world around them in the photograph looked younger, too.

Karen turned the chrome handle of the shower. Water screamed down on her head, beating away. It fell on her scalp and on her back like a shower of solid pencils landing rubber-side down. Noise and steam rushed up around her. Her reflection clouded and receded.

David stood on the terrace with a glass in his hand. He began to circulate, taking in the view over the Firth of Forth. Edinburgh looked misty in the distance of the late sunshine, like a steaming cow. He rocked back on his heels.

'Hi,' said his wife. Her body had materialised in the doorway.

'What a lovely dress,' he said. The dress was green and it clung to the outside of her body in an alluring way. 'You look like a very sexy goblin.'

She laughed. David turned back to the air, pleased. Her finger reached out and touched the piece of shirt material covering his elbow, but he couldn't have felt it. She went inside.

The guests arrived and kissed their hosts. Leslie introduced his girlfriend, Belle. Karen thought, she looks so young. 'How old are you?' she asked.

'How old? Twenty-four.' Belle looked at Karen and then she looked at Leslie. Everyone followed David's confident figure into the garden. He was laughing loudly at something Joe was telling him.

They stood on the terrace like herons. Six of them, standing around on slender legs. Karen felt like a fish in fancy dress. David gave everyone drinks and the blocks of ice sparkled in their cut-glass tumblers. The hum of traffic on the road was soft and distant.

'I hear you're an artist, Leslie,' said Karen.

'I don't know about that. I paint pictures, that's all.'

'What sort of pictures?' asked David.

'Semi-figurative, largely based on the human form.'

'Oh right,' David nodded uncertainly. 'Karen's an artist.'

'Really?' said Leslie, pointing his eyebrows at her.

'No, I'm not,' she said, wondering at the way David cast cubism and curtains together.

'What do you do?'

'Houses,' said David, answering for her. 'She's an interior designer.'

'Right,' said Leslie, nodding encouragingly.

'It's not art,' said Karen.

'Mairi said you used to be a model,' said Belle, eating a peanut.

'Yes.'

'How cool! What sort of modelling?'

'Various stuff.'

'She just used it as a springboard into acting.' David was keen to promote his wife. Partly because he loved her, partly because he didn't want people thinking he'd just married her for her stunning looks. He was a bit older than her and it could have all seemed a little seedy.

'Oh really? What were you in?'

'Oh,' said Karen, waving her glass. 'I was in *Glenbarry.* I was Nuala in *Glenbarry.*'

'Cool,' said Leslie. 'I remember that programme. I didn't recognise you without the red hair. Great.'

Karen thought the programme was a load of twee shite. Leslie thought the same, but was still pleased to meet an ex-demi-celebrity. Karen smiled.

'What do you do?' Belle asked David. 'Are you an actor as well?'

'Oh no,' said David. 'I'm a builder.' Everyone laughed, including David.

'That must be hard work,' said Belle.

'Mack as in Mack MacRae,' said Joe.

'Oh,' said Belle.

'Housing developments,' said Leslie. 'But you don't live in one.'

'No, of course not.' David lived in a well-proportioned Georgian manor.

'This is a beautiful house.'

Close commuting distance from Edinburgh. Paddock, pool, charm.

'Thank you.'

'What a lovely evening,' said Mairi. David almost said 'Thank you' again, like it was his.

'Great view you've got,' said Belle.

'I like it,' said Karen, and everyone turned to look at her. There was a pause while she didn't say anything else.

'What sort of houses do you build?' asked Belle.

'Whole range. We just cater to people's tastes.' David grimaced, and then laughed as if he had made a joke. Karen looked away, embarrassed.

She knew that the worst social crime you can commit is to want the wrong things. 'Taste' – like something you were born with. A sense that lives in the tongue: organ of speech, kissing and giving oneself away. But people can change. People can learn to want the right things. Karen had learned. She'd got used to thinking it could protect her.

Karen looked down at her wrist and the hand encircling her glass, seeing the marks of time in spite of it all. She hated the slow creep of it, the lines around her eyes and the creases in her forehead, making themselves at home. Gradually she was growing old, and one day strangers would stop looking at her.

Karen derived pleasure from being beautiful in public places. People's gazes strengthened her walking and made breathing a work of art, their attention making her an end in herself. She was justified by the eyes of passersby.

But she didn't own her own beauty. It was ready to leave at any moment, and its departure would be the death of her. Stay, Karen pleaded. Photographs of you just aren't enough. A Karen Mack who was not beautiful was perfectly unimaginable. She had never existed. Karen was scared.

Her eyes skipped over to Leslie. He was watching her and she smiled.

'Did you go to art school?' she asked.

'Glasgow,' he said, nodding. 'I just graduated in June.'

'Congratulations.' She even sounded old! He was young, and he was going to be an artist. Like doing cave paintings, she thought. I wish I'd done a cave painting. I wish I could learn.

'Will you teach me how to paint?' she asked.

He laughed and smiled. 'I'm sure you don't need teaching,' he said. 'If you're half as good as David says.'

'No,' she said, smiling back at him. His face was fresh and there was so much hair on his head. Most male acquaintances were half-bald now. They kept fit, but time was running out of their scalps and you couldn't stop that. It's happening to all of us, she thought. I wish I'd done a cave painting.

'Who's your favourite artist?' asked David.

'Um. Giacometti. Those spindly sculptures, they're the size of your thumb and yet – more human than a real person. It's the smallness of the figures. They hardly exist. That's what makes them so real.' There was a pause while Leslie felt awkward.

'Great,' said David.

Karen went inside. She stood in the blue sitting room and watched them for a few seconds. Then she carried on towards the kitchen. She stopped: she couldn't remember what she'd come in for. Had she come to get something? She went back outside, but they were all talking. People only look twice when they don't know you. She stood there and then she started down the stone steps that led from the terrace to the sloping lawn. Belle saw her and wondered where she was going.

Halfway down, she stooped and took off her shoes. They were lovely, but the heels were difficult on the slope. Karen walked between the beds of late-flowering roses. She looked quite small from the vantage point of the terrace above. She stood beside the pool and looked up, back towards the house, and saw them all standing there. They were all talking among themselves, she could hear the pleasant murmur of their voices. There was confident laughter above the fragile crystal. She saw Belle. Belle was looking at her. Karen looked back, her face tilted upwards, shaded, with the sun behind her.

Leaves were falling and the water was cold. She was growing old. The pool murmured mechanically beside her. Karen turned to face the sun, twisted her arm up behind her back and tugged down the zip of her dress. She could feel the cool air on the gaping bare skin around her spine. She moved the shoulder straps and pulled the dress right down, stepping out of it in her pants and strapless bra. She felt a little embarrassed. She looked over her shoulder with one arm folded over her breasts, but it was all right, still only Belle was looking. She grinned at Belle. She felt glad now.

She took off her bra. It left a deep pink mark like a weal around her rib cage. Invisible support. They have to make them extra tight in order to hold you up without the straps. Her small breasts spread outwards in flat relief and then hung down below her as she stooped to take off her pants. She stepped naked to the edge of the pool and pointed her hands out in front of her.

They all turned when they heard the noise. A perfect dive, splashing into the pool below. She rushed headlong through the icy water; her body turned into something else. Down and down she went until she grazed the bottom. She skimmed the floor of the pool, gliding the length of it. It was a perfect dive. Her hair spun out behind her, billowing forwards as she slowed.

They watched her go. A pale gold bullet shooting through the rectangle of blue. They had stopped talking.

'It's Karen,' said David, as if somebody would tell him otherwise. But nobody said anything.

She felt the cold water all over her and herself moving through the heart of it. She felt elated as the oxygen ebbed, and her lips were smiling as she surged up to the surface for air. Bang, her wet head emerged into the world. She gasped. She reached out her arm and hauled herself in to the ledge at the end of the pool. She hung on it for a while, just breathing and looking round, breathing in the rich scent of the roses. The water was cold and her teeth began to chatter.

She took a lungful of air and struck out into the pool. Her arm was strong, thrusting the water behind it and propelling her forwards. Now the other arm, and she was off. At the end of each stroke she drew her elbow up in a right angle, lifting her face sideways out of the water to inhale beneath it. She didn't know what she looked like.

She saw them all, framed in the torrential dripping triangle of her bent arm as she flipped her head that way for air. Hair streaked over her face. She saw them all standing on the terrace, very far away and very small, and she knew they weren't talking. She almost laughed, and then she dipped her head and was gone again.

She reached the end of the pool, touched it with her outstretched hand, turned, and started back the way she had come. She was swimming in her own wake. David and the five guests stood transfixed on the terrace, watching her. She was gliding up and down, touching the ends so calmly and turning, just swimming, but there was something powerful in it.

David put down his glass and started down the garden. He was moving quickly and his arms swung wildly by his sides, keeping his balance on the slope. As he got closer the noise became a little louder, the splash of her hands piercing the water's surface. He could hear her every stroke. He came through the roses and she saw him through her watery breath. She kept on swimming.

'Karen!' said David. 'Karen!' He sounded angry and hurt.

She went on to the end of the pool and then she stopped. She hung in the water with one arm on the ledge. He could see her legs dangling in the blue, splintered and wavering like hallucinations. Her wet hair was plastered to her head and she was looking at him.

'What are you doing?' said David. 'What on earth are you doing?'

'Swimming,' she said, and she shrugged her shoulders.

David stared at her. 'Have you lost your mind?'

'No,' she said. 'It's just that I'm going to die.'

'What do you mean? What do you mean, you're going to die?'

'I'm going to get old, and then I'm going to die. Just nothing, and nothing, and nothing.' She slapped her free hand on the water as she iterated the nothings. Nothing, splash, nothing, splash, nothing.

'We're all going to die,' said David, exasperated and feeling faintly ridiculous as he gesticulated at her in his smart but casual clothing. What a silly discussion, he thought. She just hung there, looking up at him.

'It's a fact of life,' said David. 'We're all going to die one day, but in the meantime we just get on with life and make the most of it.' He smiled, trying to cajole her out of the water.

'Yes,' said Karen. 'But nobody really believes it.' She looked at him. 'I won't be here,' she explained. I wish I'd done a cave painting. This is it, she thought, this is it.

'This isn't the time,' said David. 'This really isn't the time.' He turned and picked up her dress from off the slabs. It was a bit wet with splashes of pool water. He held it up as if he wanted her to climb out and put it on and come inside with him. It looked embarrassed. Karen looked at him.

She took a deep breath and it seemed to him to last forever, a long deep breath and she was gone, her head ducking under the water again. He watched her go, swimming past him, and he wanted to kick her. He threw down her dress and strode up the hill of the lawn, his feet sliding backwards in his smooth-soled shoes.

He had settled the guests inside. They were all in the blue sitting room, drinking and chatting. He knew they had been talking.

'Well,' said David. 'Sorry about all this. I think we'll have to start without Karen.' He laughed.

They sat and ate dinner in the dining room. The windows had been opened due to the warmth of the day.

'This is delicious,' said Mairi. 'Yum.'

They ate their chicken livers and talked about interesting things, and they all ignored the sound of Karen swimming up and down the pool. They moved onto the main course and still she kept going, up and down, somewhere outside the window. They couldn't see her. They just heard the sound of her pushing herself through the water, up and down, moving with a smooth regularity. At the end of each length there was a short pause while she stopped to turn and catch her breath, a short pause where they all relaxed for a moment before she started again.

'Is Karen all right?' said Belle to David.

'Yes, yes,' said David. 'She isn't always like this; you must think we're very strange. No, it's very out of character. She's just upset about something.' He bowed his head and paused. 'So, Belle, I hear you've lived abroad?'

After a while, David got up to close the windows and they were all relieved. You could still hear her, but only faintly now. It was more like the sound of distant waves crashing on a cliff, you could pretend it was that and not Karen, swimming up and down, up and down, just swimming up and down the pool.

Mooncalf

Lydia Robb

Sabbath. The pier is deserted but for one skipper swilling down the decks. *Anither heathen like masel*, says Granda. *The hale world's at the kirk. Hallelujah!* He turns his back to the wind, cups his hand over a cigarette and strikes a match. The acrid smell of sulphur lingers. Smoke curls up his nostrils as he descends the metal rungs to the boat.

At Gran's bidding, I'm wearing the balaclava and Fair Isle jumper she knitted for Christmas. I hate the colours. *For God's sake cratur, wrap up weel. Catch yer death in this weather, so ye wid.* The wool is coarse and itchy but I'm glad of the extra warmth.

Move yersel, laddie. Ye'll no catch ony fish, hingin aboot there wi yer hauns in yer pooches. He checks that the gear is in order. Bait, handlines, hooks. He rives at the engine, it grumbles reluctantly, sputters into life and we're skimming out over the harbour bar. I can taste the salt on my tongue, feel the wind stinging my face and the surge as we head for the open sea. I'm lulled into a dwam by the movement of the boat. When I look back, Gran's house is fading in the distance.

It was funny how we spoke about going to Granny's even when it was Granda's house. He had an early night last night on account of his tubes playing up. I'm curious about 'the tubes'. I asked him once. You could tell, he didn't like discussing it. He'd answered in a few syllables. *The War. Nerve gas*, and told me I'd understand soon enough.

Gran had sent me upstairs with a mug of Oxo. Granda's room was filled with big dark furniture and smelled of moth balls. *Put it there, laddie*, he said, pointing to the bedside table where his distorted dentures grinned from a thick green tumbler.

The other room at the top of the creaky attic stair was Uncle Billy's. You could hear him snuffling and grunting like a small animal, the crackly sound of his wee transistor muffled behind the door. I was tempted to keek through the keyhole but was frightened to. They'd locked him in because he put 'next door's' cat through the mangle. Blood and guts everywhere in the wash-house and Mrs Gibb wailing like a demented cat herself.

Bluidy halfwit, Granda fretted, *although yer Granny winnae hae it.* Gran made excuses for Billy like she always did. *Belle's cat wis sittin on his washin board an widnae budge. He didnae like that, did he?*

Granda was wheezing like a pair of bellows when I went in. *Hoch hoch.* He cleared his throat, coughed into a big starched hankie. The bedside light cast his trembling shadow on the wall behind. He clamped his fingers to the brass ribs of the bedhead and heaved himself into a sitting position. The bedsprings gave a metallic twang. He blew at the steam curling from the mug then started sucking like a baby.

The strains of 'My cup's full and running over', came drifting up from the kitchen. Gran was getting ready for her weekly jaunt to the Sally Army. She normally drags me along even though she knows I hate it. On this occasion I was allowed to stay at home because of the exams. She says the singing and praying lift her spirits and that more importantly,

Uncle Billy loves it. He's in his element when he's playing his tambourine. *Oh God our help in ages past.*

Tell ye this, son, Granda pointed to one empty pyjama leg. *There's nae sic thing as a God*. His wooden leg was scary. It was propped against the bottom of the bed, a big black boot attached to the end, the laces long licorice worms. The wooden leg makes no difference to him. He manoeuvres himself aboard the coble like an acrobat in the circus.

On the first day of the school holidays, the two of us climbed the worn stone steps to the sea-wall and battled our way from one end to the other and back in the teeth of a rising gale. Once or twice I feared we'd be blown into the waves, slapping and sucking below. Gran was furious when she found out. *Toughen the loon up* was all he said.

He and Gran never spoke for the rest of the day. After tea she made me sit at one end of the table with my books. Uncle Billy rocking backwards and forwards in his chair, a lump of snot dangling like a yo-yo from the end of his nose.

Christ, said Granda, *dicht yer snitch*. Gran leaned over with a lump of toilet paper and did the job for him. Billy resumed his rocking, his horned fingernails scratching out a rhythm on the ridges of the washboard, the semblance of a hymn keening in his throat.

Granda growled, *Dae we hae tae pit up wi this racket aa nicht?* An Gran replied, *Och, if it keeps him happy*. But Uncle Billy *is* always happy. He smiles even when he's got tears running down his fat cheeks.

I listened to the furious clicking of Gran's knitting needles, the wind rattling the windows and wished I was home.

When will we see Mum?

Granda looked over the top of his half-moon specs.

He wants his ma, he mocked. Then he changed tack. *Trust oor Liz tae merry a furriner.*

Berwick's no furrin. Gran shook her head.

It is tae me. Onywey, time she wis hame, nou the bully boy's left.

At the mention of my da, my tongue seeks out the space where I'm missing a tooth.

Driftwood spat and sizzled on the fire. Granda rose now and again and kicked the escaping embers into place. As he did so, sparks birled like fireworks up the lum. He'd return to the sideboard, winking at me whenever he caught my eye.

With the aid of two mirrors, he started to cut his hair, wielding a set of steel clippers and an open razor. Satisfied with his handywork, he combed and parted his wavy white mop into place. *Right, son*, he turned to me brandishing the razor. *You're next for the chop*. He proceeded to give me a balder. When he was done, I looked like I'd had the ringworm. Then he tied Uncle Billy to the kitchen chair with a lump of twine and gave him a short back and sides too, before plastering his hair down flat with Brylcreem.

We anchor off the 'Deil's Heid' and set to work. Granda baits the lines and lays them out in the usual fashion. We sit in silence for a long time, thinking our own thoughts in the gently rocking boat. Gulls swoop and screech, white scars drifting across the red cliff face. Granda pulls the thermos from his bag, pours two mugs of tea, washing his pills down with the first gulp. *Cheese roll, son?* He takes a bite and screws up his face. *Fit for the moosetrap, this stuff.* But the fresh air has made me hungry and it tastes fine to me. *Yer gran's forgot the chutney.*

We were just on the point of calling it a day when they come. In their hundreds, churning the water like soup. Within minutes we have a catch that would be the envy of any boy. Blue-green fishscales turn to copper in the light from a dying sun. The mackerel squirm and flap wildly against the sides of the barrel.

We're within sight of the shore when the engine coughs then dies on us. *Shite!* Granda swears under his breath then he's tugging vigorously at the starting motor. Once, twice, three times, but there's no response. The sweating and cursing make no difference. He shouts to me to fix the oars to the rowlocks. *Move, laddie. Quick. Quick.*

When I've followed his instructions, I look round and sense there's something far wrong. He's slumped beside the barrel, his forehead pressed to his knees. *Granda?* My heart is dunting against my ribs, panic rising in my throat. *Granda! Granda!* But there's no answer. A wan moon rises in the still-light sky.

Then I see him. Uncle Billy. Scuttling along the pier, head down, hugging his arms to his chest. *Uncle Billy*, I scream. *Biii–llly!* My voice bounces back on the wind and the ebbing tide. He looks up and waves. My arms flail wildly above my head. *Billy! Help!*

Then he's turning and I hear it: the tinny jingle of the tambourine. He's giving it all he's got, bashing out a tempo, his bandy legs syncopating in time to the beat, his retreating back a grey blur.

Jackson's Hotel

Simon Stephenson

The police have been here a lot these past few days, asking questions about the fawn-haired boy. I have told them nothing – that is, I have written nothing down for them. Everyone here at Jackson's Hotel, where I am the night-porter, thinks I am mute; I have always been happy to keep it that way.

Though I believe at one time it was both, Jackson's Hotel is now neither a proper hotel nor owned by anybody called Jackson. The current proprietors go by the name of Mack-enzie and run the establishment as a sort of clearing house for the marginal souls of this city. Our guests are largely depen-dent on bottles, on needles, on other people's prescription medications, to make it through the days. They fund these pursuits in the oldest way imaginable.

How I come to be at Jackson's Hotel is that when I arrived in this city, from a faraway town I'd left in a hurry, I needed somewhere cheap to live and overheard two men in the bus station talking about this place. How I come to be here as a mute is that when I entered Jackson's Hotel, Danny Mac-kenzie was having an argument about money with one of the women from the fourth floor and I stood there watching for a long time, thinking they hadn't noticed me, until the woman turned to me and said, 'An' you can stop leering an' all. What's the matter with ye? Cat got yer tongue, eh?' I nodded, about to turn around and leave, but by then Danny Mackenzie was looking at me and he asked, 'Are you here for a room, pal?'

Thinking it was getting late, and I could find somewhere else in the morning, I nodded again. At the same time I was wondering whether I might be able to get away with not saying a single word to these people.

'Well, it's ten quid the night, six if you share.'

I removed a ten pound note from my pocket and held it out to him. He took it, then asked, 'Single or sharing?'

I held up one figure to indicate single.

'Cannae speak, eh?'

I nodded, though there has never been anything wrong with my voice.

'What's the matter? Sick?'

I drew a finger across my Adam's apple and grimaced.

'Aye, that's what I thought. Well, you can have 4–B.' He handed me a key and pointed to the staircase. 'Third floor.'

I shouldered my bag and walked towards the stairs. The woman called out after me, 'You need a little anything tonight honey, you come up the fourth floor an' ask for Lisey.'

Though I did not take Lisey up on her offer, plenty of other men did that night, and as I lay on the rusty cot in room 4–B, the sound of them traipsing up and down the staircase kept me awake into the small hours.

When I came down the next morning, the desk was unmanned. Thinking to enquire what time I had to vacate my room by, I walked through a doorway marked 'Lounge'. There was nobody there to ask, though, nobody except a man who lay curled up on the floor, asleep amongst the debris of a previous night's drinking.

I left the hotel and walked around the streets. It'd been dark when I arrived, but the area around Jackson's Hotel was exactly how I knew it'd be: deathly quiet, because those of us who inhabit these places aren't usually morning people; posters on lamp-posts of somebody's missing daughter; nine or ten in the morning and the only shop open an off-licence.

When I got back to the hotel Danny Mackenzie was parked outside in a saloon car, talking into a mobile phone. I hung around, waiting for him to finish the call, but he scrolled down the window, put his hand over the mouthpiece of his phone and said to me, 'My brother's at the desk. He'll fix you up another night'

I should have just shaken my head to indicate I was leaving, had a home and family waiting for me somewhere, but I couldn't because I didn't.

Danny Mackenzie's brother Flint looked just like him, except a little meaner, if that's possible.

'Help you with something, chief?' he asked as I entered.

I nodded, showed him my key and pointed to the staircase.

'You're the deaf guy, eh?'

I shook my head, gestured at my mouth and then drew that same line across my Adam's apple.

'Aye, well, it's all the same thing to me. Five pounds.'

I was surprised, as it'd been ten the night before, but I didn't question it, because I seemed to be getting the best of it; anyway, how could I question anything when I was supposed to be mute? I now know how there's no fixed prices at Jackson's Hotel, just whatever you think you can get out the customers, which is why it went down by half for the second night, as I'd seen the room by then. I went back upstairs, and that was the only time I ever saw Flint Mackenzie, because a week later he got the jail for assaulting someone in a pub.

I spent the afternoon in my room, sleeping and waking, listening to the sounds outside, waiting for time to pass. At about seven that evening I came downstairs. Lisey was sitting on the reception desk, dressed in her working clothes, talking to the fawn-haired boy.

'Hey, mister!' she called across to me, 'Never came up last night. Something else broken except your voice, eh?'

She cackled with laughter at that, but stopped abruptly when she realised the fawn-haired boy hadn't understood her joke.

'Cannae talk at all,' she said, gesturing at me.

The fawn-haired boy turned to face me; that was when I got my first proper look at him, and I saw how he couldn't have been more than sixteen years old.

'That true?' he asked.

I nodded, and drew the finger across my Adam's apple.

'Shame we couldn't get you that same operation, huh Lisey? Give us all some peace.' he said.

She was still pretending to be outraged when Danny Mackenzie came in and asked them if they were getting paid to stand around chatting. They hustled out into the night, leaving me stood in the hall with him.

'What about you? You looking for a job?'

I shook my head, because though I have known desperate times, I have never done the kind of work Danny Mackenzie had Lisey and the fawn-haired boy doing. Besides, I was fifty-eight years old last birthday and doubted there would be much of a market for my services. Danny Mackenzie must have guessed what I was thinking.

'No, it's no that. What I'm after is a night-porter to man the desk here. You'd earn your board and lodgings, and I don't care if you sleep. Just be here to let the folk in and out, and call me if there's any trouble starts. You interested?'

I nodded, because even at the new price of five pounds a night the money I had from the town I'd left in a hurry wouldn't have lasted long.

I started that same night, and though I never got back the five pounds I'd given Flint Mackenzie, the job has worked out well enough. The comings and goings are easy enough to deal with; the girls and boys from the fourth floor handle their own customers, so all I have to do for them is press the buzzer that opens the door. I have to turn away occasional tourists, because Jackson's Hotel somehow persists in an obscure guidebook, but most of them, once they see the reception area, are only too happy to hear that there is no room at the inn.

Danny Mackenzie wasn't born with such scruples. He once booked in a genuine traveller, a Japanese businessman named Mr Hashimoto who was unfortunate enough to find his way here in daylight hours. I got to know Mr Hashimoto a little during the evenings, when he'd come to the night-desk and talk to me. He told me his company usually dealt with the Holiday Inn, but he preferred it here at 'Mr Jackson's Hotel', because it let him get to know what the people of this country are like, and Mr Jackson, by which he meant Danny Mackenzie, was such a respectable man.

I wanted desperately to tell him how wrong he was. To tell him about other citizens, citizens who live in houses not hotels and have families instead of acquaintances. Most of all I wanted to tell him how Danny Mackenzie was possessed of one of the blackest souls ever to darken this earth. Despite living mute for some months, I have shaken my head to all suggestions that I learn sign language, largely because it has always looked so complicated; nevertheless I doubt there could be any symbol or sign which would adequately convey the darkness of a man who nightly sends others into the alley.

Thankfully, there has been no trouble at the hotel and I have never had to telephone Danny Mackenzie – that, of course, would have been a challenge in itself. I have, however, slept a lot, like he said I could, and sometimes, after the bar has closed, I have gone through and listened to music on the jukebox.

The best thing about the job, though, and what has made

my time at Jackson's Hotel bearable, has been the dreams – not my own, because after a lifetime of dreaming I am more than tired of those, but the dreams of other people.

Mr Hashimoto was not alone in coming to talk to me, and in fact almost all our guests spend time at the night-desk with me. Like Flint Mackenzie that only time I met him, they seem to confuse being mute with being deaf; either that or they've never had someone they could tell secrets and trust not to mock or scold. Whatever the reason, they have treated me like some kind of priest and so it has come to pass that, in the small hours of the morning, I have got to know the inhabitants of Jackson's Hotel better than anybody.

If it's true about it being easier for a camel to pass through the eye of a needle, the people here at Jackson's Hotel have little to worry about. They do not yearn for much, and what they do want you probably already have and never give a second's thought. Nobody has ever talked to me of saloon cars like Danny Mackenzie's, mansion houses or foreign holidays, but only of getting clean and off these streets, of lost siblings and fostered children, of warm winter clothes. I have heard these tales over and over, and many times have been glad no words of consolation are expected of me, because what do you say to console someone who lives at Jackson's Hotel and works for Danny Mackenzie?

Strangely, it was Lisey's story that moved me the most. Lisey, who'd worked for Danny Mackenzie longer than anyone, who was starting to grey beneath her peroxide, who spat like a man and swore like a sailor, who joked about me being a queer for never coming to the fourth floor, about my muteness, about the old-fashioned songs I played on the jukebox.

Any time there wasn't an audience around to hear her jokes, though, she talked of William. That was the fawn-haired boy's name, William, and at first I presumed she was talking of him, but it quickly stopped making sense, because sometimes she'd speak of him in the present tense and sometimes in the past, and often mention them both in the same sentence: 'Today would have been William's birthday . . . I've not seen William all day.'

It took me a long time to realise there were actually two Williams, the fawn-haired boy and another one, a William who had died when he was still only a baby. A William who had been Lisey's son when she was sixteen and had nothing else in this world to hold onto; who knows, but if he had lived she might have been somewhere else.

Perhaps it isn't surprising I had difficulty understanding about there being two Williams, because even Lisey herself seemed sometimes to forget this. During my first weeks at Jackson's Hotel I'd been puzzled by the relationship between her and the fawn-haired boy, but when I came to understand about the two Williams it made perfect sense: she wanted to be his mother.

The others only talked of getting themselves away from here, but Lisey always spoke in the plural, getting *us* out of here. She'd take William, she said, on a bus, and they'd live in a village in the countryside somewhere. She'd get a job behind a bar, work she'd done when she first came to this city. There was some plan where William would do odd jobs around the village, but she didn't talk about that much, and I think all that mattered was for him to be there.

The fawn-haired boy was our only guest who never told me anything about his dreams. He spent a lot of time with Lisey, so it's possible he told her the name of the place he went when he closed his eyes to sleep, but somehow I don't think so. Like I've said, he was only sixteen years old and I don't think he could have yet discovered what a powerful thing it is to dream, how you can somehow keep on getting up each morning and going through the motions as long as some distant star continues to wink at you from an unreachable horizon.

I was sleeping when he came back that night. Though the bell rings beside where I lay my head, I have grown accustomed to it over the months, and I imagine he probably buzzed several times before giving up to sit down in the doorway.

It was Lisey that woke me. Coming down the stairs into reception, she'd seen him through the glass door, his shirt covered in blood, and screamed. She ran to the door and I buzzed it open, then followed. The fawn-haired boy looked to be in a bad way – the blood wasn't only on his shirt, but ran dark down his trousers, was dried into his hair and stained onto his hands. We got a second shock when he stood up and walked into the hotel unaided.

Lisey had him sit down on my desk so she could look him over. He had a cut on his hand, one on his thigh, and the beginnings of a black eye, but that was all and not enough to account for so much blood. At least, not for it to be the fawn-haired boy's blood.

'What's happened to you, William?' Lisey asked him.

'Danny Mackenzie.'

The name was explanation enough, enough to explain the violence anyway. The fawn-haired boy must have told Lisey the rest of it after they went upstairs; I didn't hear until the next day when the police arrived. They were only asking questions about Danny Mackenzie at that point, but soon they were wanting to know about a fawn-haired boy who several people had seen arguing with Danny Mackenzie in the alley that night. I pieced the story together from the questions they asked me and the accounts of our other guests.

A client had complained to Danny and he'd taken it out on the fawn-haired boy. The fawn-haired boy, beaten down into a corner by Danny Mackenzie and a dreamless world that after only sixteen years was already shattered beyond repair, had taken the knife he carried for insurance and stuck it into Danny Mackenzie.

The last time I saw him was when he and Lisey had come down the stairs and I'd buzzed the door to let them out into the night. He was carrying a battered suitcase and she clutched a carrier bag to her breast. They didn't turn around to say goodbye, but I knew they were leaving all the same.

I'd like to be able to believe they've gone to a village somewhere, a place with a bar where she can work and plenty of odd jobs for him to do, but I know that isn't true. No, they will have boarded a bus to another city just like this one, a city with an alley and a hotel that doesn't take bookings from tourists and a dozen Danny Mackenzies lining up to take advantage.

Maybe I'm committing a sin by not saying any of this to the police. Certainly, it is a sin to kill a man, to take a knife and plunge it into his heart until it stops beating; the Gideon bibles they have in every room of every proper hotel in the world will tell you that. If that man happens to be Danny Mackenzie, though, and the heart is as cold as his was, I believe there are deadlier sins in this world, sins such as sending someone nightly into the alley without even the armour of dreams.

Though Danny Mackenzie is gone and never coming back, I do not believe much will change at Jackson's Hotel. The police didn't care for Danny Mackenzie any more than anybody else did and will stop asking their questions soon enough; Flint Mackenzie is due out of jail next month and will return to claim his empire. Maybe I will learn to talk in the interim, but I do not think so. When they can trust you never to tell, people give you their secrets, their dreams. I am fifty-eight years old and tired of my own dreams, so I will continue, silent, and fall asleep into better worlds other people have created for me.

A Storm Gathering

Jonathan Falla

That Thursday night, Malik felt quite disembodied. He lay on his rush bed staring up through the darkness, nervous, slim, naked, wrapped only in silence. All bodily sensations – his profuse sweating, his weight pressing through the threadbare sheet onto the rough cords of the charpoy – all had left him. He felt that he was floating through a very bad dream. He told himself: this can't be happening to me, I am Msc of Khartoum University, the Americans will not allow another famine, they have promised!

It had been a difficult week for the little town. At the brickworks, they'd set women to stack bricks by the thousand, then paid them the price of four cups of tea; there had been a fight. Someone had been found with an antique rifle, had been beaten unconscious by police outside their house. Raiders had been seen in the rocky wastelands north of town, and the Army helicopter had caught them in the open and strafed them – but they weren't raiders at all, just nomads, who died in the sands among their punctured baggage and the smashed bones and exploded bowels of their camels.

For Malik, it had been little better. He'd promised to pay his local staff on Monday, but the bank had run out of notes. He'd had to pay in sugar, which they could trade, but he wondered how long they'd stay on. He'd promised cash very soon but, that evening, someone had stolen his radio. Tuesday morning brought delegations of village elders, tall men in white robes politely reminding Malik that they were dying and that he'd promised to prevent this. Tuesday afternoon, the clinic for malnourished babies complained that they had no milk powder for 'Allah's special infants' and what was he doing about it? He'd promised to drive to the city and collect some from the Agency doctors but his Landrover had failed to start. On Wednesday the Army radio operator had sent a message: be informed, please, that the promised seventeen tons of wheat would now be seven tonnes. Walking in the souk that evening, Malik had felt the stares, felt himself clamped and squeezed between the people's hope and hostility.

On Thursday the wheat had actually arrived, one truckload, not two, a donation from Norway. It was old, the weevils had found it; every grain was bored out hollow, a thin starchy dust rising as they spread a sackful on a straw mat. Black weevils had wriggled outwards in a ring, fleeing towards the edge of the mat. Men's faces were twisted in contempt for foreign food, foreign aid, governments foreign or otherwise, for university sorts from Khartoum – and for their promises.

'So,' they'd sneered aloud, 'what else have you to offer us? Wonderful, is it not, what these educated types can do.'

They'd turned their white-robed backs on Malik.

'I promise you . . . !' Malik had cried, his voice wavering. The elders had ignored the anxious young man in his scarlet nylon shirt standing by the disgusting heap of dust and insects. They'd stalked back to the souk in a malevolent huddle. He'd heard someone snicker.

A hot wind was rising. By nightfall the raw cement walls of Malik's office throbbed with heat. In the toilet block he washed by candlelight with brown water from a bucket. After prayers, he began his accounts but found converting wages into sugar impossible, for the price changed daily. The walls pressed in; the pressure lamp hissed, white-hot. He ate a meal of rice with cold beans in oil, hung the scarlet shirt on a chair, lay on his charpoy in the darkness and sweated. He thought of the promises the Agency had made when he took the job, and within moments that sense of disembodiment and unreality came over him. Surely, he repeated, this is not me, I am not here.

Far off, a vehicle whined, lurching down into the dry wadi, accelerating across the riverbed, heaving out again. Police, thought Malik, searching for hoarders. Or the Army chasing their tails as the bandits make fools of them. But the vehicle turned off the main street, climbed the short stony hill to the Agency house – and stopped. Now Malik thought: the Army have come for me. He lay still, telling his heart to hush.

'Malik?' The voice was female. That also seemed unreal. 'Malik? Are you there?'

He heard the steel gate juddering open.

'Sir? The foreign doctor lady is come,' his houseboy called. Suddenly, the world was urgently concrete.

'Wait, I'm coming,' Malik cried out. 'Please wait, don't go!'

Medicines! Medicines he'd promised to the clinic. A delivery, he could make a delivery!

'Malik,' said the woman with a torch, 'we've driven eight hours, had two flats and dug ourselves out twice. We're most surely staying with you tonight.'

He backed inside, pumped and relit the lamp. She was slim and handsome with a strong mouth and bouncy black hair thick with dust. A thin flowerprint skirt swung about her fine legs. Self-assured and nosey, she surveyed the unfinished cement shop he'd rented for the Agency's office and his quarters.

'So, Malik, you're nicely set up here.' Malik peered round in surprise. Behind a crude screen of grey blankets pegged over string, his charpoy skulked. Reeking clothes lay on the floor.

Steel chairs, a table, a litter of tools and tins, cardboard boxes serving as filing cabinets scattered about on the concrete: that was it.

In his rush Malik had buttoned his shirt by the wrong buttonholes; it hung on him asquint. He began refastening it, as though merely toying with the buttons. The doctor gratefully swallowed the water he'd given her.

'Some drive!' she grimaced cheerfully. 'That'll be why we don't see you in town much.'

'You have brought medicine?' he enquired excitedly.

She purred, 'What are you needing?'

'Every medicine!' Malik blurted. She became doctorish.

'What exactly is the matter?'

'Malaria is coming; there is tuberculosis . . .'

'You've tuberculosis? Malik . . .'

'Not I, all the people! The sick are everywhere. These Medical Assistants are helpless, they cry to me daily.'

'I see,' said the lady doctor.

'What can we deliver?'

'Not so much.'

'Not much?'

'I've only my personal kit, Malik; I'm here to inspect. Did you know your shirt's askew?'

Malik blushed furiously and buttoned the shirt again, sick with disappointment.

'We do have food with us,' she said kindly. 'Have you eaten?'

Waving away his help, she produced a meal of crackers, red Libyan jam and pilchards. The driver took his to the Land-rover. The woman sat at the rickety table, eating with gusto, grinning at Malik. He thought, she drives all day and still has energy, while I am washed up.

She declared breezily: 'I'd like your company tomorrow.'

'Company?' echoed Malik.

'The village health posts. We'll visit the Medical Assistants in the morning, see what they need.'

'Medicines,' said Malik sullenly: he'd promised chloroquine which had never materialised.

The doctor parried: 'Must assess them first. Any coffee? No matter, I've my own.'

He should stand and light the stove for her but she was there first, ignoring him.

'The Assistants will not be at their places,' said Malik.

'Why so?'

'They are in town, hoping for some food or some pay.'

'They'll not be paid if they're not working,' the doctor observed sharply. 'So you can guide us.'

'But I am expecting delegations tomorrow,' pleaded Malik.

The doctor frowned: 'Oh? Well, in the morning you can show us the souk; we'll round up the Assistants and return them to their villages.'

'Thank you,' said Malik. She had no authority, but the Assistants wouldn't defy her, and, he'd be relieved to see them go.

'Time for bed.' She reached for her bag. Malik wondered where he should sleep. He started tugging the dirty sheet from his bed, but she stopped him.

'I camp on the roof.'

He gawked at her.

'The roof of the Landrover, Malik!'

She walked round the table, bent down and straightened, holding a pair of Malik's underpants, which she folded, popping them on the end of the charpoy.

Malik had never known such humiliation.

They found three Medical Assistants in the souk, drinking glasses of sweet tea in an airless booth of rush matting, balanced on stools with their toes peeping from under the white robes. The doctor stood over them.

'Now,' she commanded Malik, 'the one who's saying his village chief is unwell, tell him I'll visit. That'll be diplomatic.'

She shooed the Assistants into the back of her Landrover, promising Malik she'd be back by evening. He watched the Landrover wallow across the sands beyond the wadi, then walked home. He passed women threshing some thin grass for its barely edible seed. Everyone knew he was there to relieve their hunger, and had delivered weevils. He felt the disdainful stares.

The heat grew insidiously on a wind edged with grit. Malik's nylon shirt stuck to his back; it was making his skin spotty, but he had no other. Mid-morning, the farmer's delegation arrived in ill-humour.

'Oh, Malik, your promises are worthless.'

Malik flushed angrily: he'd brought them sorghum seed, the one promise he had delivered, a free gift from the Agency!

'A gift of no value, the wrong species, Ugandan rubbish; it will not grow here.'

'It's good sorghum!' protested Malik.

'Good for the blacks of the south, maybe,' scoffed a lout in a filthy jelabiya whose spittle foamed through black tooth stumps. 'It won't grow here, as anyone but a college boy would know.'

'Anywhere but here they'd have the wit to make it grow!' shouted Malik, incensed. This was a mistake.

'Oh, Malik, you insult us as well as starve us? We shall not forget. We'll tell our people what you think of us. Then, we promise you, we'll be back.'

With which they swept out. Malik's staff stared at him in dismay, then downed their pens and departed. He thought they were running away – until he realised that the *muezzin* was calling.

At the mosque, no one spoke to Malik; he felt a hundred glances but saw only the robed shoulders turning away, murmurous. He left, more on edge than ever. A yellow dog ran at him; he cried out and the urchins laughed.

Restless and uneasy, he considered climbing to survey the town from Administration Hill. But the glare and the abrasive wind tired him. He walked under the trees to the wadi, where red kites circled, waiting for carrion. He walked to the bore-hole where fractious camels, muzzles in the galvanised tank, sucked singlemindedly. A rider appeared, stooping his animal hurriedly and calling to his friends. Someone indicated Malik with a thrust of the chin. Malik left the place, hurrying home.

The town seemed malevolently silent, ill-will hanging in the air like dust. Malik trailed up the lane to his house. His compound walls perched on ragged clumps of concrete, undermined by the rains.

Shortly after, his Secretary hammered on the steel gate calling, 'Peace upon this house!' The houseboy did not appear. 'Oh, Malik!' the Secretary persisted.

He remained outside the gate, declining to enter, glancing apprehensively downhill.

'You know,' he said, 'that the chief is dead?'

'Which chief is that?' asked his young employer.

'Of Burush,' the man answered. 'He's been old and sick all month. But his death – that was today.'

The Secretary tugged up his robe and fled, stumbling in the ruts in his haste. Malik wondered why one should know so particularly about this death. The lady doctor was inspecting Burush. What difference that might make, he couldn't tell.

He thought of his undone paperwork: it would not redeem the promises he had made. He sat in the yard drinking fruit squash, frightened of the stillness, wishing for his radio. He heard distant shouting, a fracas in the souk. Later, the Army helicopter took off and flew west.

Still the heat grew. Mid-afternoon, he heard scrapings from the office.

'Put that down!' he shouted from the doorway. The houseboy dropped the tinned milk which rolled off the table to the floor. The boy ran into the street and was gone.

In the yard again, sitting on the sloping sand by the toilet block, Malik felt bewildered by anxiety and loneliness. The high mudbrick walls gave no security; who might that be, scuffling and whispering behind them? Hearing the Landrover return, he felt a rush of warmth and gratitude to the lady doctor and hurried to open the steel gates. He glimpsed two men staring from the street corner, a third hurrying to them, gesturing at Malik's house.

The Landrover bumped into the yard.

'We've been all over!' she declared, twirling indoors to dump her shoulderbag on a chair. 'There's food for thought everywhere; those poor frustrated fellows, they're aching to work and I've promised they shall.'

She patted the dust off her flowery skirt and took water from the jar. Malik asked: 'You saw Burush?'

'Surely, and the chief, poor man, lain on his cot in a sweltering hut and flies crawling over his eyes. He's quite poorly.'

'Yes,' agreed Malik. 'He is now dead.'

She looked startled. 'Well, I called as promised and gave him an injection, though he was too far gone.'

Malik sat down hard, staring open-mouthed. She frowned: 'Now what's wrong? You want one too?'

'You gave an injection?'

'To show willing.'

'He is dead,' said Malik, 'after the injection.'

'Oh dear,' she said breezily, 'I'm not surprised.'

'After you gave him an injection, he died,' repeated Malik.

His fears took hideous shape, like some evil bulk sensed in a dark room then glimpsed in silhouette against the window. He jumped up and pulled the steel shutters tight, bolts squealing home. The doctor followed with her eyes, touched by his panic.

'It was penicillin,' she said. 'No way . . . Malik, he was three-quarters dead.'

'All dead now!' cried Malik, shouting to her driver to reverse his Landrover against the high gate.

'What are you expecting?' said the doctor in a whisper.

The sloping yard looked across town towards the tree-shaded souk. Malik stared that way.

'Oh!' he cried. His tone puzzled her.

'Malik, what are you expecting?' She was frightened.

'Coming now,' he whispered.

'Who?' She took his elbow and began, 'Promise me nothing awful . . .'

But Malik promised nothing, only pointed.

'Dear Lord,' breathed the woman, looking out past him.

Across the little town, a tawny curtain was advancing. It stretched from the mountains beyond the wadi on their left, to somewhere far into the desert on their right, and from the sandy ground to somewhere thousands of feet above them in the heavens. At this moment it divided the souk perfectly in two, one yard in full sun, the next obscured. The curtain was quite opaque, as thick, as heavy as velvet. It was made of fine dust, millions of tons hanging in the hot air. The desert was up on its feet, and was coming.

It approached silently, smoothly, with the steady purpose of massed soldiers in leather armour. The dust drew across trees which melted from sight. It devoured houses, and you expected shrieks from inside, but there was only the clatter of a thousand shutters. Malik and the doctor watched, mesmerised. A jeep struggled down a sandy backstreet with headlights blazing, until the yellow curtain drew over the vehicle and the lights turned bilious before disappearing. On a roof nearby, a hatchway opened and a man appeared. He glanced at the approaching dust, turned his gaze on Malik and shook his fist. Then he was enveloped and gone.

'Allah be thanked.' Malik's eyes shone. He smiled.

'*Thanked*?' said the doctor, astounded.

'They cannot get us in this. Tomorrow we go early, quickly, we go away!'

'Who's wanting to get us?'

But Malik rushed about bolting everything, yelling to the driver who hurried inside. They pulled the doors tight behind him.

'Light the lamp!' Malik ordered the doctor, then recalled that the kerosene was finished. 'Candles, in there.' He covered the typewriter, files, water jar and his suitcase of clothes. Then he sat down.

'What do we do?' said the doctor, flapping her hands helplessly.

'Please, be comfortable,' he gestured cheerfully to the bed. 'That is best. Now we must wait.'

The candlelight seemed to thicken, then curdle. There was silence – until the tin roof began to heave and clang, the shutters to strain and squeal in their steel frames. Beneath the door, puffs and curlicues of dirty orange dust streamed in. Through the tiniest chinks, dust penetrated in little jets. It entered the roofspace, dribbling down through holes in the ceiling where bare wires hung. It found cracks in the solid walls and seeped in. The house seemed to bleed internally.

Malik saw the doctor fumble with the collar of her shirt, trying to pull it over her mouth. He saw that she was scared.

'Malik,' she whispered, 'shall we suffocate?'

He gave her a tea-towel wetted with a scoop from the water jar. The doctor pressed this over her mouth and nose. 'Thank you!' he heard, muffled.

After which, all three sat in silence, sunk in thought or sleeping. The candles burned away while dust drifts gathered on the floor and a film settled on the room until all was a uniform colour, as though they sat in a sepia world. The driver said, 'Last year my neighbour's children disappeared in a *haboob* like this and were not seen for two days.'

'Dear Lord, Malik!' the lady doctor whimpered.

But Malik sat quietly, watching the last candle flame wave gently in its halo of dusty fluorescence, and he wished that the storm might last forever.

Vesuvius

Ella Henderson

'We're buildin' a volcano,' Liam contributed loudly to the general teatime cacophony.

As usual no one heard him. It was always the same: no one listening and everyone shouting down the telly. Time for 'scaling up'. He had developed a technique of 'scaling up' or 'scaling down' with which he attempted to regulate the amount of attention focused on him.

He waited until his father had finished studying the sports columns of *The Star* and was flipping through the main news, seized possession of the tomato ketchup and bellowed, 'We're buildin' a volcano!'

The Star twitched irritably at the volume of this piece of information. His brother who had always done everything he had done – only better – ignored him. His sister was concentrating on the mobile on her lap under the table.

'That's nice! Where are ye daein' that? Doon the resi?' His mother sat hunched on her chair as though she were cold, even though it was June. She smiled at him vaguely.

'Na!' He was indignant. 'In the school. We're all tae bring newspapers for the *paper mashy* and the one that brings the maist paper gets tae ignite the volcano. Will ye gie me the auld papers, Da?'

The Star was unresponsive.

'The bairn's speakin' tae . . .'

'Shit!' A sharp, painful squeal from his sister diverted attention from him to her.

'You seen a moose?' scoffed Sean.

'We dinnae hae mice!' remonstrated his mother vaguely and none too confidently.

'He cannae gae oot the night!' shrieked Leanne. 'He's jist texed me. Got tae much hamework! That'll be right! He'll be oot wi' yon bitch, Simone.'

She banged up the threadbare stairs and slammed her bedroom door.

'Dinnae dae that! Treat oor hoose wi' respect or you'll be oot!' bawled *The Star*.

Liam relinquished the ketchup bottle and accepted defeat with resignation. But that night when he was in bed, in the quiet-without-the-telly, Vesuvius slipped into his mind. He could see the smooth conical outline, almost phosphorescent under the stars, like a glossy holiday poster in the travel shop down the centre. At any time it could blow its top and the fire would shoot high into the dark. The scary film music would start up and get more scary as black smoke blotted out the stars and filled his nostrils with the stench of thousands of rotten eggs. Then the steep sides glowed red as the molten lava poured over the sides like hot strawberry jam over hot chocolate-sponge pudding. He ran before the molten lava, leading the townsfolk of Pompeii down to the sea where they all swam with dolphins in blue Mediterranean waters which were suddenly sunny and sparkling and warm . . .

The few copies of *The Star* which he had taken from the wheely-bin were redolent of onion and cigarette ash and Liam knew that they would compare unfavourably with the crisp piles of newspaper which some members of Primary 6 would be bringing in. He decided to call in at the newsagent on the way to school to beg for old newspapers. He was not altogether optimistic about his reception at Jackson's as he half knew that Mrs Jackson half suspected that he had lifted a large box of milk chocolate from the shelf last month while she was gossiping with a customer and had forgotten to pay for it. However, she not only gave him a large armful of old newspapers, she also supplied him with a black sack to put them in.

'It's the least I can do,' she remarked with pious smugness to his neighbour, Mrs Petrie, with the arms like the slabs of corned beef. He felt them watching him through a haze of cigarette smoke and it made him awkward and clumsy as he bundled the papers into the sack.

Miss McGregor had to concede that he had the winning bundle. The whole class were soon ripping paper enthusiastically, stirring the shreds into wallpaper paste in an old enamel tub, and, under strict supervision, constructing a large conical shape with a promising hole at its apex through which the fire would burst and the lava would flow. They left it to dry and proceeded with the rest of the day's work. Miss McGregor was a young and enthusiastic teacher who favoured the thematic approach and the whole day's work was inspired by her thoughts on Pompeii. As far as Liam was concerned, discus throwing came a very poor second to the usual period of football and long division could not be improved by the fact that he was having to divide 4,250 figs among 75 Pompeian schoolboys. He'd never seen a fig but his grandmother had once given him Syrup of Figs for constipation.

'That amount o' figs'll gie them all the skitters,' he whispered to his mate, George, who promptly blew a very loud raspberry. Miss McGregor kept him in at break instead of George. George came from a 'nice home', which weighed heavily on Miss McGregor's scales of justice.

He occupied himself at break by looking at one of the books on Vesuvius from the neat pile on the table. It was about the eruption that took place in the year AD 79. According to the book, the townspeople had been utterly unprepared for the eruption and the molten lava had enveloped them so fast that they had been preserved in the lava flow doing whatever they were doing. One woman had been baking bread, marvelled the writer, and there was a picture of her lying next to her oven to prove it. The book explained why the people went on living there despite the danger. It was because the volcanic soil was very fertile. It showed pictures of smiling slightly tipsy-looking Italian farmers, grinning behind mounds of harvested grapes with Vesuvius looming in the background.

In the bus on the way home, he punched George for not owning up about the raspberry and then he told him about the woman who had been caught in the lava flow baking bread.

'You could hae bin daein' anything!'

'What if ye were in the bog and WHOOSH ye were flushed awa' wi' lava?'

'Lava in the lavvy!' They were hysterical.

'What if ye were SHAGGIN'?'

The woman in the seat in front of them turned round and glared at them. They spluttered laughter and George fell off the seat into the aisle. George and the woman got off at the same stop and Liam watched him as he walked past his own front gate and crossed onto the other side of the road so that the woman wouldn't find out where he lived. He watched him until the bus rounded the corner to plunge down the hill towards his estate.

At teatime he decided to go for it and scaled right up.

'I didnae need your stinkin' auld papers, Da,' he threw triumphantly towards *The Star* across the tea table. 'I got my ain AN' I'll be lighting the volcano.'

Predictably *The Star* was laid down long enough for him to receive a clip round his ear that made his cheek burn. But as soon as he had steadied his lips, he put in his bid for the last word.

'AN' ma teacher says that if parents skelp their kids they can get reported tae the European court an' probably get capital punishment.'

His mother sent him up to bed before *The Star* was laid down again, but he managed to take his plate with him and, as he lay in the darkness munching happily, he reconstructed the 'trapped in the lava scene' to his satisfaction. Miss McGregor was eternally scowling over long division on the blackboard; Jimmy Petrie, the bully, was sitting in the bog with his *designer* jeans forever splattered with lava and forever wrinkled around his *designer* trainers; Leanne was frozen in the act of *daein' it* vigorously with Jim Elliott in the Elliott garden shed while Simone, standing in the shed doorway, was never able to do anything to stop them; his mum was sitting at the kitchen table with her hands wrapped round a mug of tea, eternally waiting for nothing to happen, while his dad had *The Star* forever plastered to his face; George was kept in for a never-ending breaktime for blowing a raspberry just as the eruption took place and he himself ran past them all to the warm sea and the dolphins forever and ever.

In the morning Vesuvius was dry and sitting on a small table in front of the class. It had been painted bright Celtic green to simulate grass and was dotted with white, blue, yellow and red 'flowers'. In among the 'flowers' were little 'sheep' made out of wisps of cotton wool and matchsticks. Liam thought of the volcano he had imagined and felt an intense disappointment.

'Like Teletubby Lan',' he muttered in disgust to George who immediately started singing the Teletubby song. Liam moved away from him so that he wouldn't get the blame. It was important that he gave Miss McGregor no excuse to stop him from triggering the eruption.

Around Vesuvius were little flat-topped houses made out of matchboxes and other small boxes and painted a sparkling white with little red roofs. Liam thought they looked like the houses in the new private estate where George lived, but he didn't have time to say so because Miss McGregor had started issuing commands in her penetrating early-morning voice. She arranged the children carefully into a photogenic pose behind the table and took photographs of her model with them in the background. Predictably, Liam was stationed out of sight at the back, but he came forward quickly when she sang out gaily, 'Time for the eruption!'

She sighed, put her hands stiffly and awkwardly on Liam's shoulders and planted him in front of Vesuvius. From under the table she produced a large jug of what looked like thick cold gravy. She reached into her briefcase and produced a short spindly sparkler, a box of matches and a taper. As she stuck the sparkler firmly into the lump of brown plasticene which she had used to seal the crater, the silence was broken only by Catriona Murphy's sniffing. She lit the taper and handed it to Liam.

'When it's half-burned,' she enunciated with emphatic slowness, 'you empty the jug down the sides of the volcano so that it goes all over the houses.'

Liam's hand was shaking.

'Don't be nervous,' she added charitably.

But Liam was not nervous. Fury was smouldering inside him. This fake, pretty little hill with its fairy sparkler sticking out of it like the Teletubby horn, this pretty world, which adults like Miss McGregor were always try to flog to unsuspecting children, was the world to which he never had belonged and never would. Where were the people shuddering in the little houses? The unemployed das, hiding their faces and their poverty behind the sports pages of *The Star*? The mums half away to never-never land on their valium? Where were the schoolchildren with the non-Nike trainers and the shame of free school meals? Where was he? Where was the real Vesuvius with its quivering black rage and evil sulphurous smell?

Though his hand shook, he lit the sparkler. It made a faint hissing noise and little spangles dropped prettily in among the 'sheep' and 'flowers'.

Miss McGregor clapped loudly and, on cue, so did all the children. She handed him the jug but his shaking hand could not grasp it and he allowed it to fall to the floor. The gravy-stuff splashed all over Miss McGregor's skirt. She uttered a little shriek and rushed over to the sink in the far corner to mop it, followed by a host of little girls. Liam seized the moment. He lit all the little cardboard houses. There was a wonderful mass conflagration of the fake and the false. The flowers blackened and the little 'sheep' shrivelled up in the heat. The mountain loomed magnificently through fire and smoke. The smoke detector screeched; the fire alarm wailed. It was superb. The children were marshalled outside. Glancing backwards, he saw the janitor throw two buckets of water over the flaming Pompeii.

He could give offer no satisfactory explanation for his behaviour and the Head had 'no alternative' but to send him home. She phoned his parents and told them to expect him. He heard snatches of her side of the conversation through the partly open door.

'SHOCKED and disappointed . . . Miss McGregor tries to do her best . . . VERY best . . . VANdalism . . . ARSE on' (he felt disbelief) '. . . looking for your supPORT . . . we have funds for the correct uniform . . . soap and water . . . GUARantee better behaviour.'

Then she walked him to the bus stop, yanking him on a chain of recrimination and reproach. On the way they passed the janitor carrying the remains of Vesuvius to the skip.

'I expect your parents will be very angry and will ground you for a very long time,' was her parting shot.

George would have been grounded, he thought. *His* father did not know about modern methods of disciplining his children. He tried to remember what Miss McGregor had said about the European Court of Human Rights, but he hadn't really been listening to her. He considered running away, but he couldn't think of anywhere to go.

For once his parents were waiting for him. His mother looked as she usually did – vaguely disappointed and more than a little confused. His father was sitting in his normal chair but *The Star* lay folded on his knee and in his face the real shame and the real disappointment and the real humiliation were unmasked. Liam felt a hot pain welling up inside him before the blistering tears scorched down his cheeks as he stood silent.

Da put out his hand hesitantly, as though he wasn't quite sure where Liam was standing, and ruffled his hair.

'It's all right, son,' he whispered. 'It's all right.'

That night in his dark room, Liam did not see his shining black mountain erupt. He did not hear the rumbling from inside it, nor smell the sulphurous stench, nor see the hot, red lava. Nor did he rush into the warm, blue sea, full of dolphins. His mountain had somehow collapsed into an ignominious, ill-defined hump of burnt-out matter. He saw himself in blue denim overalls, working in the warm Mediterranean sunshine, working with rake and hoe till his hands blistered, working the fertility in the ash, so that in the shadow of the mountain there would once more be vines heavy with grapes.

Drying the Man Out

Sue Rullière

Brenda observes her husband across the kitchen table. His watery blue eyes – the ones she fell in love with ten years ago – are weary and unfocused. Greying, thinning hair falls around his scrawny face, still creased from sleep. He stirs his mug of tea twenty-seven times. This is, Brenda notes, five times more than usual. Mind you, earlier in the week he'd stopped at a mere eleven. Just stopped, and put his spoon down. She'd almost asked him for an explanation.

Tom raises his voice above the whirr of the washing machine and asks Brenda to pass the milk. He takes the carton with a rough, bony hand and pours clumsily. Brenda used to find his hands masterful. How many faulty toilets have they since explored? How many blocked drains have they probed? There must be a drier, more savoury way of earning a living, she insists. But plumbing's what I do, says Tom.

Tom's cornflakes are swimming in milk. In pursuit of maximum sogginess, he submerges those floating on the surface with the back of his spoon. This done, he scoops and slurps. Brenda stares into her tightly held coffee-cup.

'It rained in the night,' says Tom, glancing at Brenda.

Brenda folds down the inner cornflakes packet several times, ensuring air-tightness. She closes the box and slots it back on the shelf, between biscuit tin and teabags. The 500-gram pack is a perfect fit. When Tom once bought the larger size, it made life very difficult for a while.

A drip is forming on Tom's nose. Brenda looks away. There must be a tool in his toolbox for dripping noses.

Tom wipes his nose on the sleeve of his pyjamas and chases one last remaining cornflake round his bowl of milk. Biting her lip, Brenda spreads margarine thinly on crisp, dry toast. She sometimes pours milk away before breakfast, hoping to limit cornflake-chasing. But Tom always goes and buys more, there and then, with a coat on over his pyjamas. It isn't the answer.

Errant flake captured, Tom raises the bowl to his lips and sucks up the surplus milk. He gulps down his tea and rinses his mug at the sink. He doesn't bother to leave it upside-down to drain.

'I'll go for me bath then,' he mumbles, padding out of the kitchen. His bare feet leave a trail of damp prints on the floor.

The washing machine falls quiet for a moment, contemplating its next move. Brenda listens as Tom goes slowly upstairs: sixteen heavy steps, taken without ambition. She cuts her toast into two neat triangles, which she starts eating from the sharpest point inwards. Always from the sharpest point inwards. She braces herself for the sound of sloshing as Tom soaps and rinses. All attempts at persuading him to use the shower have failed. 'If you want to save water, you can share me bath,' he said once. She shudders and wipes a stray crumb from her lip.

Beside her, the washing machine begins its spin cycle, working itself up into a frenzy. Its relentless juddering reverberates in Brenda's head. With teeth clenched and fingers drumming, she pictures Tom as a giant cornflake immersed in hot water. Every time he has a bath he gets soggier. That is the problem.

Brenda met Tom at an office party. He'd fixed a leak, exchanged his spanner for a beer and got chatting to the girls from Accounts. Brenda couldn't take her eyes off him: this strong, sturdy man with power over burst pipes and eyes as blue as the oceans. She giggled, drained her wineglass and walked straight up to him. 'My basin's blocked,' she announced. 'When can you come and fix it?'

The first time they made love was in the bathroom. The second time was in the bath itself. She had pipes changed, taps checked, cracks filled, overflows replaced – anything to get him into the house. She plied him with cups of tea and his favourite water biscuits. When they tried making love in the bedroom, to avoid hard surfaces, Tom said it didn't feel right. So she had a carpet fitted in the bathroom and they came to the sound of running water.

Brenda told no one. He was her secret lover who mended leaks and made her drip with desire. She'd never been happier. The girls at work teased her, guessing there was someone, but never guessing who.

One day, when Tom was checking the ballcock in the cistern, Brenda said they should get married. 'If you like,' Tom muttered, without looking up. Brenda booked the local Registry Office. They couldn't get married in a church, she reckoned. Not after all that bonking in the bathroom. She bought a suit, in pale blue, and a huge floppy hat. The girls at work were beside themselves with curiosity: 'Who is he? What's he like? What does he do?'

'You'll see,' Brenda replied smugly.

On the day of the wedding, it rained solidly. All day. Brenda's hat became floppier than it was meant to be. There was no avoiding it.

The girls arrived straight from the office in high heels and a state of excitement. They greeted Brenda with a yelp: 'It's the plumber! Brenda! What the hell are you doing with the plumber?'

'Well . . . he's studying to be a marine biologist, actually,'

Brenda lied, unexpectedly. She looked across at Tom, standing awkwardly to one side, wiping the rain from his face with the sleeve of his hired suit. His hair was matted and stuck to his scalp. Why hadn't he brought an umbrella? He could cope with water in pipes, it seemed, but not with the sort that fell from the sky. His blue eyes looked grey in the rain.

Half an hour later, it was over. Brenda watched flakes of confetti float briefly in puddles, then drown. She tried in vain to revive her hat.

The following day, Tom moved his things into Brenda's house. She made space for his clothes and his books on DIY. His towels filled the airing cupboard and his razors cluttered the bathroom. He brought with him bottles of pills and a strange-smelling dandelion tea – to help with his waterworks, he said.

There was no time for a honeymoon. Too much needed doing in the house. Brenda wanted the whole place decorated, each room a different colour. Tom said he had customers waiting, but she explained that the house took priority. So he made phone calls, bought tins of emulsion and got on with the job.

One by one, the rooms took on new hues: Spring Shower Green, Honeydew Yellow, Watermelon Pink. Brenda rushed home from work each evening, eager to see what had changed. A wet kiss from Tom was received on the cheek. Then she checked for flaws in the paintwork and counted the empty mugs that charted his progress from one wall to the next. If he drank less tea, he'd get more done, she commented dryly.

Tom had just started on the bathroom – a delicate shade of Sea Spray Blue – when Brenda first noticed the damp patches: on the wall above his side of the bed, on one of the cushions on the settee, on the leaves of a pot-plant she hadn't watered for ages. There was condensation on the windows and a musty smell. She held a hair-dryer to the damp patches and turned up the heating, in an attempt to dry the place out. There was something not right, she said. It must be to do with the paint. Maybe in future he should stick to plumbing.

Gradually she realised that Tom himself was over-moist. When he walked barefoot, he left wet prints in the carpet. His eyes watered, his nose ran and he had too much saliva. It was as if he hadn't dried out properly since the wedding. She urged him to cut down on tea and baths, both of which he took to excess. But that was just the way he was, he said; you can't expect to change a man.

Brenda saw her dreams beginning to trickle away down the plughole. If only she'd married an electrician, things could have been so different. She became suspicious of the bathroom, insisting they make love in the bedroom, without sound effects and with a towel to protect the sheets.

But Tom couldn't function like that. He needed contact with water. It was his undeclared passion. He was having an affair with it, right under her nose, yet she was powerless to stem its flow. His manliness was draining away. She had a wet, drippy husband.

Tom appears back in the kitchen, still damp from his shower. 'Can't you even dry yourself properly?' Brenda implores.

'I'll put the washing out,' says Tom. He empties the machine of its load: four days' worth of their separate lives combined in a sodden, chaotic mass.

Brenda watches him walk in sandals through dew-damp grass to the far end of the garden. His white shirt sticks to his back; the clothes basket balances on his hip; his jeans hang loosely from his waist. She sips her black, sugarless coffee.

Beneath the grubby plastic washing-line and a tree heavy with apples, Tom stoops over the basket. He untangles each item in turn and rearranges their lives in a row, with wooden pegs. His brushed cotton shirts hang limply in the breeze beside her billowing polyester blouses. Brenda winces at the disorderly array of unmatched socks: stripes mixed with diamonds, brown with grey. It makes putting the things away afterwards so tiresome. But Tom just won't understand.

Brenda rinses her coffee-cup and leaves it upside-down to drain. She gazes, unblinking, through the window.

A glint of a smile appears in her eyes.

The washing-line's sagging now, like the tree. Tom's left his sandals beside the basket. His feet are clamped to the line between a blouse and a sock. She counts ten clothes pegs, one on each toe. He's hanging with his arms folded across his chest, head skimming the ground, gently swaying in the breeze. Moisture from his body is trickling off him into the grass. His face is puffed up and swollen. Liquid's spouting from his gaping mouth, like water from an overflow pipe or some ornamental gargoyle – it doesn't matter which.

Still staring, Brenda slowly dries her hands. He might at least have pinned himself higher up, closer to the post, so as to keep his head clear of the ground.

Blue dye starts seeping from his jeans, staining his shirt and soaking into his folded arms. It streaks down his face and drips off his hair. The ground beneath him turns blue as it sucks the colourful liquid deep within itself. Blue apples appear on the tree. She wonders what blue apples taste like.

She's warned him, of course, about mixing coloureds and whites. He should have listened. He's only himself to blame.

She fears he'll take longer to dry than the other clothes, being so wet to start with. But the sun comes out, strong and warm, sucking the final drops of moisture from his body. He hangs there, paper-thin and brittle, rustling in the breeze. Brenda frowns: ten pegs seem wasted on something so light.

She goes upstairs to brush her teeth.

New Shoes

Esther McLeod

She looked down at her feet standing in her new shoes. They didn't look like her feet and the shoes didn't look like they had in the shop. In the shop they'd looked just right; plum-coloured suede soft enough to sink your teeth into and the strap with its gold buckle making her ankles even thinner. She hadn't hesitated at all before she'd said, 'Yes, thanks, I'll take them.'

But that was months ago and felt like a different life. Now, in the wardrobe mirror, they looked like they were trying too hard, straining to make her tall and elegant and she couldn't even straighten her legs properly when she walked. Desperate was the word that came to mind. A desperately-trying-hard woman with tight knees, but trying hard at what?

She felt like taking them off, and her tights, and her skirt, and her clingy top that made her skin cold, and her amber beads that made her neck hot, and her make-up, and then last and best of all her rough lace underwear. Between the sheets she could lie still and slowly heat the bed, aware of the others in the background, their voices moving around the house, distant and separate from herself.

When she'd been ill she'd never got up, unless to journey to the bathroom. She'd moved slowly as if already old and frail, and returning to her bed felt like a homecoming. She'd slip her hand into the cool dark under the pillow and feel the smooth tight sheet as the comfortable edge of her safety. All she had to do was lie there, not talk or respond or even think, just lie and let the random shots of pain flicker inside.

But now she had to go out. In these shoes. She practised walking towards the mirror; heel down first and tilt the hip, pelvis forward, shoulders back, look bored. The more she posed the better it worked, but she needed a mirror to pose.

Chris looked in round the corner of the door, his eyes on her legs stalking across the room. 'Great,' he grinned. 'Is that catwalking?'

She stopped, hand on hip and scowling, 'If you like.' He smelt of lemons and alcohol, his chin shiny blue with the second shave.

'Well, that's the babysitter here. Kids have already got her in the bedroom bombarding her with all their stuff. So . . . you ready?'

'No.'

'Alison, you look gorgeous. Really.'

She smiled at him for trying and for a second he looked relieved and much younger. Then he went off to the kids' room for goodnight kisses.

Alison got her coat and shouted her goodbyes from the front door. If she went into their bright room strewn with books and toys and their beds waiting like little nests, she knew she'd be lost. And Chris, his patience grinding, would have to start all over again, 'Come on, Alison, enough's enough. You're over it now for Christ's sake. The doctor said that weeks ago, absolutely fine. It's just you, you have to force yourself and get on with it. Really.'

Outside was cold and dark, the pavement slick, although the rain had slowed to a fine mist that hung in halos round the streetlights. Going down the steps she gripped Chris's arm and held on. He held the bottle of wine trying to read the label, 'No, it's okay,' he said. 'Thought I'd picked up the wrong one,' and then he squeezed his arm, crushing her hand close. 'It's nice to have you hanging on to me like that. Clutching me.'

Easier to smile and say nothing. She concentrated on the pavement as it rushed up too fast and made her ankles jar. She heard her steps clattering along, like some parody of a woman, and she wondered if she'd have to speak or if she'd be able to get by with just smiling the whole night.

Too soon, they were there. Chris rang the bell and the door was opened by a dark-haired woman smiling them into the light and heat and noise. Chris kissed the woman on both cheeks and as her hand rested on his shoulder Alison thought it looked very big for a female hand, fine black hairs running across the wrist and a little beyond the watch strap. She tried to remember what the woman's name was, but the voices and music buzzed in the background and the sweet smell of clary sage oil burned and thickened in her head, and she kept breathing in until she was all air and could smile again. She moved forward and gave the woman her coat and a smile with the kisses and didn't say anything.

No need, the woman didn't stop to draw breath as she led them through the hall past the cloakroom and into the kitchen of spotlights and stainless steel and many people. She slotted them into a small group, her big hands waving around, and left to get them drinks. Chris seemed to know the other guys, both dressed from head to foot in shades of brown, and the tall girl with a drooping head of curls and a transparent top showing tiny breasts. Alison readjusted her smile so it wouldn't get stuck and tried but couldn't catch the words they tossed about.

Someone handed her a drink, a tall glass of thick red liquid flecked with black seeds. It reminded her of iced soup, and as she sipped, her throat and stomach heaved against the chemical taste like bubblegum and meths. She swirled it round in the glass for a moment or two then stepping back, placed it on the counter top and pushed it away with her fingers. Picking up someone else's newly opened bottle of beer instead, she wiped the top thoroughly with her palm before drinking.

She leaned back against the cold steel and watched. An open doorway led through to the sitting room, long black couches with people sitting there. Some slumped into the leather with their drinks rested on their stomachs like they'd been there for hours and couldn't bring themselves to move, while others perched on the edge of their seats, their legs bent and stunted beneath them. They all talked and talked, like they were the best of friends and wanted nothing more than each other's company, and everything they said made them laugh and say more, their voices mixing and cutting in an incessant flow. Perhaps they were only repeating a phrase, or the same meaningless word like a crowd scene of extras. Had she been a better actor she could have slipped in among them, but that ability had left her, and besides there were enough of them already, they didn't need another. An extra extra. She hadn't said anything at all yet, and the longer she didn't speak the harder it was to utter a word because it was never the right one, never important enough to break the silence.

A girl squeezed past brushing against her in a wave of perfume and dark hair. 'Sorry,' she smiled over her shoulder and kept going. A pretty face, that no doubt Chris would find soon too and end up dancing with or talking to, close and earnest in a dark corner. He'd moved into a different group standing by the fridge and catching Alison's eye beckoned her over to join them. She stared back but didn't move. The fridge was tall with a glass door and a variety of bottled beers to choose from. To get one would entail walking five paces maybe and then she'd either have to join Chris or turn and walk the five paces back and she knew her steps would be rusty and awkward, like her words if she had to speak. It was easier to stay put and just pretend to drink from her empty bottle.

Without warning, the guy beside her turned and raised very straight dark eyebrows at her and said, 'Hi.'

She could tell he liked her; people raise their eyebrows when they greet someone they think attractive, something to do with letting more light into their eyes, either so they could see better or so they looked better, she couldn't remember which.

'I'm Jeff, by the way. I work with Mark . . .'

This meant nothing to her and she waited while he went on. 'And you? Are you a friend of Elaine's?'

Elaine, that must be the woman who'd let them in, whom they'd given the wine and kisses to, but could she say she was a friend? It didn't feel very honest and she was in so much doubt it seemed safer to stick to the truth and it was such a short simple word to start with.

'No,' she said.

'Mark then. You know Mark?' His eyebrows went up again. He was trying to help her; she could see that but all that came out was, 'No.'

'So you came with some other people then? Some other friends?'

More, she had to give more. 'I don't have any friends here. I came with my husband.'

As he laughed a spray of spit flew from his mouth and landed in a spatter across her chest. She watched, waiting for the last, minute bubble to burst and sink with the rest into the cold fabric of her top. When she looked up he'd turned away and was talking to the woman on his other side. Now they'd spoken, she felt quite friendly towards the pale-blue expanse of his back, the dark short hairs on his neck and she angled her body towards him. The woman he was talking to kept darting her glances over his shoulder, more puzzled than friendly, but Alison smiled back.

'You all right?' Chris's hot hand gripped above her elbow. Pulling her arm away she pretended to take a drink of beer. 'You don't look it. Come over and talk to Elaine for a bit. She's really nice, y'know, you'll like her.'

Alison watched the muscle of his jaw flinching while his eyes held a softer, searching worry. 'Please,' he said finally, and she moved closer, leaning in, and allowed him to propel her across the floor into the circle of people. Bright under the beam of the spotlight shining on the heads, the faces distorted into planes of light and shadow like masks, each mouth open and noisy. A man opposite wore tinted glasses and she saw two of herself reflected, her forehead and nose looming large and white, her eyes hidden in their dark hollows.

'Love your shoes, Alison,' Elaine said and everyone looked down at her feet. She glanced, too, and they still didn't look like her own; they were too far away. She felt unsteady without Chris's arm there, in danger of falling with nothing to hold.

'It's okay,' she smiled although she hadn't really staggered. They all kept watching her, waiting for more. 'I'm just going to go to the . . .' she turned and made her feet go one in front of the other, stiff and shaking across the floor.

'If it's not free, use the one upstairs,' Elaine called after her.

The hall was cool, clear of cigarette smoke, only the sweet oil heavy in the air. She leaned back against the wall with her eyes closed just breathing, in and out until the shaking stopped. Such faces they all wore in there, knowing what to say and how to act, how to be. She must have known all that at one point, she'd laughed and danced with men she'd newly met, talked and teased about . . . what? What was it she couldn't remember? Like trying to find her way back into a dream looking for the sense it held, and only catching a glimpse in time to watch it dissolve and slip from her reach. And now, where was she now if all that was a dream? She opened her eyes and waited to see. She looked up through the stairwell, up through the cupola into the dark sky above the glass and felt safe for a moment.

Suddenly the music from the sitting room jumped in volume and a whooping joined with the dance track. Although the toilet door in the hall stood open, she started up the stairs, her thighs weak and trembling and each step sinking in the thick carpet. At the top, so many doors, all panelled and painted white, she didn't know which to take. The first she opened was a box room, piled high to the ceiling with cardboard and plastic and a heap of squashed dusty shoes on the floor.

The next was a bedroom. The master bedroom, she thought as she clicked on the light and saw the expanse of cream carpet and the king-sized double enthroned in the middle. With the door shut behind her the music died to a muffled beat and she heard her long sigh steady in the quiet.

On the wall hung black-and-white prints, close-ups of bare skin curving into creases and crevasses of hair, isolated sections it was difficult to place. There was another white-painted door in the corner, and as she crossed the room she caught her reflection in the tall dark window doing the same: a small woman moving through bright empty space.

The door led into a white-tiled bathroom, hotel fresh in its polished chrome and glass, towels folded on the rail, fat and white and waiting. She closed the lid of the toilet and sat down, took off her shoes and her tights, her skirt and top, put her beads on the glass but let her underwear drop on the floor with the rest, and stepped into the shower. Twisting it as hot as she could bear, she stood with her face turned up to the spray rubbing hard at her make-up and pulling at her skin. In the mirrored tiles she looked back at herself, her eyes pale in their circles of waxy black. She shut off the water. Tried drying herself with a towel too soft to absorb much. Still damp, she crossed the carpet, lovely on her bare feet, switched off the light by the door and got in between the cool sheets of the bed. It spread around her, vast and welcoming, even the unfamiliar scent was soothing. She could feel the pulse from downstairs, separate and distant, and imagined herself safe and suspended high above their heads.

The Girl Who Died In Her Sleep

Douglas Noble

There was a tremor in the thin meat crescent of Malachi's closed eye. His soft black fur ruffled in small waves beneath the action of a hand brushing over him. From Malachi's throat came a rumbling sound, and he stretched his body back toward the touch. He purred deep within himself.

'I wonder what he dreams of?' There was a voice then, a male voice, not the voice of the one who was stroking Malachi.

There was a moment of sparkle, a shine. It moved back and forth across the cat's fur. The little glint of a ringed finger. There was a stone set in the ring: sapphire, or tinted glass. The blue of it in the light, showing up like white fire. Sparks. Bright even beside the skin of the hand that stroked him, that pale skin, that sort of pale.

Malachi purred as Ava stroked him. She felt the shift of his ribs beneath his fur, beneath his skin. The ring on her finger glinted as she moved her hand, moved her arm, but it glinted in such a different way to her dress. The dark-red silk ribboned with highlights. The strands of brightness traced the curve of her, the long lines of her body, of her legs. It lay tight about her, held up by impossibly thin straps, it drew in the light of the room, warming her paleness. The silk seemed to make her glow. It filled her eyes and widened her smile. He thought. Noel thought.

He sat beside her on the low bed, sitting awkward with his long legs twisted under him. It was the first thing he'd noticed as he came in. The low bed. He sat next to her, looking at her, trying to work that one out. The bed on the floor, the pattern of the cloth that covered it, yellow and red. Noel tried not to look at the spot where her dress had ridden up a little higher against the white of her smooth thigh. At least he imagined her thigh felt smooth.

'I don't know, I think, I think that if we could ever really know that then we'd just, ah, just be cats.' She gave Noel a slow sort of blink and he had to steady himself with the wineglass. The red wine she'd poured for him moved about its glass in little waves. Up on the wall there was a picture of a skinny girl that Noel almost recognised. Something about the way she was standing, or lying, he found it hard to tell which. Noel tried to look about, to take in all the things she had in her room, but he kept looking back over her. It was when she moved a little, when she stretched herself, the fine lines of her neck changing, or her hair falling over one eye. It was the soft shift of her breath on her breast, the lines of light changing in the silk. It was the stroke of her fingers on the lazy cat, the elegant tracings of her fingers as she stroked it, the designs, the patterns. The glint of her ring, the patterns through ruffled fur.

'How d'you mean?' Noel asked.

Ava looked up from Malachi, stopping the movement of her hand for a second. 'It's just, well, if you know as much as someone's dreams, then really, I think, you're pretty much going to *be* them anyway.'

Noel nodded. 'Right,' he said. He didn't know what else to say.

Ava resumed stroking the cat, and her eyes went down to him, nestled warm in her lap. Noel gripped his glass, stem trapped between two fingers, uncomfortable there. His eyes kept on her, when he tried to glance away he only felt more awkward.

'Mmm?' she queried, directing the sound towards the cat. 'What you say?' Malachi opened one eye slowly and gave her a long look.

'Doesn't look like he's saying much,' said Noel, desperate to say something.

'No, he's saying plenty. Aren't you? Aren't you?' She laughed lightly, the sound floating above her.

'It's funny,' she said, 'when he does that. Do you know what he reminds me of? This time a girl in my school, she was trying to, she fancied this teacher. She was always trying to give him the eye. That's what she would say: "Watch me give him the eye," and she'd do this y'know totally over-the-top kind of thing, drawn out for ages. I mean, really, she must have been doing this the lengths of entire lessons. It's just that. It reminded me of that. Always did.'

'And did she?' Noel asked.

'What?'

'The teacher? Did she ever manage to?'

'Who? Karen? Oh, no. No, she never did. But, I mean who gets what they want at that age? I'm sure I wanted to have a pony or something, or be a princess. It never happened though.'

'Oh, I don't know.'

Ava wrinkled her nose at him. 'But really? No, I mean it. You never do. It's those things that get you all through life, they say. The things that get you up at night, wishing you'd done something a bit different, or sooner, or at all. Those things that stop you getting to sleep. If you'd only . . . you know. I sometimes think my memories are like those old crime-scene photographs that you see. The ones that turn up on programmes about forensics, or miscarriages of justice. It's like you can look at these pictures of air crashes, or slit wrists, or whatever, but there's nothing you can do. You can't go back and warn them, like, don't take that cab, or don't go home alone. It's like that with memories. There's nothing you can ever do to help.'

Ava stopped speaking and started to rub Malachi's stomach again. The cat purred and stretched. Noel didn't know what to say. His free hand gripped the covers, twisting the pattern into something new.

She looked up. 'But now what must you think of me?' She picked the cat up off her lap and held him in the air for a second, facing Noel. 'Ask Malachi,' she said, smiling. 'He'll vouch for me.' Malachi grabbed at the sheets with his claws and bolted from Ava's hands.

'Maybe not,' she said. The cat disappeared behind the side of the mattress. Ava fell back onto the bed with a sigh, letting the fall knock the breath out of her.

'But, God, I'm tired.'

Noel smiled, slow on him. 'Yeah, I suppose,' he said. 'We've been on the go for, how long?'

'Urggh, too long, I think.' She covered her eyes with her hands for a second, and then pushed herself up into a sitting position. 'Still,' she said, 'it was worth it, no?'

'Yeah, it was.' Noel's voice dropped to a low, warm hum. The words melted together – 'Idddwazzz.'

Ava stood up, and turned to face Noel, looking down at him. Noel put his knees up almost to his chin and hugged them, looking up at her. His eyes moved past the skin of her legs, the soft fabric glimmer.

'I'm going to the bathroom, to get changed,' she said, her voice soft, not quite drowsy. 'You're going to have to share the mattress, at this side.'

'Right,' said Noel, 'but I've not, ah, I've not brushed my teeth yet.'

Ava raised an eyebrow. 'Did you bring a toothbrush?'

'Well, no. No, I didn't.'

'So, then how were you going to?'

Noel looked a little confused. 'Oh,' he said, 'I suppose.' Ava smiled.

'Right,' she said. 'See you in a bit.' She turned then, and for a second, in the twirl of that action, there was a little raising of her skirt, and Noel's eyes, without any thought, darted towards this fresh flesh, this new intimacy. Then Ava was gone, out of the room. The door clicked shut behind her.

Noel sat staring at the chipped paintwork for a couple of seconds before he set to work, untying the laces of his boots, pulling the laces from their holes. He could hear Ava puttering about in the adjoining room, the sound of water running. He'd be in bed before she got back, he'd be under the covers quickly. He noticed Malachi eyeing him evilly as he took off his shirt. Fine, thought Noel. It was strange that the cat should look at him like that. He'd never done anything to hurt it. Noel stood and slipped his trousers down his legs, letting them crumple in a heap. He pulled back the covers and slid between them, feeling the crisp new cold there.

From behind him he heard the creak of a door, and he turned, seeing the gleam of her skin for a second before the click of the light switch clothed them both in a sudden darkness.

'Where are you?'

'Uh, here.'

'Uh-huh.'

He felt her step over him, on to the other side of the mattress. The blanket barely stretched between them. She tugged at it.

'Stealer.'

'S'my cover.'

Noel looked at her back, seeing it now blue in the weak light. Above the thin cotton of her nightdress, he could see the first few notches of her spine, dented with a deeper shadow. He could feel the cold on his own back, and pulled at the blankets.

'Nut. You're no getting it,' she said.

'Then I'll have to move closer.'

'So?'

Noel moved closer, trying to keep from touching her, his arm awkward at his side, knees digging into each other.

'Tell me a story,' she said, her voice suddenly heavy with sleep.

'Like what?'

'I don't know, don't you know any stories?'

'No, I . . . I can't think,' said Noel. 'I mean, I suppose I could, I could tell you about the time my mother, the time I remember lies for the first, uh . . . time.'

'Okay then.'

'Right, ah. No, the first time that I remember lies, and this was my mother who told it. Well, my little sister, you know my sister? Well, she and I, ah, we must have been arguing, having an argument about something or other. We were little, after all, just kids. Anyway, Jeannie called me a sod and my mother must have heard her because she comes up and tells her not to say it, not to say that word because it's bad. So my sister says why? What's it mean? If it's so bad, well, why? And my mother said, and this is the lie, that it's a word for someone who drinks too much. But even then maybe, we knew that was a sot, you know? A sot. We know that now, I mean. That's not what a sod is, I mean . . .'

All of a sudden Noel became acutely aware of the way he was lying behind Ava. He almost choked.

'So, ah that's the first lie I can remember.'

'Is that all?'

'Ah, yeah.'

'Then you've been lucky,' said Ava, and reached back and

took his hand. She squeezed it softly. They lay together like that, for a little while, until something else happened.

Afterwards, they lay steaming in the cold air. From somewhere Noel could hear the steady padding of a cat's footfalls. He looked at Ava, his eyes used to the light but not what he was seeing. The angles of her, the shapes. They still lay tangled in each other; he could feel her stroking him, her hands on his hip, on the base of her back.

Noel looked at her eyes, the lids that he had kissed. She blinked slowly, lazily, her eyes becoming everything for a second.

'Hey, you,' she said.

'Mmm,' he said in return, falling back towards her. They kissed again. Skin pressing against skin, fingers tracing the impression of spines as if they were playing the clarinet, or the oboe.

Noel opened one eye and saw Malachi staring at him, expression unreadable. He felt Ava's mouth twist into a grin beneath his own. She made a noise then, an old noise, contented. It sounded almost like a purr. Malachi watched them.

Ava laid her head upon Noel's chest. When she spoke he could feel it. It was like she put the words into him, directly in, like with an injection, or a knife.

Looking down all he could see was her back, the shape of her shoulder, the hair on her head. She could have been anyone, he thought, anyone at all. He couldn't make out what she was saying, he couldn't think. Malachi had moved away and was now sitting up on a chair, looking down on the two of them, flicking his tail. The feel of her voice was sleepy. Noel couldn't help but look at the poster on the wall. In the half-dark of the room it looked almost familiar, reminding him of something he'd seen once, but he couldn't remember it, couldn't remember where. The picture was some art print, with a duplicated signature at the bottom. It showed a girl, either standing or lying down, with her arms raised over her head. Noel could see the dark shapes of her eyes and lips. Behind her, or beneath her, there was a dark striped shape: a blanket or towel, some kind of sheet. It haloed her pale form, or gave her dark wings, but in the half-light Noel couldn't tell.

'Who did the picture?' he asked Ava. She lifted her head and looked at him. He felt the shift of her against his skin.

'Um?' She was looking at his eyes.

'The picture – the wall,' he said. 'It seems, I don't know, familiar. Who did it?'

'Egon Schiele,' she said. 'Why? D'you like it?'

'I don't know. I think I saw something that looked like it once. I'm not sure.'

'I see,' said Ava, and she settled herself once more, this time at his shoulder, her lips brushing against the thin skin of his neck. When she spoke she sounded different to him. Too close. There was a deepening chord of sleep in her voice too, Noel could hear her slipping away, and in himself too, he could feel the ebb of him as he started to fall.

'I've always liked that painting,' Ava said, her voice drifting now and then. 'When I was little, well, I had a towel that was just the, just like the one in the painting. The background. I remember, me and my brother would tie towels around our necks. See, our house was ah, next to this other . . . house. There was a tunnel, like a wind tunnel. We'd get these towels and hold them over our heads and catch the wind, catch the air in these towels. When we were little, and the wind would push us back, and we'd fight against it, fight until we lost, we lost our grip . . . on the towels. And the towels would just, ah, whip back, fluttering behind us, like . . . like wings.'

Her voice had gotten more and more quiet, and by the last word Noel could tell that she was already asleep, only speaking out of a duty to her story. Noel could feel the difference, the new way of breathing she had, the rise and fall of her bosom against him.

Noel's eyes stuttered open to sunlight and for a second he couldn't remember where he was. The ceiling above him was so unfamiliar. He sat up sharply, dragging the blankets with him, and remembered. On his right Ava lay, uncovered now, skin white in the morning. Noel thought of old china. He looked down at her. He knew where he was. He knew who she was. He just didn't recognise her at all.

It was all to do with the way she lay, he thought. It was all to do with the way she held her arms.

Noel wondered what time it was. The colour of the light seemed washed out, sallow. It could only be early.

He looked down at her, her face, the lines of her neck, the shape of her breasts, the way in which she held her hands. He couldn't feel anything.

She lay on her back, her eyes closed, head tilted to the left. Her hair was hidden beneath her head, tucked under, secreted away. Ava had her right arm stretched up, bent at the elbow, her fingers rested against her cheek, just under her ear. Noel couldn't tell if she was smiling, he couldn't make up his mind. Ava's left hand was clenched into a tight fist and held just above her navel, except for her forefinger, pointing. Her small breasts seemed to lie vanished into her ribcage. Noel hesitated, unsure whether to touch her or not. Eventually he drew back.

He didn't know. He didn't know. Once he had seen a photograph, a long time ago it seemed. The name of the picture was *The Woman Who Died In Her Sleep*. It showed the body of a young woman, torn open and sewn back up, autopsy scar snaking up her torso. Looking down at Ava, Noel couldn't help but think of it. He couldn't think of anything else.

He looked down. All he could see was meat.

There was a soft sound and Malachi jumped onto the bed. He seemed to come out of nowhere. Slowly, very slowly, the cat started to walk towards Noel. Malachi came to Ava, and hesitated. Then he placed a forepaw on her, and started to walk over.

Noel looked at the cat, eyes wide and empty of understanding. Malachi stopped on Ava's stomach and glared at Noel. It's like he knows what I'm thinking, thought Noel. Then, still looking at him, the cat unsheathed its claws and scratched Ava, and suddenly Noel found himself staring into the eyes of a new woman.

'Oh, good morning,' she said.

Striking Out

Isabel Walter

She has been awake for hours, waiting for it to be the next day. Now a sallow light is groping its way around the curtains, nudging the room into shapes and shadows. Objects jostle for attention. She can't make sense of them at first, she doesn't know what they will be. Last night it had been so dark. But she was glad he'd kept the light off. And after all they are just ordinary: a bedside cabinet, a wicker chair, a wardrobe bulked in a corner.

He has hunched the duvet over, leaving her half bare. She looks washed out in this light, almost see-through, skin pulled taut as porcelain over joint and knuckle. Her body still takes her by surprise, the way it has billowed and swelled, the curve of her breasts, the balling of buttocks and hips. It is a woman's body, it looks as if it belongs to someone else. She has never had so much flesh before, smooth and firm like butter straight from the fridge. In short skirts and jeans her thighs chafe together and tiny red pinpricks grow where the sweat pools. When he found them he had fingered them lightly, curiously, as if they were infectious. But her belly has staved in, cupped between the sharp points of her pelvis. It's like he has hollowed it out with his touch.

She thinks there should be some trace, some staining at the edges, a smudge or smear from his hands. She didn't expect to look so white and clean when she feels so soiled, as if something has been scuttling over her skin.

She had thought it would be last night. She'd already told her mother she was staying with a girl friend. He'd asked her twice before and she'd wriggled out of it, keen as a kitten with clean-paw excuses. But she knew not to keep them hanging on, not to be a tease. It was all they talked about in the toilets at school. It wasn't nice to say yes the first time – that was slutty. But to keep on saying no, time after time, when you'd been with someone a while, that was frigid. That was tight.

Lick of lipstick, curl of mascara.

'That Elaine, she was with Tony last night.'

'She's slept with half the footie team since October!'

Laughter.

'Yeah, Elaine's a slag.'

'At least she's not a tease, though.'

They'd look over then, to where she was towelling her hands.

'At least she's not a tight stuck-up bitch.'

That's what Tom had thought she was. A tight stuck-up bitch. Tom had said she was cold and he hadn't needed to touch her to know. But things had been different with Tom. He was always trying to burrow into her head, he wanted to get so close. He'd said they were soul mates, and had a way of making her tell him things, even things she didn't want him to know, he made it seem right she should tell him. One afternoon in the summer she had climbed with him to the top of the law. You could see the whole city falling away below you, and the hills across the firth plump as cheeks and freckled with shifting shadows. The water between had glittered and stung. But he'd said they should lie down, so their world was pared down to grass and sky, a sweet turfy smell and the clouds bowling past high above them. She had hitched her T-shirt under her bra to let the sun at her skin. They were eating ice creams which dribbled in the heat down fingers and face and neck. He had leaned up on one elbow to look at her.

'So, are you on the pill, then, Maggie?'

She didn't move, kept on watching the clouds. 'No. Why should I be?'

He reached out a finger and traced around her belly button. 'Well, you know . . . I was thinking, maybe it might be a good idea.'

She waited a bit, chewing on her lip while she chewed over his words. 'You could always use something.'

'Oh, come on, Maggie, it's not the same like that. It doesn't feel right. You know.'

Damp had begun to seep sluggishly through her clothes. She tried to think of the right thing to say. She knew if she looked at him he would guess it, he would see it in her face, it was like she was always opened up to him. But in the end he'd guessed anyway; he'd started laughing and said, 'Maggie Henderson, you're a virgin, aren't you? Tell! Tell! Aren't you! *Are* you?' Then she'd wanted to bury her face away from him, he diminished her so, the way her older brothers could, and he was still laughing. 'You are! I knew it.' When she did look at him something in his eyes made her guts cramp. 'I could be your first. Oh come on, wee Maggie, let me be your first!' He doubled himself up by her knees. 'I'll be gentle with you, I promise, Maggie. Oh, let me!'

He'd made out to be playful, but she'd seen a greed in him that scared her. And after that she could never say yes to him. He'd held it as a trophy to claim as his own. She'd wanted it not to matter so much.

But she'd known as well how it would be if she kept on saying no, how it would grow and become something big and press down on her, one more thing to set her apart, to make her different, to make her somehow wrong.

* * *

Stuart hadn't thought she should go on the pill. He'd smart blue eyes and was decent and straight; she hadn't had to ask him to use something. He was older than her, a good few years; she'd wanted someone who'd know what to do. He even had his own flat in a whole other part of the city. He'd black hair and a wee earring and a leather jacket which she'd worn on the way back to keep warm. It smelt of dust and cigarettes and the nape of his neck. They had stopped at the fry bar by the dock, just like normal. He always wanted chips after a night out, and he'd buy her a chocolate bar for her bus home. Last night he'd bought her chocolate just the same, but she hadn't been able to eat it. Something was bunched like a fist inside her. She'd told him she'd save it for later and dug it deep in his inside pocket. It must still be there.

Last night there'd been a gig in a room above a pub; someone he knew was in the band. She'd lingered at the back while he lost himself in the crowd. She was shy around his friends; they made her feel schoolgirly and green. She'd sipped beer from a bottle, leaning against the windows and watching feathers of snow flurry in the orange of the street lamps below. When they turned up the lights he'd fought his way back to find her, his face shiny with sweat and pleasure. He was a little drunk.

'What did you think?' He tucked her hair behind her ears to study her the better.

'It was good. Kind of sparkly.'

He smiled, and took both her hands in his. Softly, 'D'you want to come back tonight?'

She nodded, but something skipped in her, and she looked quickly down into her drink. He caught up her chin and lifted her face, eyes on eyes. 'Hey. Are you sure this is what you want? No pressure.'

Yes. She was sure. She wanted it over with, now. She looked at him straight and remembered to smile. 'Yes. Sure.'

He'd relaxed then, happy as a puppy. Things were so simple and easy with him. 'Another drink?' She'd shaken her head and watched him thread his way to the bar. She didn't want to get too drunk. She'd heard stories about girls who got too drunk, girls who did things they regretted, who didn't remember stuff in the morning.

But she could remember it all, unglossed by alcohol. Their clumsiness had taken her aback. She had expected it to be like swimming, to have a pattern and flow, but they'd seemed to snag at one another. Maybe it was her fault. Maybe she *is* a tight stuck-up bitch.

When he'd touched her at the first he'd said she was cold, but she'd felt cold, she'd been goosebumping all the way through, she couldn't seem to get warm. It had made her feel grubby and pawed-at, like someone else's newspaper left on a train. It had made her think of a rhyme the boys had used to sing when she was small.

My Bonnie lies over the ocean
My Bonnie lies over the sea

She had known it was dirty, even when she didn't understand it. She had known from the way the boys sang it, their tone had made her skin shrink and she'd wanted to put her hands over her ears.

My Daddy lies over my Mummy
And that is how I came to be.

She must have been four or five, playing out with the other kids on the street. Anna was seven and had told Maggie what it meant behind the garages in giggles and fumbled whispers.

She remembers the indignation and disbelief that had marched her straight home. Her mother had been in the kitchen mixing bread. Sun was falling hot and yellow as egg yolk from the high windows behind her, blanking her face like a cut-out.

'It's not true, is it, Mummy, you and Daddy never . . .'

Her mother had lifted and folded dough, lifted and folded, lifted and folded. Her silence had entered the space between them like an eavesdropper. When she finally spoke her tone was low and cold. 'It's not nice to talk about such things.'

When it was over he'd said, 'You don't have to be such a bloody martyr about it.' Then he'd left her in the screwed-up sheets while he showered. That had made her feel unclean on the inside as well. She'd gathered up her clothes and pulled her T-shirt back on for comfort. Then she'd clenched herself right up at the edge of his bed. But in the end he'd come back damp and put his arm over where she was coiled and slept with her. That was the nicest part, the sleeping together. She likes the warmth of another body beside her.

Now when she holds herself very still she can hear the huff and slip of his breathing. She flexes out the flat of her palm to feel his heat through the covers, the soft rise and fall of his aliveness. Then she shifts carefully to the edge of the bed and stands up. He doesn't stir, still heavy with last night's beer. She puts on her clothes but they are cool with sitting out in the air all night and don't stop her shivering. She checks her pockets for purse and keys before slipping quietly down the stairs.

Outside, cold and brightness slap at her. She's giddy with tiredness and the sudden sun. She feels matted like an animal, her hair is knotted with sweat and sleep and she wishes she could brush it. She remembers suddenly how he ran his fingers slowly through its length as if it was something beautiful and thinks how it will be like this all day, suddenly remembering things, little things she will stow away and keep to herself.

She's never been here before, right out on the city's edge where it presses up against the sea. At the end of his street she stops to get her bearings, pursing her eyes in the low light. The main road curls above her but it's Sunday, too early yet for a bus home. She could stop in the shelter to wait, but she feels restless, like she wants to keep on moving. Instead she turns down the hill to the shore, walking quick as if it will shake off the way she's feeling.

The sky is perfectly clear, blueing from the pallor of dawn. She can tell by the light that she's near the sea. The park behind the waterfront is marbled with frost and the grass crackles under her step. There are puddles frozen white and puckered like warm milk left to stand. She has to be careful in her heels. The air feels brittle with cold, like it would shatter if she goes at it too fast. But the cold is good; it has a cleanness to it.

When she gets down on the beach, the sea has the same clean feel about it. It's stretched flawless and flat, a grey canvas pegged between shorelines. Rock pools are blistered with ice. There's a fresh salty twist to the air, the cold snubbing at the stench of dead fish and seaweed. Out in the air her body feels chafed and scoured out inside and there's still the feeling of insects running over her. The sea glints ahead of her. She wants its salty cleanness for herself.

She scans the horizon. The only figure in sight is a solitary dog-walker, climbing slowly back up among the streets. She begins to peel off her clothes, T-shirt, jeans, bra. She folds them and places them high up on the beach, above where the sand is scuffed and there are drools of black weed and netting. They'll stay dry there.

When she's completely naked she walks out to where the sea

begins. The wet sand feels flabby beneath the soles of her feet. It takes her a wee while to wade in, the water is so cold it burns, it doesn't tickle like in summer but knocks the breath out of you. The waves are tiny and flat, slopping feebly at her flesh. When she gets in up to her waist she strikes out, kicking hard to feel the muscles tug. She swims out and out until the shivering stops and she feels scraped clean by the cold.

From here she can almost make out her home. The houses seem so small. Later there will be Sunday roast, in the dining room with cloth napkins and the best cutlery and everyone avoiding each other's eyes. It will be the same as always, as if nothing has changed, nothing is new. And now she has the beginnings of a different feeling inside, like you get when you find something, and an emptiness turning to hunger. She thinks of the café on the main road, of how she might sit in its steamy warmth, taking buttery bites of teacake between mouthfuls of hot black coffee. She dips her head under the water, to wash off the smell of last night, of smoke and beer and sex and the scent of his leather jacket, and begins the swim back to shore.

Wee Fishes

Anne Callaly

Sometimes I lie soaking in the bathtub trying to remember. But I can't.

Sometimes when I hold my breath and keep my head under the water, I *imagine* that I can remember. I imagine what it must have been like. Lying there, at the bottom of the sea, my hair streaming and tangling around my face. Trying to call out and the noise of my own voice trapped inside my head. And then the deathly silence of it all. But I can't imagine it. I can't even begin to. I wasn't there when it happened.

Dip dip dip
My blue ship
Sailing on the water like a cup and saucer
Tit tit tit
You're not it

Instead, I can hear every sound amplified through the walls of the bath around me. Sheena Easton on TV in the next room, the tap dripping into the wash hand basin next to the bath.

Drip drip drip
You're not it

Like being in a submarine, listening for the enemy. Up again, *Gasp!*, and then back down under. Under the water, counting to twenty with my breath held and my cheeks puffed out, bursting to take a gasp of air. This is what the world must sound like from the womb. I could be a wee bairn floating around, happy as Larry. I can hear my da in the back yard shouting at our next-door neighbour.

Paddy, ya durty wee shite!

The football must have finished on the telly. It's a bad day for everyone when Rangers get beaten.

> *Would ye keep yer fuckin' scummy mongrel dug away fae ma gerdin, or al kick yer hole all the way back tae whatever scummy midden ye came fae?! Oh aye?! You an whose army?*

And on and on he goes. Ranting and raving. It's not as if we have the Chelsea Flower Show out there. He always seems to be angry. Angry with everyone. My ma says he wasn't always like that. I once heard her say that he wasn't like that with my wee brothers and sister. She doesn't mention it that much.

Tickly tickly on yer knee
If you laugh you don't love me

She always calls them that, them being *wee*, that is. They wouldn't be *wee* now. They were older than me when it happened. How come? Because I didn't even exist then, that's how come. They'd be big and strapping now, causing trouble on the estate and having my parents up to high-doh. *I*'d be the wee sister. I'd be the favourite.

Ickle ockle
Message in a bottle
Fishes in the sea
If you want a pretty maid
Then please choose me

I can hear my ma clattering around the kitchen; her sister Agnes there yack yack yacking away in the background. She'll be over for the afternoon to scrounge some money and eat us out of house and home. They'll be smoking fags and drinking tea, and Agnes will be sitting there like Nell Gwyn with one raspberry tit hanging out and a bairn that's fallen asleep at the pump.

> *Yack yack yack. Did ye hear the latest on Jackie Coulter's man? Beat the livin' daylights out of her, and her only just out of the infirmary after the last hidin' he gave her. Took three polis to pin him down before they carted him off in a squad car in one direction and her in an ambulance in the other. Yack yack yack.*

Ma will be tut tutting and calling him a bastard. Her mouth will be set in that thin line she's always had since the day they fished her out from the sea half dead from the cold.

You shall have a fishy
On a little dishy
You shall have a fishy
When the boat comes in

They never found the boat, though. It's still rolling around at the bottom of the sea along with a tartan picnic satchel and the empty cans of lager. Covered in moss like a green hairy monster. Crabs and fishes going about their business as if the boat had always been there. Crabs and fishes and the three wee bairns. All smashed to bits. Aye, so were Ma and Da before it happened. Ma and Da. Having a good laugh, probably singing the latest Sheena Easton hit at the top of their voices before the boat capsized.

My baby takes the mornin' train,
He works from nine to five and then La La La

Both totally steamboats on a hot summer's day.

It's roasting here in the bathroom too. Indian summer outside. Indian summer in Glasgow? I always wonder what the Paki man who runs the shop thinks of that. We'll all be falling around like skittles complaining of the heat and he's still sitting behind the counter with his green cardigan buttoned up to his neck. Mr Singh. Lovely Mr Singh. I like Mr Singh. Never said a bad word to me, even the day he caught me stealing the Hubba Bubbas. He's always smiling. Although most people say he's a bit of an eejit and was bundled off to Glasgow by his family to marry a cousin who was so ugly that they couldn't find a husband for her in the local mosque here. He must have nearly died from the shock when they unveiled her on their wedding day. She's always picking on him, the ugly old bitch. Rattling away in her foreign garble. Barking at him from one end of the shop to the other.

Hark! Hark!
The dogs do bark

I don't know *what* she's saying, but you can tell she's giving out laldy to him about one thing or another, and him just sitting there with that stupid smile on his face. He probably doesn't understand a word she's saying. Pakistani with a Glasgow accent can't be that easy to follow. If my ma spoke to my da like that, he'd boot her up the street. But it's hard to get much conversation out of Ma anyway. She wouldn't be the world's biggest chatterbox. She'll be sitting through there with Agnes now. Agnes will be running marathons for Talkers Anonymous and Ma will just be nodding away adding a few sound effects and the odd *Ugh-huh-ugh-huh, Nooo!* and *Bastard* to show Agnes that she's not snoozing. Mind you, you'll hear Ma say more in her sleep. Hear her battling her way through some nightmare in the middle of the night. Making the biggest racket at the top of her voice.

Gary! James! Mammy's over here! Just gie's yer hands!

And then it's lost in a flood of sobs and my da's shouting at her *Shut up! Shut up!* and Ma's shouting *Danny! Danny! The weans are in the water again and the wee bairn Fiona's clinging to me with her wee arms roond ma neck.* And Da's still yelling at her to shut her face before he shuts it for her, and then I don't hear any more because I bury my head beneath the sea of blankets wishing the bairns had never been born and singing myself to sleep to shut out the din.

Mammy sent me for some water
Water from the sea
My foot slipped and in I tumbled
Then three jolly sailors saved me

They were both pissed that day. Just having a day out in the rowboat on a nice summer's day. Ma, Da and the three wee weans.

> *One said he'd buy me silks and satins*
> *One said he'd buy me a guinea gold ring*
> *One said he'd buy me a silver cradle*
> *To rock the dead babies in*

Bad Behaviour Sailors

Jonathan Falla

They put the Dialectologist in Room 19 and he appreciated the plain, pictureless white walls, the scrubbed wooden floor with one thin oriental rug. The windows were large with mosquito-meshed windows and sliding louvres. The bathroom was down the hall. It was not smart, but then he was not paying the money that the oil companies were paying, not dollars. Oilmen got a balcony; the Dialectologist got no balcony. Oilmen got a telephone; the Dialectologist got no telephone. He was not sorry; he did not want to be disturbed. He bathed, taking his usual fastidious care. He put on a clean pale-blue tropical suit, snipped two unsightly hairs out of his nostrils, touched his mandible with cologne, then descended to the lobby.

The evening was hot and close, the lobby noisy with Texans, also British acting like Texans; in 1963 they knew no better, though this was Trinidad, and to some minds still British. The oilmen lolled in the lobby with their long engineers' legs jutting inconveniently between the low tables; the boys bringing drinks had difficulty, had to push by the palms that rattled in protest. Mosquitoes floated through the evening and alighted silently on backs of hands, drilling for blood. The oilmen slapped and blew smoke at them, smoke from cigarettes they'd been forbidden all day in the oilfields.

Their colossal Texan shoes were noisy on the bare floorboards, their clean shirts already clung with sweat, their hair was plastered to their heads from tepid showers after a day in the San Fernando oilfields. They were hungry and thirsty. They called for more bottled beers, cracked loud jokes and leaned forward to smack each other on the shoulder. When the Dialectologist came down the broad wooden stairs he found just one vacant armchair – wood, with a woven rush seat – at a table in the lee of a towering and dusty fern. The oilmen took no notice of him but he recognised Milburne, a chemist at the University. They nodded to each other. The Dialectologist ordered lager, and waited. Three-quarters of an hour yet till dinner – but he was not waiting for dinner.

He sat still – unless a pricking on his forehead told him that a mosquito was sucking. He watched the front door. After ten minutes, he saw movement in the darkness outside, a glint of dull metal. The door opened and three young men came in. Two were very black, one of them tall and strong, the other a slightly made teenager. The third young man was more delicate yet, with East Indian features and coal-black hair slicked down with cheap and heavily-scented pomade. None wore socks and their trousers were clean but frayed. They were carrying tuned steel drums, 'pans' they called them, drums for a steel band. They looked uncertainly at the boisterous oilmen filling the lobby who gave them not a glance. Then they set the 'pans' on the boards near the front door.

Reception regarded them thoughtfully, about to demand of them their business. The musicians could feel it coming, were ready to shrink, to retreat. But before Reception could speak, the Dialectologist got to his feet and crossed the hallway with his crisp, precise step, smiling his welcome.

'I'm so glad you could come.'

The young men returned his smile, relieved. They shook hands.

'Let's go upstairs. Would you like rum? A beer? It's imported.' The Dialectologist turned to Reception. 'Three beers to Room 19.'

He led the three black men up the stairs. Reception watched them go.

In Room 19 the Dialectologist indicated the bed.

'Please,' he said. His visitors looked at the bed, the plain green cotton counterpane, the fat bolster, all as yet unpressed.

'So, Sir, may we enquire, where is Madam?' said the Asian. They all looked at him, interested to know where was Madam.

'My wife?' their host parried sharply. 'She's in London.'

'She duh like go roun' de islan'?'

'No. She doesn't travel well.'

'Yuh all 'lone?'

'Yes,' smiling but curt. 'Please.'

He waved at the bed again; his visitors sat down, the Asian on the far side obliged to twist to see the Dialectologist, who said: 'I'm most grateful to you. I need specimens, you see.'

The three men looked at each other with another uncertain smile.

'I'm told one of you is a story-teller.' They started indicating each other. The Dialectologist said, 'Yes, but one of you in particular?' They smiled and pointed to the taller black man.

'Wonderful,' said the Dialectologist.

There was a knock on the door. The Dialectologist called, 'Come!' and the Asian, on cue, sprang to open the door, revealing a boy bearing a tray with three American beers and glasses.

'Roomservice, Sir,' he said.

Roomservice took two steps into the room, then froze. He stared at the European gentleman in his pale-blue tropical suit, at the three young blacks sitting on his bed.

'On the bedside table,' commanded the Dialectologist. Roomservice deposited the bottles and glasses. He stood holding his tray, regarding the white man and the three blacks. The Dialectologist pressed a shilling into the boy's hand.

'Tell Reception that I want no disturbance for the next hour. None, you understand? I don't want the maid turning down the bed, nothing at all. I'll lock the door.'

Roomservice backed out, still surveying the group, his look flicking from face to face. After the door closed, there was a silence in which no one's eyes met. They peered at the floor, they studied the wardrobe.

Until the Dialectologist said: 'Right, then.'

At his gesture, the Asian served drinks then sat down again. The three men sat on the bed clutching their beer, the Asian still twisted round to watch.

There was a wooden suitcase-stand by the window. The Dialectologist dragged this to the middle of the room; his three guests jumped to their feet to help but he waved them back to the bed: 'Best leave me to it.' He positioned a chair either side of the suitcase-stand, placed the massive clockwork tape-recorder in its wooden case on top and opened it. He stood the heavy chromium microphone on a folded handkerchief against vibration. He took from his suitcase a spool of new tape and threaded this into the machine with neat and precise fingers. He grasped the key and wound the clockwork mechanism thirty times. Then he began to speak:

Oh, when I was in love with you,
Then I was clean and brave.

He watched the recording-level indicator, a curious green light that swayed like an electric imp under a magnifying lens. He touched the controls, speaking again:

And miles around the wonder grew
How well did I behave.

He looked up; the three young men were studying him. He felt himself blush, but smiled. The three visitors glanced at each other warily. They watched in silence as he briskly tapped the microphone, then appeared satisfied.

'Right,' said the Dialectologist. 'Who's first?'

The guests exchanged more guarded looks.

'Don't be shy.'

They prodded the younger, smaller black man to his feet and he shuffled towards the chair in front of the tape-recorder.

'Done anything like this before?'

'No, Sah, me kyah tell waddah say.'

'Tell me a story. Whatever you like, maybe an old story, "Anansi". Or maybe something from Carnival this year; you went to Carnival? You went in a masque? How did the band dress – Cow Band? Fancy Indians? Tell me about it.'

'We play Bad Behaviour Sailors, we fix dat foh weself!' the youth suddenly looked animated, his friends laughed, the Dialectologist laughed with them.

'Bad Behaviour?'

'Mad-bad, man!' hooted the taller black. 'We playin' William Tell, Bad Behaviour varshn!'

'Bad Behaviour Sailors! Excellent!' he said, leaning forward to press a button. 'Tell me about Bad Behaviour Sailors.'

Later, the Dialectologist went downstairs to order more beers. He looked excited and a little flushed. He stopped at Reception and said:

'Three more beers for Room 19, please. No, four beers.'

Reception – a portly black – said nothing but stared at the Dialectologist a long moment. He then wagged a finger at Roomservice, the gesture oddly muted, and muttered, 'Four beers,' while glancing at a door nearby, a door with frosted glass which stood a little ajar. As the Dialectologist followed his glance, the door opened sharply. There stood a thin woman in a thin unlovely dress with thin straw-coloured hair hanging perfectly straight and lifeless. She was grey-eyed, purse-lipped and hollow-cheeked as though sucking on something very disagreeable.

'You,' said the Latvian proprietrix, 'I wish to speak to.'

'Ah,' said the Dialectologist politely, indicating her office, 'Shall we . . . ?'

'No, we speak here.'

The woman's nostrils flared. Reception eyed her apprehensively, shifting his weight. An oilman, standing at the desk to write someone a memo, looked up.

'What can I do for you?' tried the Dialectologist, bewildered.

'You can leave the hotel, please.'

'I'm sorry?'

'Indeed, and you will leave this evening. I do not want you in my hotel.'

A silence. Another oilman was staring now. The Dialectologist felt a cold, disorienting fear as though he had been caught at something and should know what but didn't. She suddenly spat into the silence: 'You are a pervert!'

He blinked, frowning and bristling. 'I beg your pardon?!'

'You think I don't know, locking yourself in your room with black boys? Just pack your cases.'

The Latvian eyes were glacial. She folded her arms waiting for him to crumple and sob. But the 'pervert' began to retort: 'I am a scientist, a linguist with the University, I am collecting . . .'

She screeched: 'I don't wish to know what you are doing! I see very well what you are doing. You are doing perversions with black boys in my hotel.'

'I'm not doing anything of the . . .'

'I have my regular guests, these respectable gentlemen!'

She nodded at the respectable oilmen sprawling in the armchairs of the lobby. Several were peering towards the tirade at Reception's desk.

The Dialectologist mounted a counter-attack.

'This is preposterous! I will not listen to such accusations. I have rights, I know who to call . . .'

He pushed past into her office and picked up the phone. He pulled a pocketbook from his pale-blue tropical suit, glaring defiantly at the Latvian woman in the doorway, jutting what jaw he had.

'I wish to speak to the Chief of Police. I'm a personal friend.'

He saw her feel for the doorframe behind her, and he felt stronger – until the Chief of Police deflated him like a knife in a car tyre.

'You know, old man, I can't actually help in this case. English laws don't apply in Trinidad. Actually, you're a guest in her private house, so to speak. Do let's have a drin . . .'

The Dialectologist put down the phone. The Latvian raised her eyebrows and smirked. There was movement outside the door and the young Asian drummer passed by.

'I tell them, Madam, just get out,' cried Roomservice, righteous as a janitor expelling tramps.

The musicians shrank as the Latvian woman pushed forward, her left arm jutting like a fencing foil, her voice keen with triumph.

'The door is there. You come back and I call police!'

The oilmen all scrutinised the Dialectologist and his black boys. He saw a Texan stub out his cigarette and snicker. He felt their contempt, he suddenly felt his blue tropical suit to be prissy.

'Damn!' he exploded, his voice rising in pitch. 'This is completely insulting! You're a foolish woman, a very foolish woman. I am well known at the University!'

Which reminded him: 'Milburne!' he cried towards the palms. 'Milburne, tell her, will you . . . !'

The chemist stood up smartly, at this instant discovering his hunger and walking swiftly into the dining room. The Dialectologist watched in dismay, feeling the beginnings of panic.

'Milburne, for God's sake!'

'Very well known, I see,' crowed the Latvian. Her arms were crossed again, her eyes shone with malice, her head was tipped back and her sharp chin pointed at him. 'Well known for what, I don't want to know. Remove your bags in the next half hour or my boys throw them in the street.'

The Dialectologist was trembling, uncertain whether it was shame or injustice made him shake so.

'I won't stand for it!' he twittered. 'I'm acquainted with the Chief Minister; I'll call him here and now!'

'Call who you like,' she retorted. 'Just take your scum away – and their tin pots.'

The Dialectologist's boys stood by their instruments at the door. He stumbled towards them, his shoes snagging on the coir matting.

'I am most terribly sorry,' he gasped with mortification. 'This is quite appalling. I'll have this in the papers, I can tell you. I won't let it rest, I'll be writing to Government House.'

'Forgeh dat, man,' said the tallest black.

'Certainly not . . .'

'Nobody go 'ffend da oilman, nobody wan' scare he dollar.'

'But she can't . . . !'

'Hey, man,' said the black, 'we gonna give yuh one tune.'

With which, all three picked up their steel pans, slipping into the straps with a flick of head and shoulder. They had wooden sticks in their hands. The Dialectologist half-raised a hand: 'She won't have it.'

But the youngest grinned at him: 'Hey, we Bad Behaviour Sailors, man, we give she William Tell!'

They hefted their pans, they took a wooden stick in each hand, they attacked and they assaulted the lobby with music. The tallest beat a tattoo, the Asian replied, and they were drumming, thundering and beating hell out of the William Tell Overture. Everyone froze, the oilmen put their drinks down and their hands on the arms of their chairs ready to run for cover. The hammered notes crashed and resounded from the windows and the walls, the floorboards shook and the pot plants shimmied. Reception put his hands on his Reception counter and grinned broadly. Roomservice showed his teeth. The waiters beamed, one began to shuffle his feet, a moment later there were three waiters shuffling and hopping, while in the door of her office the Latvian woman stared in astonishment, her mouth working it seemed silently. She was shouting at them to stop, she turned white with disgust, puce with anger – but no one heard her.

Now all two-dozen oilmen stood up. They didn't flee to dinner, they stood and faced the pan-men, beaming hugely, beating their big oliman paws on their thighs. Milburne the chemist reappeared in the doorway of the dining room, his starvation on hold. Faster and faster beat the steel pans, louder and louder still, the players' hands blurred with speed and frenzy, William Tell riding mad-bad, furious and delirious through the close, mosquito-ridden tropical night, loosing off at those Austrian apples left and right, till the tune thundered to a close, all six sticks together: bang! bang! bang! – and the two-dozen oilmen, three waiters, Reception, Roomservice and the Dialectologist burst into cacophonous applause, clapping their hands.

'Wonderful! Wonderful!'

'Out! Get out now! Get out of my hotel!' screeched the sour-faced Latvian proprietrix.

'Boo!' called an oilman, bellowing with laughter.

'Boo, boo! Shame!' roared his friends, stamping with delight. 'More, play more!'

'Get out!' she screeched ashen-faced, gibbering, barely able to speak through her shaking lips. She cuffed Reception's shoulder and the portly man jumped in fright, then hurried round the counter flapping urgently at the pan players. The three young men bowed as one to the Latvian, then marched out through the double doors held wide by Roomservice and Reception, out into the steamy San Fernando night. Behind them, a last, falling chorus – 'Boo, shame!' – dying into laughter as the oilmen took themselves in a body to the dining room for their dinner.

A furious *slam!* of rattled glass. The Latvian had shut herself in her office.

Of an instant, the lobby was quiet and still. The Dialectologist was almost alone. Only the waiters moved between the deserted armchairs, gathering bottles, glasses and ashtrays from the low lobby tables, while Reception busied himself ostentatiously with registers and ledgers. From the dining room, however, came loud talk and uninhibited mirth.

Suddenly hungry also, the Dialectologist followed the crowd into the dining room. His usual small table was vacant and he sat down. Absentmindedly he tore up some bread and nibbled at it, musing, while the maids busied around the oilmen.

After a few moments, he realised that he was not being served. The maids were avoiding his look. A small black woman of indeterminate years tried to dodge past but was too close to him. He reached out and caught hold of her.

'Bring me the soup, please.'

'Oh no, sorry, Sah, Madame tell we not to serve you.'

'Ah,' sighed the Dialectologist, 'I see.'

He let the maid go. He was very tired. Glancing through the open doorway, he saw that the Latvian's office remained closed. He tore apart and ate all the bread on his table, crumbs sprinkling over his pale-blue tropical suit. Then he started on the bread from the next table.

Mango

Fiona J. Thackeray

The threat of callous heat was already swelling in the air as a young mother and her baby walked in the shade of white walls. Valia stopped silently by the heavy gates, 7.50 a.m. At 8, the noisy unlocking, the guard's unhappy recognition. She looked back at him like yesterday's ghost. His reluctant eyes conceded and with a sigh he stepped aside to let her in.

The car park at this hour was empty. Great trees spread their boughs, throwing generous shade. Back on the hill where she used to live, the trees were all cut to make room. The tin roof drank up sun all day like a basking dragon, breathing back all the heat at night. Sweat crept from every pore as, twisting in the sheets, she kept her weight off the parts that hurt. She never slept to the end of dreams under that roof. And Luiz, rankly stewing beside her, could sleep through the Eternal Fire. A blessing, some would say, but Valia saw it was his weak point.

Beneath the old mango in the centre of the car park was a bench. It would be her place again today. Shifting Joaquim onto her knee, she let her breath out slowly and rearranged the cloths he was wrapped in. He opened his eyes for just a moment.

A cleaner, polishing fingerprints from the brass of the public doorway, eyed her suspiciously. Valia looked away. The guard came from unlocking the ladies' lavatories, crunching on the pebbly path.

'There's no wind today, Senhora. You won't see any mango fall from this tree.'

He was standing over her, hands on hips. She sniffed and looked down, tweaking the cloth over Joaquim's cheek. The guard shifted his weight impatiently to the other leg. He didn't know why she had to come here, of all the places with mango trees in town. Another sigh.

'We close at 6; you have to go then. And don't bother anyone.'

With a rough flick of his key bunch he paced back towards the gate.

Under the tree it was peaceful. The Museu de Arte Sacra was an old building. Its trees, too, were old – magnanimous shelters. Many people came just to kneel in the Museum chapel and meet Father Timoteo, famed for his benedictions and compassion. Valia knew it was a special place, holy and forgiving. The best thing was the peace. Where she had come from, so much noise and tension. Always some fight or siren, shots sometimes, Pagode music and mothers screaming. Here the tall white walls deadened the traffic drone, and people spoke in low respectful voices. Here, at least for a while, she was safe. No one would look for a slum girl at the museum.

She had put her faith in God. There was no choice of refuge for someone like her. But God would provide for her, if she waited for Him long enough. He would draw the white walls in close and she could vanish in the big city. He would stir up a wind for a mother and her baby in need. No big storm, just a few gusts to make the branches sway. And a fruit would fall. It would be her mango, not stolen, but freely given to her in a public place from a sheltering tree.

Spying the glossy leaves above the wall two nights ago, the

idea had come to her. Such a tall tree: a mature one. All she could see were the higher branches. But it was the time for mangoes. By now it must be drooping with heavy fruits. Maybe it was a vision – she liked to think so – a sign for her to go where she would be cared for: to this peaceful, pure place, out of sight. Craning back her neck, she looked up into the sturdy canopy, a sooty green and sunlight rash. She could disappear in its shade. Bending down the outer twigs, fat mangoes, green with blushing bottoms. She knew how the flesh would yield to her bite, the fibres lacing her teeth, the juice soaking her chin and neck. Smoothing the baby's cheek, nodding, she had only to wait in faith.

Gliding quietly into the car park was a shiny car with tinted windows. A man in damp linen stepped out to open the door for a woman with a handbag. She took his arm with a crinkly smile, and they strolled to the entrance. Valia pulled her shirt over a rosette of dirty-looking bruises, suddenly ashamed. The woman's lilac blouse sleeves fluttered halfway down her forearms revealing fine, liver-blotched wrists, like a leopardess. A rumour of flowery perfume trailed her. Behind this, Valia thought she could smell smoke, but she couldn't tell from where.

Joaquim was waking now, wrinkling up his face as the hot day seeped in on his lullaby dreams. His eyelids were smooth like fallen petals as he slumbered. Now, folded back deep into the sockets, they bared his eyes to the day. He stared silently into her face, worked his gums, switched focus up into the mango branches. He was, for a moment, bewitched by pendulous fruits and patchwork shadows. Then the crease across his nose returned, and the first faltering sputters of his cry. Soon his mouth tautened to a vent, bewailing his empty stomach.

Her nipple stoppered his anguish; the tight little mouth softened as milk flowed to his belly. Valia hunched shyly over her son and looked behind. The guard pretended not to stare.

By noon the car park was crowded. The leopard woman had left; families and couples had been and gone. Now a few people sat on benches and walls. Bodies drifted from one scrap of shade to another, slinking from the heat. They barely noticed the slight figure waiting for a mango to fall. They chatted, swatted flies and complained about the heat. Gradually they gathered their momentum to go.

Weary old women came on foot, knitted together in twos or threes. Crowded on a long bench by the Chapel entrance, they were waiting to receive one of Frei Timoteo's blessings. They fanned and shaded themselves with pamphlets, swabbed at mizzled brows. Their crumpled faces were icons of enduring faith, cracked as antique lacquer.

At long intervals, a heavy wooden door admitted one blessing-seeker. In her hallowed moment with the Frei, each woman knew every ounce of suffering in her life would be rewarded. And emerged glowing, cleansed by the Frei's wisdom. Drifts of scorched scent escaped each time the door was opened. To Valia it was a torment, though she knew it must be incense.

The sooty smell was from her childhood: all those times when police came to the hill in the night. Kids saw them first, from where they flew kites on the rock. No uniforms, but that didn't fool them. You could tell the police anywhere. The kids ran upwards, bursting to tell. But before they got far, the first gunshots cracked in the air, rattling tin walls. Reeking fuel emptied around the lower shacks then a quick getaway, as if it never happened. The first time, Valia couldn't believe it. After that she expected nothing better. She remembered smoky amber glowing on the hillside, panicky voices, running figures. And in the morning, the gloom of wet blackness pervading the remains of homes built only from debris anyway. Steaming stumps and twisted metal. Crouched among the char, black faced and silent, those who had lost a little, which was all that they had.

The baby stirred. She stood to stroll around the compound, bouncing him gently in her arms. Beneath an acacia she stopped for a moment. Joaquim gurgled. She was freckled by the tree's dissected shade, filigree fine after the mango's dense cloak. She tried to resist the impulse to stare at the women and the Frei's door. That smell was in her mouth now, acrid and sooty, lining her tongue with dissolved bitterness.

From the duty box, the guard passed her an irritated look. He spooned rice and beans into his mouth from a foil tin. Under his arms sweat patches spread, leaving a map of blemishes on his grey, badged shirt. Valia hummed a tune to block out the thought of beans in her stomach. He looked like he could cause trouble with a full belly and nowhere else to spend his energy.

They sat back under their tree, Joaquim restless with the heat. Valia made a game for him with acacia pods. Rattling them, then hiding them behind her back, humming. Valia smiled with those wide, lively eyes mothers make for babies. He giggled. His flawless face beamed, then grew solemn, seeking the pods and the noise. She let the silence linger, watching his expression. When she shook them for him again, he screamed with delight, and tried to grab a pod.

Out of the museum trailed a small group of schoolchildren clutching merchandise: postcards and posters with images of sin, and hellfire, assorted saints and Christ bleeding for our souls. The kids were glad to be out, too long under the oppressive gazes of martyrs. Two girls, dragging satchels over the sandy ground, came to sit on a low wall beside Valia's tree. They crouched close together in jeans and grey school T-shirts. Whispering – a crucial debate about a boy, the one loitering near the guard's box. They nudged each other, little high-pitched shrieks and forbidden laughter escaping. Valia used to be the same with Ana, teasing the guys with their clapped-out old Vespas, all standing round like they thought they were mechanical geniuses. Outside Ana's dad's bar they would fix each other's hair, dancing around in shorts and high sandals, trading precious secrets and desires. That was until Luiz came along and her belly began to swell the first time.

Now the schoolgirls opened a caramel bar, a drooping tile of sweetness, fused by the heat to its paper. Neither girl had the patience to wrestle for its sticky promise. They cast it onto the wall and went to join their group. Just in time, as the teachers came pacing from the exit.

The mid-afternoon sun punished everyone until their pores wept into submission. Valia felt it keenly. Her 'Jesus is Love' shirt damply clung. Such smiling faces, when they gave her that T-shirt at the Universal Church of God is Love. She and Luiz used to go on Wednesday nights. The church was all right until they had to wave money above their heads to show how much they wanted to be saved. Soon all the money Luiz didn't drink would go to Pastor Julio. And what was left to feed two children with? No wonder her little girl had got sick. Valia began rocking with her son. To and fro, rocking out all her resentment for the past.

A bee came to investigate the caramel, which melted now into the dimples in the stone. It made a curious dance around the sugary pool, nudging with its legs before taking off to circle again. Gingerly, it landed and tasted the edge of its caramel lake. Valia stood abruptly, and set off around the compound with Joaquim, too hungry to watch the bee. She couldn't bear to be tempted to scrape up leftovers like that. Her son was getting irritable. Bouncing him impatiently, Valia paced from tree to tree. A jaggedness edged her voice now as she tried to quieten the baby.

Pacing couldn't calm either of them. They returned to the

bench. The baby was noisy now. Valia slumped heavily against the mango's trunk, unresponsive to Joaquim's wails. Maybe God was deserting her. Maybe she deserved it, tainted as she was with her sooty shadow of guilt. But the babe was an innocent. If she let them find her, he would be left alone in the world. Valia began to curse and cry. Silent tears curling down her nose, hot breathy oaths muttered into her lap. Joaquim, crying louder, drowned out the sound of bad words from his mother's mouth.

She cursed the blessed women by the Frei's door, she cursed the greedy tree, keeping all its fruits, the Frei, too lazy to come out and help people in need, the guard's malign face, and the baby who wouldn't stop crying. Then she cursed God, who turned a deaf ear, and herself, for getting into this mess, sinning, hungry, nowhere to go.

The last cars swung out into the road, with friendly waves and beeps. The guard closed the gate, leaving open the small pedestrian door. He turned to look for her. Valia made up her mind, bracing her feet in the dust.

'After 6. Time to go, lady.' Swinging his keys again.

Valia sat still, looking straight ahead.

'You heard me. Time to go.' Again she stayed still. 'No wind, no luck. Try somewhere else for mangoes.'

She sat still as the tree.

'Merda!' he spat on the ground. He had been expecting this all day. Should never have let her in.

'Move it; you can't stay here.'

Valia shook her head. 'No.'

'What d'you mean "no"? I warned you this morning. You think this is the sanatorium or something?'

Valia took a deep breath. 'I need to see Frei Timoteo.'

The guard looked outraged, 'You can't! He's busy. You want to see him, you've got to queue up with the others. You saw them there earlier.'

'I have to see him. Tell him a young mother is here with her baby. Tell him they need help.'

'No. Look it's not possible, just move it.' This in a lower, intimidating tone.

'I'm not leaving till I see him.' Valia was nervous but with the determination of the desperate. 'I need him to confess me.'

The guard gave an exasperated sigh. He turned away from her and marched to knock on the heavy wooden door. He rubbed his forehead agitatedly. As the door opened, she could see him raise his arms and shrug his shoulders in gestures of helplessness, explaining the nuisance woman outside. He shook his head and looked back towards her. A balding head peered around the door.

She understood everything now. God was angry with her, that's why he didn't send wind to make a mango fall. She had come here, the worst type of sinner, to this holy place, expecting shelter and heavenly fruits. What she deserved was to burn in hell. All she could do now was to confess to Frei Timoteo, throw herself on the mercy of God.

The Frei was crossing the sandy space in grey robes, lit then shaded by sun piercing tree canopies. Arriving under the mango, he smiled and said,

'Good evening, Senhora. The guard tells me you need my help.'

Valia was stuck for words. She looked at her son, quiet again, looking back at his mama.

'Tell me your name,' said Frei Timoteo.

Valia looked up into his face, lined and wise. His eyes were grey and dappled by the light pattern at the mango's fringe. He was nothing like fat Pastor Julio.

'Valia.'

'May I sit down, Valia?'

The Frei sat on the bench leaving space for Valia to think.

He saw Joaquim's petal-eyelids close. Folding his hands in his lap, he waited for Valia to talk. He was a man who could wait for a long time.

And so she told him the story of homecomings and fear, of unfocused eyes, anger and *cashasa* fumes on the breath. She couldn't stop there; it all came stampeding from her mouth. Out rushed the swaying pauses, sickening anticipation and flesh blenching as punches gained rhythm to become a battering rain. She told of hot tears, of bones that throbbed, and ink-stain blood that spread under the skin. She spoke of heaving snores and darkness coming. More, she mentioned gasoline pouring, precious things bundled and a sleeping child clasped. And now a door closed, a rock or two quietly placed, and a match, flaring, dropped casually as a handkerchief. She finished with the start of a long, hot journey.

Closing her eyes, tears escaping between the lashes, Valia could smell the Eternal Fire sharper than ever. The smoke tainted her own hands, clung in her clothes. Pastor Julio would have screamed about the Ten Commandments, shame and sin, and the Devil turning us to his own work.

Frei Timoteo told her God could see all her suffering. He sent for the guard to bring a ladder to the tree.

In his office of wood, the Frei pressed some coins and a square of paper into her hand. The paper had a name and directions written on.

'It's a quiet place, too,' he said.

Valia set off across the city, her sleeping babe in arms. She was feeling lighter, despite her sack of mangoes.

Tumshie McFadgen's Bid for Ultimate Bliss

George Anderson

Don't talk tae me aboot sensualists.

You name it, thirll be a website furrit.

Tumshie McFadgen took things tae extremes, though.

One o Tumshie's heroes wiz Harpo Marx. According tae a book about him that Tumshie read, one o Harpo's favourite things wiz tae lie back oan a hammock in his garden whilst having the soles o his feet tickled by the string o a kite being flown by his wee laddie.

Tumshie wiz fur a slice o that, bit drew the line at requiring his ain wee boay tae dae the kite flyin'. It wid take ages tae raise wan, bit dinnae think he didnae consider it. McFadgen didnae normally dae things by hauves.

Tumshie spent months working oot how tae re-create the sensation for himself.

At first he hud this system o pulleys and that which administered a glide o string oan his expectant feet. He parked himself oan a sunlounger instead o a hammock, though. There are limits.

Bit it wisnae making it, and Tumshie concludit that whit wiz actually missing wiz the poetry. It wisnae jist the feeling o string that wiz required. You had to actually know that it wiz from a kite in flight, in order tae enjoy the full wistfulness o the moment.

So oanyways, the crowd o boays he hud went aboot wi since the school hud always known he wiz a sensualist. It aye hud tae be the richt amount o vinegar oan his chips. The richt fags. The correct shade o paint oan the motur or oan the lobey woh.

He had very particular thoughts oan whit should be swallied when and wi whit and the correct procedure fur hay-in a bit naughty wi a burd.

But the trouble stertit when Tumshie tried to combine a few o these sensations at the yince. He came up wi this notion o cross-pleasuring.

Whit wid it be like, he postulated, tae experience the maximum whoopie in all five senses at the same time?

Moon River Thompson wiz wan o the boays he ran wi, an it wiz him thit telt me aboot it.

'Hiv yer cake an eat it?' he queried Tumshie on hearing the plan.

'Shag it, lisen tae it, feel it up, talk tae it and generally buy the T-shirt by way of sensory enjoyment? You'll git intae bother, boay. Mark my wurdz. You'll get intae bother.'

Bit Tumshie wiz not tae be diverted.

He stertit aff wi a big lang list o braw situations to see whit wans he could combine.

There wiz the funny bits in films and comedy sketches. The sound o big Jimmy Page coming back in oan the guitar after that funny hippie bit in the middle o 'Whole Lotta Love'. There wiz the feelin o silk boxers oan his bahookie, an the smell o gidd coffee.

For a wee while there he agonised ower where bevvy should come intae the equation – The smell o beer an the taste o whisky? Should it be that sensation or the actual feelin o gettin pished.

Bit in the end he biled it doon to five things – wan tae cover each sense.

Wan. Touch. Well that wiz easy, he wid get a knee-trembler aff his current principal squeeze, Lumphanan Lizzie Maguire. Fine big healthy girl. No a pun o her oot o place.

Two. Taste. A mouthful o the Caledonian Eighty Shilling. God's ain beer. The only thing Edinburgh's oany gid fur. Makes ye sing like Frank Sinatra. How an ever, it wisnae jist as simple as awe that. The moment o peak flavour hud tae be achieved. It was a particular part o the aftertaste he craved – no the full-on rush o the first second. The flavour went into a sort o journey fur aboot five seconds before settlin doon and it was aboot two seconds in that Tumshie liked best. There wiz an awfa complex ratio o malty/sweet/bitter/fruity an ah don't know whit tae be considered.

Three. Sight. Erchie Gemmell scoring THAT goal against Holland in 1978. Again, it hud tae be timed right. Hitting the ba wisnae guid enough. The ba in the net wisnae guid enough. It hud tae be that moment when the ba jist hung tantalisingly ower the keeper's heid, seeming tae brakk awe the laws o physics. Hovering. Hinging. Mocking. Saying: 'The wee boy thit hit me is an ugly wee red-haired party fae a wee insignificant cuntry, bit ye know whit ye can dae? Ye can get it right up ye. Because I am the finest-struck ba that ever there wiz. Look on me and know, the agony it is to seek perfection, and find it, when it's too late.'

Sorry, man. Goat a wee bit poetic there furra minute. Where wiz ah? Aye . . .

Four. Smell. An this wan wiz difficult tae pull aff, wi the beer being sae close at hand, bit he wantit a sniff o freshly crushed basil leaves. Haw dinnae think the boy wisnae sophisticated and cosmopolitan by the way. Sensualist fae wae back, like ah said.

Five. Sound. An this was a hard decision fur Tumshie tae make. It finally came doon tae a particular snatch o Scotty Moore's vicious rockabilly guitar oan 'Mystery Train'.

Noo some fowk wid say that this approach to pleasure wiz courtin disaster fae the aff. Such conspicuous consumption disnae go ower weel wi some fowk. An treating sex in such a recreational fashion wid upset wan or two, am sure. Mibbeas some o yis, and am mebbe in this camp masel, wid regard it as sacrilegious to give anything less than yer full attention tae a Scotty Moore solo. Whatever ye think yersel. Bit I'm here tae tell you, it was a bluidy disaster awe roon.

Tumshie's main problem wiz working away oan the timing so that he orgasm'd just as the beer hit the right flavour, and Erchie's shot reached its apex, an the basil burst its sweet juices, and Scotty hit his stride wi the trebly, crunchy riff.

A tall order by any account.

Bit Tumshie wiz a perfectionist. He wondered about nano-seconds of difference awe, his gob, ears, peepers and snout wirr a good two foot closer tae his brain than his thrapper.

Or wait. Whit if the maximum effect could be gained by each o the rushes coming on yin after the other, rather than at the same time. Awe within a coupla seconds. Building up tae a crescendo.

Sort o like a barbershop quartet giving it 'Heloooo, helloooo, hellooo' until they hit one big harmonised chord of bliss.

Wan experience piling oan anither until a mighty wall o bliss hud been built oot o awe the different bricks.

'Christ, man, geez peace,' Thompson telt him in the pub one night as he agonised out loud. 'You'll be thinkin o ware-in tight shoes tae take them aff jist at the richt time a gnaw.'

It wiz a joke but dinna think Tumshie didnae think aboot it.

Bit gnaw. He decidit tae be realistic. His first targit wid be tae get awe the sensations tae kick in at aboot the same time, give or take a second.

If he managed that, then mibbeas he kid make it his life's

work tae refine it doon tae all at the same time. An mebbe efter that he could dae it again with five in a row.

He could compare!

Five in a row in quick succession with all at the same time!

Christ, this wiz pioneering stuff, he thocht tae himsel.

An if if wiz easy, it widnae be worth daen, he kept telling himsel.

He kept telling Lumphanan Lizzie a gnaw. It hud become obvious early on that she wiz going tae have tae administer no jist a guid seeing tae, bit awe the ither things as well. In order tae experience the bliss tae its full capacity, Tumshie wid huv tae be free o such things as switching oan videos, hittin the pause button oan the CD and twistin a wee green leaf under his neb.

'This is going to take one helluva slide rule and ready reckoner, Tumshie,' she telt him, bit at first she humoured him, and they experimented.

They hud a few tries wi her gein him the business, an then keeping things gaun wan-haundit while fumblin wi awe the ither paraphernalia – trying tae time the start o the fitba vid, the music and awe the rest. Bit eventually she took a scunner tae it, an fact o the matter, she took a scunner tae McFadgen, which come tae think o it, wisnae awe that surprisin.

So he goat the dunt, and hud tae start fae square wan, finding anither lassie, an training her up forbye.

Getting a girl was difficult but do-able. Bit at the first mention o what cross-pleasuring entailed, they tended tae shoot the craw sharpish.

Tumshie wiz at his wits' end.

He jist couldnae find a partner prepared tae show a bit o willin.

But in the meantime he hud actually sortitt oot everything else himsel.

There was wan major breakthrough. He hud had a video o

the Gemmell goal made by some audio-visual company. They had pit 'Mystery Train' oan the soundtrack and synchronised the correct bit o guitar wi the ba hingin in the air.

An through repeatit experimentation Tumshie learned the proper sequence for sucking on the straw fur the beer, and crushing the basil.

So he was back tae the problem o who his assistant in this great sensualist endeavour wiz gaun tae be. He considered hirin a prozzie, bit gnaw he thocht that wiz a bit weird.

Wid ye credit that, by the way? He thocht that wiz weird.

But eventually it dawned oan him thit it wiz gaun tae hae tae be a DIY knee-trembler, a self-service seeing-tae, and indeed a naughty o the roll-your-own variety.

Over to Annie Palm and her five lovely daughters, he concluded intae his pint wan night.

This wiz a major crossroads on his road tae ruin, by the way. For now he was oan his own. Regardless o how unwilling or sceptical his paramours hud been, he did at least huv their companionship tae see him through the trials and tribulations o the bid for ultimate bliss.

Now he was oan his own.

Well, fur years he tried it, and Thompson said he goat quite close a few times, bit when attemptin the full five, he only ever achieved three o the sensations in anything like the same coupla seconds.

And deep in his hert, am sure he knew, that tae dae oany o these pleasures justice, ye huv to concentrate oan jist wan at a time.

Bit he kept at it, and it drained him an you know, he was jist a shadow of the man he used tae be.

He began tae worry that there wiz something rang wi him. Well, it's obvious tae you and me thit there wiz something rang wi him, but what he meant wiz that he had shortcomings that meant he couldnae pull this feat off. He began tae think the world wiz full o fowk thit kid dae this, but jist didnae waant tae. Here wiz him desperate, an no able tae pull it aff.

He wondered if meditating or some ither Eastern religious guff would help him crack it.

Until one day a terrible realisation dawned. He had conditioned himself so much that he couldnae actually enjoy oany o the things on their ain oanymair.

A pint was now a frustratin reminder awe his failure, an no a simple pleasure at the end of a day.

If truth be told, he didnae actually like basil oanymair. Scunnered wi it he wuz.

Early Elvis tracks now left him unmoved. He began to see the sense in some o that really rank Vegas stuff.

But the most disturbin thing wiz he couldnae hae an orgasm withoot thinkin aboot Erchie Gemmell. At first he could manage with just aboot any small red-haired Scotland veteran – Harper or Bremner fur instance. Bit eventually it wiz nae Erchie, nae chunce.

An it was shortly after admitting this tae Moon River Thompson that he disappeared from view. Nobody knows whit happened tae him. He jist went.

Bit the video was gone as well.

Ain't Misbehavin

Barbara Clarke

Mama says we going to eat to oblivion the day old man Blue gets his self dead, gets his self all sliced up. I say where's oblivion? she says just eat; goose fat glistens on her lips, her cheeks swelled with meat, red in the grey pigeon light of evening; she says I don't know what's coming, she combing through the flour with one hand like she sifting for gold but she all the time watching me. But I know cause angel she speaks to me.

When she comes at night, my angel, she touch my face as though washing a new-born baby, kisses my eyes quiet from crying, feels like butterflies dancing, like it's raining, says sweet Rosy Brown dream, but that's because up there I cry, cry so bad, used to anyhow, but all the while the weeping smothered me, where life flickers like a lone flame, a tiny light, same they use to light the lanterns at Halloween.

One night I lay watching, rain touching the night, seeing my reflection, seeing all those tears inside; and outside I wiped the blue glass smooth, moved the wet across as if parting grass in a river; the tall bull rushes that cut my legs when I am crouched down listening with frogs, and there my smile watching me. I smile a while, fix it on the glass looking in, looking at my smile I see a half-moon curve that makes me warm, then she says it, my angel, 'Let me feed you here,' and I see her lift her hand half cupped holding berries, small black berries, juniper. I shiver, think of ghosts and know that no one died just yet and I just listen, loosen my mouth so it hangs softly, might even look a little pouty and then I go on looking for the shooting star which falls when some-one dies, so I can be ready to jump right under the bedclothes crawl into the darkness that smells of old skin. I tell them all, uncle Jose, Mama but they don't even let me finish, I say that word angel and they are onto me again, get me all tied up, tan my hide they call it, say 'Sister you need that beatin till your soul is spared, praise be.' They make me stand up for a long time, my feet swell, my head tired and hanging till I start to dream and bubble at my mouth with dryness, the bright sun making liquid of my sins. Then they love me like the lost one, feed me chicken breast and sour milk made into jellied cream and then they drag out the tub fill it with soft water and soap my body let me lie down and float awhile, rubbing all the old ways, touch the scars of history, the devil marks of times gone before.

But she comes back to me. We say nothing just lie awhile cooling off in cotton with the emptiness of night. She says to me let's sing, but if I let one drop of sound pass my lips I'll be taken down the stairs put in the dark room that smells of pepper and stale plums, the shelves all lined with pickled nuts and apricots, their swollen flesh sets me thinking of lips cut off, smiling lips sliced off silent, swimming, smiling in the juice thin as old men's lies.

Sometimes my heart beats so loud I think they'll hear, but they don't. I play dead, let her kiss my face where I sometimes dream my mother washes me in oil, rubbing and rubbing, then bends down close enough to taste a while. I dream, my tongue wriggles out my mouth touching and I wake up screaming, that sweet-smelling tender flesh sour as old leather coated in cobwebs and beetroot skin. She comes back again and we say nothing. I lie remembering the sweetness of outside, the earth heavy, the damson scent lingering like her breath when she passes through the room. Sometimes I know she's waiting for me because of that smell, it lingers just long enough for me to follow. I lie practising death singing a soft lullaby and angel comes with marguerites and foxgloves. I make garlands wrapped in red cloth and put them in my secret place where I keep magic stones and paper with black words scattered over, underneath the slats my bed rests on, the slats Jose cut for my own bed.

Jose brushes Mama's scarf round my hands, breathes heavy like I think he might die, heavy breath like the old woman who slept in church at night. But Jose does not die, is not struck down for all his fast talk and touch; sins of the flesh which God can see, in fact turns a blind eye to, there is no goodness. But she calms me, tells me he might fall down dead, might one day fall down, slump heavy, like the giant dolls they dress as clowns and pump up full of air, they can pretend to dance with you; they have them at fairs in spring and fall, but this time when he gasps for air, crushes me, it's like he's punctured, a knife has slithered into his sweating back and I fall asleep seeing him falling, falling. A small cut that at first doesn't even bleed, too deep, but then I cry out to her no. I think of Jose in the afternoon lighting a fire and he bringing apples in honey and a tray of peach cake, we sit breaking up twigs and putting them gently into the flames, the light melting into dust fine as stone is soft. He holds my hand and we sit there like they do in songs only there isn't any moon, just some old man like they say in the Bible, old men cradling their young keeping them safe and warm and then it's gone can't remember anymore of that good time. Sometimes I'm so afraid, if I remember it too much I might forget it altogether, because it's such a long time ago I can't even remember my own face from then.

The words I keep black and printed on paper fine as silk

don't come from the Bibles, they are words about gold and beauty and silver plates of chicken wings and cherry paste the dark ripe cherries too precious to take to market, picked when the moon is half open, the kind saved for feasts of the dead the resurrected, carnival times.

One day she says to me I'll lie down in such splendour and one day I'll get so much freedom I'll begin to drown and I can't imagine what that is. Freedom the word stays heavy, cloys my breath and then she's gone. I feel the rope wrapped round my feet and then feel the belly weight of sadness. When she speaks of freedom I know the word is bigger than the world and all the space between the moon and me. The word chokes, makes me feel I'll faint with fear and longing, she knows that's what I feel and still she goes on tormenting and I can't run away not now. With the early milky light comes the scratchings in my mind, insects crawling in the roof, falling where I lie.

Old man Blue comes to get his rent, pushes past Mama with his fist held high, doesn't see she has her knife she uses to peel fruit skins, all shiny sharp sitting on the ledge by the empty can of tea. She stands, keeps the table between them, makes sure he walks round so her back is against the open door. He says I want that money, his eyes watering with his need for beer, and he dances round the table, sits awhile, then unfolds a cloth and lays out eggs, their skin faintly blue and she sighs moves her hand to take them. Afternoons by the well, waiting for the boys to come with their green-painted buckets to draw out the crystal water. Old man Blue comes by and looks me in the eye, says words softly, feels like snails melting on the tongue and I spit into the well, make a wish of torment. Later I bring candles, like they say, wait for the north star. With the candles a wreath of sage and brown berries to imitate the eye of the beholder, set them on the hearth of stones taken from the desert, and then light the fire, so a heavenly smoke is lost, gathering with it our thoughts into one long thread of touch. But it isn't any good. I lie practising for death feeling the spirit move like Mama said it would, but I feel it in my belly not in my heart. It flicks like a bird dancing on the edge of an early morning pond tasting the magic of sunlit water, my soft belly swelling like a pudding the fancy kind I have only ever heard about, the old days of plenty when water pours out sweet as wine, red as blood. Then the dark brooding silence and she is gone, my spirit angel is still.

Cold of morning and I have freedom, came last night just as she said, never fancied it meant without her, always thought she would be there; this freedom is not what I had intended, no sense of sweetness, but fragile as a leaf left on the wild sea. Old man Blue's been back, tells me I'm the devil child, sends for the priest who comes with prayers spoken as if he curses and purple silk embroidered cloth he hangs around his neck, thick with vines and a lamb limp, with garlands of purple grapes, its throat cut. The priest, his voice coarse as gravel, brittle as old women's bones, grinds me down to kneel, with only shame to cover my face, a thin veil of tears to weaken the blows he offers in a way to calm my mother's fears, the punches driven from despair, a beating that may just end all that is to come.

The word, his will be done, is a long road, blue earth scattered with black smooth stones and fallen grass from where the scythes have cut. And in those hours of freedom I think of Mama's milk, I've smelled it all those years dried onto cloths wrapped round her breasts at night, tasted it in memory, seen those drunk baby faces crooning in her arms wishing it could be me forever, the only truth.

Sometime I thought it was angel calling, but the wind teasing the leaves in a place of tall houses painted sugar pink and ash, houses all a top the other, loud sounds, all confusion, till up close I hear the drum and music like I don't know and people crying out with sheer passion to be alive, it is the night, when usually it is a time of silent fear. They call out 'You gal dancing?' and I get swung round in arms of old men who sidle up to feel my proud hard belly, slithering words with promises of love. But their voices fade and I am hearing her, the angel, listening hard and making shapes from shadows but there is nothing and then I am standing all alone the old woman sweeping and sweeping, all that's left of music.

I miss her like the kisses in the morning I imagined would be coming if Mama was there to wake me and imagine it is her when old man Blue flops his belly over mine. My old self is disappearing, the paper dolls from times too far gone to recall, a sense of dust, and smells of sour dough and dead mice withering out of reach. Morning finds me slumped against an old man, his mouth foaming from a little too much beer. Blue room with a coverlet of rose cotton, this word love, the image of me reflected from a mirror leaning on the table, a sense of shadow wrapped in my arms, holding onto. Old man Blue, his laughter echoes as he seems to crush my bones like chicken wings, he biting down and sucking every last drop of marrow fat and in my arms folded in a damp cloth, the child and in her there is light, fragile as moon light and nothing wanting but the reflection of winter coming.

Christmas at Waipanoni Falls

Janette Munneke

Way up in the back blocks, that's where it was. Way, way up, if you follow the river right into the bush, just before you get to where it becomes a tiny trickle falling over bits of rock between the trees. He lived in a tiny bach up there, so they said. Sylvester, the old folks called him. Silverfish, we named him, because he was just like one, shimmying away out of sight whenever a human being came near. The wildman of Waipa Falls. Months would go by without anyone ever seeing him. That one time, when I was about eight years old, a whole year had gone by. One Christmas to the next.

'You boys seen old Sylvester lately?' Nan asked, while the men were there digging the pit for the hangi.

'Na, don't reckon I've seen 'im since *last* Christmas,' Uncle Pita said, not being slow to stop and lean on the shovel. 'Yeah, I remember, we was up there looking for a branch for the Christmas tree for the marae. 'Member that, Hone?'

Hone stopped digging too, and sat on the edge of the pit, for which pit was too grand a name by three-quarters. One shovel full each, I reckon. At this rate it'd be nightfall before the slimy slabs of pig flesh, which Nan had been up since dawn skinning, could go into the ground, let alone be ready to be hauled up in clouds of steam huffing and snorting as if they were still alive.

'I remember. Not a sight to forget easily, 'im standing there in his birthday suit, holding that eel in his hands like a lover. Nearly as tall as him, too.'

Nan must have seen that my eyes were nearly popping out.

'Hone, that's enough of them tall tales. You'll give them kids nightmares,' she chided. 'And get back to your digging. I'm sorry I asked now.'

'Oh go on, Ma, now that we've stopped, isn't it time for one of those beers you got in the river? 'Sgonna be a real scorcher today, I reckon.'

With one fluid movement, the men stretched themselves out of work mode and into tea-break, and ambled off down the path to the water's edge. Nan flicked a fly off the meat and went inside, returning shortly with a damp cloth to lay over the basket. Ra turned and looked at me and I nodded.

'Nan,' he called. 'Hana and me, we're goin' bush. It's gonna be a while before the dinner's ready at this rate.'

'Did you feed those chooks?'

'Yeah.' Ra pulled Granded's old army helmet onto his head.

'Well, take Boy with you. And don't you go for enough so you can't hear me call you when the hangi's cooked.'

I patted my hip and Boy got up from the verandah and loped towards me with the same sort of stride as the men had used to go to the river.

It was a lazy day, the kind that takes forever to pass, even if you are having fun, the men too lazy to dig the pit, Nan too lazy to hurry them up, Boy too lazy to walk far, the sun taking its time to climb up into the sky.

Out of the small clearing around the homestead and under cover of the bush, it was cool, dark, dank-smelling. Ra paused only to ferret around for a stick to hold in his hand like a shepherd's crook, smoothed the bark off on a sharp rock, and strode out for the river's edge. We could hear the men's voices and Ra looked back at me so I knew to be quiet. We crept up a small bank, just upriver from where they were, and first Ra looked and then me. Uncle Pita was lying down on the bank, Hone propped up against a tree in the cool. 'Reckon it was fifteen foot long, that monster,' Pita was saying. 'Yeah, right, fifteen foot, it must of been. Now if that was as tall as Sylvester, that'd make the man, what, about, fifteen foot tall?' Hone chuckled, but I couldn't see what was so funny.

'Ra,' I asked when we were a safe distance away, 'how tall is Dad?'

'Oh, he's about six foot three. And a half. Or maybe three-quarters.' Ra was a whole year older than me and his class was doing fractions that year.

In the bits where I could take my eyes off the path, I used my fingers to count up the difference between six foot and fifteen. Even without the three and a half or maybe three-quarters, it was a mighty lot. I wondered if Ra had heard, but if he had, it didn't seem to be stopping him.

We pushed on upriver, knowing we had to make as much ground as we could before the sun got too high and forced its searing rays between the branches of the rimu and kauri trees. Then the morning freshness would be gone and it would be too hot for exertion, even under the green canopy.

Boy didn't share our knowledge or our enthusiasm.

'Ow, shit.' I swore, tripping and nearly falling over him. He had slumped down on the path ahead of me. In the dappled light his mongrel brown coat barely distinguished itself from the patches of shade, and it didn't help that I was still counting.

'Ra!' I called. 'Ra!'

There was no response from up ahead. I tugged at the scruff of Boy's neck, but he just puffed and looked at me with big loopy eyes.

'C'mon, Boy, c'mon.' I said, but even I didn't think I sounded very hopeful.

I gave up and sat down beside him.

'Ra!' I shouted again. A fantail flitted out from a beech tree, followed by another. They always come in pairs, Nan would say. She said it every time. 'Fantails come in pairs, trouble comes in threes.'

'That's us, Boy,' I said, leaning back on him. 'You, me and Ra. Trouble.'

'Whatcha doing?' Ra's voice made us both jump.

'Boy's tired. He stopped.'

'Bloody dog.'

'Don't swear at him. It's not his fault.'

'Well, it's not mine, so who does that leave? Eh? Bloody girl, that's who.'

I stuck my nose in the air like a girl while I tried to think of an answer.

'Bloody, bloody, bloody,' he said, and started to run off.

'Ra, where're you going? Come back. Don't go without us.'

'To get some bloody water for the bloody dog.'

When he came back he was carrying Grandad's old army helmet, half full of water. Some of it sloshed out onto the path where it was soaked up as I watched. The drips that fell on my feet were like a balm.

Boy slurped noisily out of the helmet, licking up every last drop.

'Here, watch it, that's my exploring helmet,' Ra said, pulling the helmet from him. Boy made a half-hearted attempt to pull it back, and all at once we were up and walking again.

I sighed. My feet were still pretty tired and it seemed like a long time since breakfast.

'Here,' Ra said, holding out an apple. He pulled another from his other pocket and bit into it.

'We can walk in the river bed now, if you like. It's shallow here. Just don't bloody slip on the stones.'

The water, barely a trickle, was still cool, the stones grey bedrock. It was hard going but worth it for the relief from the heat. Trees curved over the river, soaking up as much of the wet as they could to survive; ferns stretched over the banks and tiny fireflies dipped and dived on the surface.

'Hey, Ra' I squealed, 'what was that?'

'Ssssh!' He grabbed my arm and I dragged my gaze from the water to see what had caught his attention.

Just up ahead was a greywacke outcrop; the trees cleared around it and it made a perfect sunning spot . . . for a silverfish. For there he was, the legend of the bush, stretched out in all his glory on the rock. I stood on tiptoes to see if what Uncle Pita had said about his height was true, and slipped and sat down hard on a stone in the riverbed.

Tears sprang into my eyes at the pain, but stayed suspended there in fear.

'Shee-it,' Ra hissed, still staring at the rock.

I looked up too, and for a moment the world went silent as a fifteen-foot wildman towered over me. At least that's how he looked standing stark naked on top of the rock.

We stayed locked together for a moment, me sitting wet, Ra and the silverfish staring at each other.

Then Boy yelped and leapt up in the air and came splashing down beside me, whimpering in the water.

'Ra, he's hurt. It was a eel, Ra, that's what I saw, he's been bit by a fucking eel!' I shouted.

Ra turned and looked, but couldn't hold his snooty face for long at the sight of poor Boy cowering in the water.

'Bloody dog,' he said, picking him up and heaving him out of the water. I scrambled after them up over the ferns and onto the bank. Boy lay where Ra had put him, whimpering and shivering. He looked so pathetic I was afraid to touch him in case I hurt him more.

'What do we do, Ra?'

Ra walked all around him till he stopped at his hind quarters.

'Shee-it,' he said again.

I moved to his side so I could see what had impressed him. Boy had a gash the size of one of Nan's best kumara stretching nearly right across his hip. Through it I thought I could see the white of the bone.

'Go and stand there in the sun a minute. You're shivering,' Ra said.

I didn't move. I knew what happened to horses when they were injured like Boy. I wasn't leaving him.

'Go on. I'm just going to let him rest a minute while I think what to do.' He stopped speaking and looked up at something behind me. 'On second thoughts, come here, Hana.' He held out his hand to me and I couldn't help it, I looked over my shoulder. It was him, the silverfish. I'd forgotten all about him. On level ground he didn't look so tall. Only about six foot three and one-quarter I reckoned. All the same I backed over so I was standing next to Ra.

'Youse bloody kids. What the fuck are you doing here?' His voice was harsh, like Dad's on a Sunday morning after a night out at the pub. 'Can't a man get some bloody peace around here?'

Ra didn't seem to be going to answer.

'You had bloody peace all year,' I told him. Ra punched my shoulder, but I was only stating the obvious. He wasn't so frightening close up. Nan would have been pleased to see he'd put some old trousers on, but he hadn't thought to have a bath or comb his hair since the last time someone visited, I reckoned, going by the smell.

'Get the fuck outa here. Go on, go!' He waved his arms about and started coming towards us. He walked like a man who'd been on the beer all night, and I thought he was going to trip over Boy.

I moved between them.

'Hana!' Ra almost squealed. Silverfish backed off as if I'd been going to hit him.

'Our dog's been bit by a eel. We can't go anywhere till Ra thinks what to do.'

Silverfish seemed to notice Boy for the first time. He walked around me to get so he could see Boy properly and crouched down to look at his wound. Boy whimpered and exerted himself enough to lick Silverfish's hand.

'Bloody dog!' Ra hissed, and I knew he was thinking how useless is that – a dog who licks the hand of the enemy.

I was starting to dry off and getting a bit fed up with waiting for Ra to come up with a plan. Besides, the apple hadn't filled much of a gap and I suddenly had a vision of a plate of steaming pig meat and sweet sweet kumara . . .

'Can you help him, Mr Silverfish?' I asked.

'M-Mr Sylvester, she means,' Ra added, coming to stand by me.

Silverfish looked from Boy to us, up at the sky and back again.

'C'mon,' he said, and picked Boy up in his arms. We followed him along a path further and further into the bush, until Ra was starting to get edgy, I could feel it coming off him. Then the bush cleared a little, had been cleared at least, and there it was, the house of the silverfish, not much more than few bits of board propped up with an old sheet of corrugated iron for a roof. He laid Boy down on a clear patch and held up his hand for us to wait. In a few seconds he came out with a small battered saucepan full of something that looked like the mud in the hot pools at Rotorua. He smeared it on Boy's wound.

'This'll help,' he said, then went and stripped off four of the big plantain leaves like the ones the men would have used to lay over the hangi. He laid them over the smelly stuff and then wrapped a shirt around Boy's hindquarters, tying the sleeves neatly together around him. Boy was looking at him as if he'd found his guardian angel. Ra was fuming, but I couldn't see why. Boy was looking much better, and now all we had to do was get home in time for the hangi . . .

Of course, neither of us knew the way home, and Boy couldn't walk.

'C'mon,' Silverfish said again, picking Boy up. They were the last words he spoke until we were nearly home. All along the river bed, all along the path through the bush, Ra behind him, me behind Ra, Boy in his arms. It seemed like the journey was going on forever. We passed the point where Boy had stopped for a rest, and I wondered if I could make them stop for me to have one now.

Then suddenly Ra did stop and I could see Silverfish coming back towards us.

'I put him down under a tree,' he said. 'You have to get someone else to carry him now.'

I could smell the hangi. It smelt like home. Christmas. Family.

'I been tickling that old eel for years,' Silverfish said. 'He's not used to having company in his river.' He began walking off.

'Mr Silver, Sylvester' I called, 'the hangi's coming up soon. Come and have some kai with us.'

'Nah, I can't.' He shook his head as if he was trying to convince himself.

'Go on, mister,' Ra said. 'There's always plenty to eat, 'specially at Christmas. Too much for us.'

'Boy would like you to come,' I said.

He looked as if he wanted to come, I swear he did. Then a cheer went up from beyond the bush as in the clearing the hangi was taken up. Ra and I both turned towards it, and when we turned back he was gone, like a silverfish into hiding.

Ra looked at me and I looked at Ra. Then we both broke out running and didn't stop till we were safe on the verandah.

Glossary

bach – term used in the North Island of New Zealand for a holiday home, hut
hangi – a kind of oven made from heated stones buried in a pit
kai – food
kumara – sweet potato
marae – meeting-place
rimu and kauri trees – native trees of New Zealand

Terminus

Jas Sherry

Shona wraps the pink bubblegum round the tip of her tongue, inflates her chest, then pops a bubble. A flamboyant squiggle puts a finishing touch to her artwork.

Here's one coming, shouts Cath.

Is it a forty-seven? Shona asks, from behind the shelter.

Can't make out yet, says Cath. Hope so.

Same here, says Shona, throwing away a dried-out ink-marker.

A bus moves steadily up the hill towards the terminus, number and destination coming into focus as it approaches its journey's end.

Is it him? demands Shona.

It is, it is, squeals Cath. Look he's giving us a wee wave.

The bus eases to a halt next to the graffiti-daubed shelter. The doors swish open to set free the group of returning bingo-players. Night, driver, they chant, as they exit into the left-overs of the evening. When the group's chatter has finally dissolved, Cath and Shona re-emerge from the blindside of the shelter and edge towards the entrance of the bus. The doors stay open. The two girls gaze up at the driver. Shona wraps the pink bubblegum round the point of her tongue, pops a bubble.

Night, driver, says Cath.

Night, night, driver, Shona echoes, chewing hard on her flavourless gum.

The driver stays inside his cab, intent upon the details of his logbook. The two girls shuffle awkwardly inside their new shoes. A final fragment of bingo laughter rises and falls into the distance.

Are you coming in or not? asks the driver.

Suppose so, responds Cath.

What if we don't have the correct fare, Mr Driver, sir? pleads Shona.

The driver's head swivels. He holds their eyes for a short dramatic beat. Stop messing about or I'll report you to the inspector, his voice stern and abrupt. The two girls giggle. In unison they step up and onto the worn platform. The doors swoosh, sealing them in. The driver continues to scan the detail on his clipboard.

Make yourselves at home, he says at last.

The girls usher themselves inside. Traces of perfume and stale tobacco linger in the turgid, unventilated air.

What's the destination, driver? asks Cath.

He reaches up and begins to scroll through a range of destinations, then returns to his clipboard. The two girls perch themselves on the seat closest to his cabin.

It really pongs in here, Shona complains, as she opens one of the small window vents. As she does she catches a glimpse of the driver's eye in the carefully angled mirror.

How does Private Party sound? he suggests. The girls look puzzled. As a destination, he adds, beginning to emerge from his cabin. He loosens his shirt collar and pulls down the knot of his tie.

Sounds very . . . intimate, says Cath.

Are we going to have one? asks Shona.

I love parties, declares Cath.

The driver looks down at them. He smiles and shakes his

head. Shall we? His upturned palm inviting them to move to one of the longer seats at the back. As they re-settle themselves, Cath whispers something into Shona's ear. She slides sideways, leaving a narrow gap between them.

Excuse me, mister, says Cath, there's a seat here; help take the weight off your feet. And some feet off your height, Shona adds. They yelp like hyenas. The driver carefully considers the obviousness of the space. Waiting for the laughter to subside, he sits on a nearby seat.

Cigarette? he asks, pulling a silver case from the inside pocket of his uniform. Cathy takes one and puts it to her lips.

Not for me, says Shona. Is that real silver? The driver nods and snaps the case shut.

He taps both ends of his cigarette on the smooth reflecting surface, before sliding the case back into his jacket. From another pocket he produces a lighter and clicks on the flame. Cath leans forward, scanning his face, noting his brown eyes straying to her breasts. She draws hard, exhales two streams of smoke through her nose.

Thanks, she says, coyly, leaning back and crossing her legs. The driver, likewise, leans back into his seat and emits a series of elegant smoke-rings. A moment of silence passes between them as they observe the brief lifespan of circles.

I thought smoking was forbidden on buses, Shona interrupts.

A lot of things are forbidden, the driver replies.

Like?

Lots of things. Small detail, the driver answers, cryptically. A playful smile appears on his lips. The girls resist the urge to giggle. The driver continues to create circles of smoke, his concentration absorbed by the rings' wavering form.

I always think of Adam and Eve when I hear that word, says Shona.

Friends of yours? the driver asks.

Y'know what I mean. Stories you hear at Sunday School: the Garden of Eden, forbidden fruit and all that.

You believe in all that, Shona? the driver says, fixing his eyes on her.

Maybe some of it, she says, looking sideways, hoping Cath might help. You're not meant to believe in everything.

I suggest you make up your mind, the driver says.

You know what I'm trying to say, Shona says. The word . . . forbidden.

You have a degree in theology? Or philosophy perhaps?

Cath puffs out a small 'o' of smoke. It gyrates in front of them.

Right and wrong and things, Shona perseveres.

And what, exactly, do you mean by 'right and wrong things'?

Being good to people. Not hurting anyone. The stories might not all be true but they tell you how to behave or . . .

Do you believe in hell, for instance? the driver asks, still managing to keep a formation of smoke-rings afloat. Cath throws a frustrated glance at her friend.

How long have we got? she asks.

As long as we need, says the driver, his hands opening like flowers.

Won't they send the inspector to find you? Who's stolen our bus? Rescue parties and all that.

I wouldn't think so, he smiles.

Does the garage never close then? asks Shona.

Not really.

He holds the girls in a long stare, not so much at them as through them. The girls divert their eyes to the adverts posted above the seats. Shona points to one and they begin to giggle. The driver throws his stub to the floor, crushing it with his foot, his left hand caressing his beard. He keeps his eyes on the flattened stub.

Tell us about the forbidden, then, says Cath.

Not able to, he replies. I would recommend Shakespeare, though. The girls share a silent 'what?'

Friend of yours? asks Shona.

He shakes his head. What I'm saying is, you'll find more to do with 'rights and wrongs and things' in one of Shakespeare's plays than you'll find in any dog-eared Bible. The Bible's so . . . one-dimensional. The two girls stare at him.

You sound like my big brother, says Cath.

What does he do when he's at home?

You mean what does he work at?

Whatever.

Well, he doesn't do anything really. He fell out with my parents years ago. Dad called him a flakehead, and he called Dad a fuckhead. Something like that. Anyway, he left. Split to Amsterdam. Up and went. Liked his pot did Joe. Listened to Bob Marley non stop, posters all over the walls. Still there, as if waiting for him to return.

I liked him, Shona says, he was a really nice guy. People get so uptight sometimes.

The driver looks up from his stub. What's any of this got to do with Shakespeare?

Nothing. I mean . . . never mind, says Cath, her eyes a bit moist.

You married? asks Shona.

The driver looks along the length of the bus. Some wee boys are hanging about at the doors. He strides down the aisle, they see him coming and scatter into the safety of the nearby woods. He returns to his seat.

Are you? Shona persists.

Used to be. Until it died.

What did?

Everything.

You're in a funny mood tonight, says Cath.

A long day inside the sweatbox. Sorry if I'm not good company.

You said you'd bring some pictures, says Cath. He doesn't respond. She repeats her statement at a higher pitch.

Hold on, he says, moving towards the cabin. Shona and Cath's eyes meet. Shona signals that they better leave now but Cath whispers no, she wants to see the pictures. Shona shakes her head, saying quietly. I think there's something wrong with him. Go, if you want, says Cath, but I'm staying. They hear the cabin door click, the driver coming back, holding a thick, matt-black folder. He chooses the space between them.

Their arms and legs brush against the rough heavy cotton of his uniform. Cath uncrosses her legs and leans into him. Shona slides a bit closer. Glancing sideways, she detects the onset of grey among the wiry hairs of his beard; his aftershave, rich and sickly, his Adam's apple, as it bolts up and down, a small animal caught inside the throat of some wild beast. And Cath's thigh, packed next to his, a hand continually dropping on her knee. She looks down at her own knee, bony and innocent.

And who's this? asks Cath, with an excited tone. The driver sighs and contemplates the photograph.

That's my young sister. Taken in Scarborough. Nineteen seventy-something.

Like pokey-hats, does she? says Cath.

That's a ninety-nine, actually, says Shona. What age?

Then, seventeen.

Where is she now? asks Cath.

New Zealand, last I heard.

Do you keep in touch?

Not really.

Shame. I keep in touch with Joseph, the brother I told you about. There are ways.

She's got your eyes, remarks Shona.

That was then, he says, more to himself.

How come there are no colour photographs here? asks Cath. How come they're all black and white? Seems so old fashioned, I think. God, I hate those old films my parents watch. No colour to them. I just can't watch a film if it's not got colour.

Shades of grey, the driver mutters.

How come there are no pictures of you?

He inspects the surface of the print closely and answers, I'm the photographer. I took all of these. I only take photographs of people I know: friends, relatives. Sometimes, the odd stranger, but only for the sake of composition; moments that demand to be captured. It's not meant to be a family album. It's a record. An art. My statement. He turns over the last leaf of the volume, checks his watch, brings his hand up to toy with his beard.

You going now? asks Cath.

I suppose, he says.

Are we not . . . ? Cath completes her sentence with an upward glance of her eyes.

Upstairs? says the driver. I should really be making tracks.

Next time, then? says Cath, rising from her seat.

Tell you what, how about tidying yourselves up a bit and I'll take a few shots. Photographs I mean. You deserve to be in the album.

You mean both of us together? Cath asks.

I'm not sure . . . says Shona.

Quick, run upstairs I'll get the camera.

The girls squeeze past him, the cocktail of rich aftershave, tobacco and sweat stronger than ever before. At the base of the stairs, Shona spots that the cabin door is very slightly ajar. But the driver hurries them up the winding stair to the top deck, his eyes keenly following their ascent. Take a seat, he calls. With you soon.

On the top deck, Shona holds Cath's hand. It'll be okay, Cath assures. He's a nice guy, honestly. I'm not sure at all, says Shona, let's go home. Cath looks at her with an expression of disappointment, disgust. Always the same with you, she says, I'll do this, I'll do that but when it comes to the bit you always crap out of it. Well, I'm staying. At least I know how to enjoy myself.

Shona surveys the windows that surround her. To one side is the growing shadow of the woods. The nearest habitat, a few hundred yards away: a row of flats. She can see a light on. Now and then a figure moves back and forward across the lighted frame. A kitchen, perhaps. Someone about to prepare a late-night snack. Down the hill, from where the bus had emerged, the street stands empty, bathed in the yellow haze of streetlights.

Cath applies a fresh coat of lipstick using the darkened window as a mirror. She offers the tube to Shona. Hurry, he'll be here in a minute.

What happened? Shona asks.

When?

Y'know, the last time.

I told you all about it. He was nice. Very nice.

I think he's creepy.

Be quiet. He'll hear you and then he won't be our friend. I told you. He's just a bit lonely. Better than any of those creeps that you hang around with at the Youthie. He knows how to treat you and stuff. I'm telling you. He's great. She moves to the rear of the bus and settles on the back seat, loosening two buttons. Well? she says.

Shona moves towards the top of the stairs. From the back of the bus Cath's voice pines, 'We're ready'. Perched at the edge of the top step, Shona catches sight of the driver as he glides up the steps: his bald patch, the collar of his shirt wide at the neck. In his left hand he carries a black case. In his right, an object, silvery and long. She tries to catch her breath in the pungent air. Near the top, he tilts his head, gazing sharply into Shona's eyes.

Tell Me a Story

Kate Percival

Once upon a time there was a woman who lived in a fine gabled house which had a fine garden which swept round three sides. The other was taken up by the garage. On each side of it was a similar villa, though hers was set further back from the road and somewhat apart from its fellows, on a long wide road that led out of town, and underlined her suburb like a straight line.

Her husband was a company man, who took a little trouble over the cut of his suit and hence set himself apart from his fellows. With a passive but profound commitment to work he attended his office six days in seven, and worked, frequently, until the large box-like building whose windows slotted in like glass in a projector was silent and dark. In fact he preferred it that way. He departed the company building at ease, content. He was successful. He was comfortably off. He had a pension plan. He returned home in twilight as the days shortened, dovetailed into autumn. He returned home to meals with his wife.

His wife tended the garden. Gardening is a cumulative activity. The little she put into it was significant. A seedhead snapped off and binned was denied its progeny populating the lawn. The plug plants from the garden centre buried haphazardly on the terrace secured themselves with new roots and satellite leaves, high-street jewels held in the claws of the rough bouldered rockery.

She had a rockery. She had dwarf conifers, and rectangular rosebeds. She was not a woman who embraced change. She had a slight problem with even the slow rate of change effected by the plant kingdom, and tended to over-prune, in order that faster growing shrubs and trees might longer keep their initial shape. In this she was quite successful, and she went indoors after an hour in the garden with a sense of satisfaction and contentment, and a bin-bag full of clippings.

The woman loved her husband, who had changed not at all. Not since their first meeting at university. From old photographs you could see that he no longer wore his hair so long, but the change had been so gradual as to be unnoticeable. She hadn't noticed it. She loved him.

Autumn became winter, winter became spring. She weeded the large garden for half an hour every morning, to keep on top of it. With the addition of two hours a week from an odd-job man, who could turn his hand to anything – lawns, patios, paths and pests – this pocket of time was sufficient.

She liked the garden.

She liked weeding best. As the days lengthened she began to weed different weeds on different days. Hence, Monday was dandelion day, Tuesday hairy bittercress, Wednesday chickweed and so on. The garden did not burgeon with life – it was not a dynamic, vaulting, heaven-climbing life force. It was quiet, it was browns and greys, opaque whites, occasional spots of petalled colour and thin abbreviated blades of green.

She liked its detail and its scope. Bent down on a cushioned kneeler she saw little conglomerations of lumpy soil, angles and facets on the chopped gravel, brown lines on broken leaves, still hinged, which flapped awkwardly in an occasional breeze. Hairy bittercress she found by the glint of its tiny white head, seed arms outstretched, a thin minimalist candelabra against the tablecloth of ground-hugging green moss. Moss was Thursdays. It formed continents on the oversized boulders of the rockery. It pushed up towards the house as though a buttress.

She liked the rosettes of bittercress, the way they pulled out so easily, shallow anchored as they were. She threw them like brides' posies over her shoulder, and they dried grey and dusty on the path, white roots shrivelled. On occasion one would be thick and fleshy, a survivor of her hawk's eye. Or one was purple, merging with the trodden path, elusive.

One day the woman and her husband went on holiday, and the garden was not tended for a week. While they were away, she sensed that her husband's thoughts were elsewhere. When they spoke his eyes seemed to miss hers, and alight on her hairline, or an earlobe. The hotel was good, and the break enjoyable, but the loss of her husband's attention troubled her. It was not so much the lack of attention itself, but its novelty. She found it unsettling. They returned home early.

In her absence, as always, native flora had crept in, and on her first morning in the garden, some time after her husband's departure for the office, she took stock.

The bittercress had spread across the main bed, dotting it with its tiny white spindly flowers. It looked like lace, a filigree of family groups. Dandelions, unseen on their departure, dominated the lawn, each flower a radiating cluster of bright yellow, blunt-ended spatula petals. Low in the tussocked uncut grass, taller near the rich soil of the borders, each party of two or three stems angled inwards to flat-fingered leaves.

She went to the garage. She retrieved the small trowel and the long handled secateurs. She rested them on the front path, returned to the house and fetched the small pruners from the cutlery drawer. There they shared space with sharp-bladed knives and cleavers of varying size, used for bread and meat.

From the kitchen door she followed the path that looped

her property. As she passed, she confidently clipped off flower heads. Her decapitation policy was enormously effective. Systematically she went on, through every border and every island bed. Amazingly, from the same skeleton that normally carried a light-weight of mixed lipstick-coloured hybrid roses, a wonderfully subtle and tangled tapestry emerged. Untouched species – dandelions, spiky thistles, cotton-seeded willowherbs – formed a living warp and weft that gently held the fallen roses.

She told the odd-job man not to come back. For the rest of that week she concentrated her attention on particular plants on different days. Herbaceous perennials she dug out on Tuesday and Thursday. Celandine with its stars of yellow flowers spread over the ground. When she pulled out a dry brush of heather the celandine, disturbed, revealed white tuberous roots, old ladies' thick stockinged legs. Carefully she poked them back into the decency of dirt.

The change in her gardening approach seemed marginal – a mere shift of perspective. And once the groundwork was done it was remarkably maintenance free. Paradoxically however, the less time she needed to spend in the garden the more she wanted to be there. Seeds would arrive each day, borne in by the wind, and added to the growing colonisation. She watched their progress eagerly.

Finally she turned her attention to the trees. They were the largest plants in the garden. Huge plants with tough knotted trunks, which split and forked until they disseminated at their height into nothing, just tiny flags of waving green. She stood at a distance from each abrupt upright, and concluded that these were indeed already weeds. With her artillery of secateurs she removed all spindly growth and other irrelevancies. She felt strong. She felt powerful.

The evening sun caught their shortened shapes and she was stood in the midst of their monstrous shadows when, at his usual time – late – her husband returned home. His body, bent, split diagonally the black line the road made at the bottom of the garden. He passed her without a greeting, and entered the house through the front door.

She stood and watched him go in. She took stock.

She stooped, picked up her tools, and went in after him.

You See Patterns When You Close Your Eyes

Morven Crumlish

When I arrive, there are children playing in the street; I have to weave through them to get to the front door. I didn't think children played in the street anymore, but here they are on scooters and bikes; there is even a hopscotch grid chalked out on the pavement. Hopscotch! That one's before even *my* time. I wonder if it is this middle-class street, a 1950s time warp, parents who ban television and Gameboys. More likely there is a hopscotch revival going on, coloured chalks and stencils and rulebooks sold at great expense, in conjunction with branded junk food.

It makes me feel old, not knowing. Makes me realise how far away I am from the world of childhood, now I'm the sort of person who would start a sentence with, 'When I was a girl,' and wouldn't notice young, clear eyes glazing over.

Maybe if I had children it would be different. Then I would be part of their games; they would rush in from school and tell me about their days, tell me their dreams, share themselves with me. Or it would be, 'Mum, I need money, just for *stuff*,' and I'd be a mug and give it to them, then Denny would give me a hard time for that.

I am wondering what Denny's children would look like, practising saying 'our son, our daughter' in my head, when the door opens, and I am faced with the poet.

He does not look how I imagined he would. He is my first poet. He does not have waving, white hair down to his shoulders, he wears neither a cardigan buttoned up wrongly nor eighteenth-century-style foppish velvet and flounce. He looks just like a man, older than me, but not quite so much older that I don't even register his maleness. Automatically I assess if he attracts me, if I would be likely to attract him. If Denny knew I thought things like this, he would kill me, probably. He thinks he is the only man who can keep me happy, says he is the only man who would put up with me.

When I met Denny, I did the initial assessment, and while he scored high on all counts, I supposed that he would never be interested in me. Especially not that night, I had just finished my finals and my hair was still unwashed and my fingertips inky, the clam of nervous sweat meant that there were handprints on my pint glass. Not attractive. An unwashed drunk and a bluestocking. Not his type at all. But somehow, we got together, somehow I was his type, and now here we are, three years later, still together, all the somehows latching together like a puzzle, a buffer zone around us, keeping us in.

It was Denny's idea that I went for this job, with the poet. I work full time anyway – Standard Life! I'm still with Standard Life! The temp job that seeped into permanence. How many dreams are shredded with the confidential waste, I wonder, and is there a database of that? But this job, this will get me nearer to art, literature. Writing, even just physically writing instead of the flicker of the computer screen, boxes to fill in.

We were in the pub, we met an old lecturer of mine, who told me about the poet, how he needed a secretary, just for transcribing, some filing, some correspondence. Evenings, weekends. Nothing too structured. Denny said it would be good for me; we need the money, I thought, though I didn't say that. I agreed, yes, it would be good to be around people who think again. Sometimes I think my brain has just seized up since I graduated, or maybe it's fallen out altogether, I left it on a bus somewhere.

The poet and I drink coffee in a bright kitchen, trees out the back window, a piney wooden table. I pour the coffee, find milk and sugar. A milk jug, sugar bowl. It is fun to play in someone else's kitchen, not having to rinse fag ends out of mugs, not clearing a space among the roaches and skins and (if I am really lucky!) the soft porn on the coffee table. This house has cookbooks in the kitchen, magazines and dictionaries in the sitting room, a wall of novels in the hall, cartoons and terse witticisms in the toilet. There are words everywhere. I don't know if they belong to the wife, or if the poet keeps them around him; maybe he feels he can absorb the words, maybe there is a calming in the stillness of books.

I want to ask him if he needs me to read for him, but I am too embarrassed. I am not sure how to approach the subject of the poet's blindness. At the moment I am pretending I don't notice, and to be honest I don't, really. He doesn't look straight at me is all, but then who does, these days? Even Denny – but when Denny looks straight at you, you know it doesn't mean anything good. When I talk to Denny I look into the corners of rooms, and when we fuck I close my eyes and store up his gentleness and his need for me in pictures in my head, use them later on.

The poet gives me the job. Does he like my voice, or is he persuaded by the recommendation of my lecturer? I spend the spring evenings, and Saturdays, writing down everything he says, Sundays transcribing it all with the Braille typewriter, and he sits and reads through my notes, his fingers tracing his words, which have become my work, businesslike bumps on the paper, columned, tabulated. I don't know, didn't know this was how you wrote poetry, but I don't ask questions. If it takes him this long to write a poem, then good, I'm in this job for long enough!

I barely see the wife. Sometimes she is around to let me in, but often she goes out, or she holes herself up upstairs in the bedroom, with the television or her stereo. We have the study, a large, empty room downstairs, next to the kitchen. It gets the sun in the evening; the poet tells me he likes the feel of the sun on his skin. I try to imagine it, feeling warmth without being able to see the way colours are brighter, and shadows sharper. I try closing my eyes, but I see red and orange and green blotches, or geometric patterns like linoleum, and I don't know if he sees them too, or remembers them from when he could see. I feel stupid, don't know how to put it, so I just don't mention it. When I find myself saying things like, 'I see,' I want to slap myself. Denny says I am pretty stupid, the guy is blind, so he just doesn't see anything; he doesn't understand why it confuses me, why I have difficulty distinguishing what I see as a result of refracted light and nerve endings doing their job and what I see in my head. Just as clear sometimes. Made-up pictures, whole lifetimes. Like dreams, what are blind people's dreams like?

All these questions, but I don't want him to think I'm rude or prejudiced or ignorant, so I just keep them to myself.

Summer comes, and I am still visiting the poet. He has told me he is writing a book, which makes sense at least, so I am filing all his notes, because that's what all the stuff I have done up till now is, just notes. I have a little machine that makes labels with raised letters for the front of the wallet files; the poet can read these with his fingers, which are very sensitive. When he meets me at the front door one evening, he shakes my hand, and his other hand holds onto my upper arm, which is bare. He is more tactile, it is a blind thing, I think, and I don't mind it as I might with an older man who could see. He says, 'Well, summer is really here!' and I don't know what to make of his allusion to my exposed flesh, I don't know what

Denny would say, then I see the wife behind him, smiling, so I suppose it is okay for him to say these things.

There has been something of a heat wave, for round here, anyway. I can't really wear shorts, my legs are rather bruised, so is my back, my stomach, but I can bare my arms, they don't look too bad, and now they have a bit of a tan. I spend the whole weekend with the poet, sitting in the garden, and I can hitch up my skirt, let my poor pasty legs see the light of day, without worrying about what anyone will say. The poet wears shorts, and sometimes sits with his shirt off. He has greying hair on his chest, his stomach is hairy too, and a little too pillowlike to be erotic in any way. His arms, though, are quite muscular. I wonder, briefly, if it is from using a wheelchair, then I remember he is blind. Not in a wheelchair. Despite this job, my mind is still not with me, not entirely.

I notice things like when he has had a haircut, and when he is wearing a new T-shirt; he thinks it is funny that I am so interested in his domestic issues. He calls me his muse, and tells me I should get back to my own writing. (When would I have the time? There is Denny, Standard Life, but I don't want to hurt his feelings, so I just agree with him.) Sometimes, we just sit and talk all day, and I barely get any work done at all, I feel a bit guilty, still being paid for this time, but after all, it is the poet paying, the poet talking. Really, I am just around to do as I am told. Anyway, I like talking with him, he listens to me, and when he starts talking again, it's about whatever I was just going on about. It makes a pleasant change. When I talk to Denny, he tells me to shut up, or I think he's listening, then he just launches into something completely unrelated. Being with the poet makes me realise how tiring it is, being with Denny, how much energy it takes up, sharing space with him. But I love Denny, and I wouldn't want him to change, or it wouldn't be love.

It is August, the heat has risen, it is oppressive and thick, the air smells of the drains, we need a good rainstorm, but it won't come, won't come. I get to the house Thursday evening, wearing my dark glasses, but when it is him that opens the door, I can take them off. If it had been her, she would have given me that look of pity, and disbelief, and I would have had to say I walked into a door, or something. It is tempting, just to come out with it – Denny slapped me, I pissed him off, he's frustrated, it's too fucking hot – just to see them look shocked, see the sympathy fold up into cold disgust, just to shut them up. Because I don't need a women's shelter, or a police helpline, or a cup of fennel tea, or whatever. I know what Denny is like. I choose to live with him, I love him, and if he hits me sometimes, at least it shows he is there, he cares about me: he loses his temper, but he never means to hurt me. He's always sorry afterwards, like a little boy.

I sit down at my desk and I'm arranging all my things, when I see that the poet is crying. At first I don't think it is crying, I think maybe his eyes are just smarting, maybe he has drops for them or something, but then it comes out, this whole story. The poet's wife has left him! It seems all her nights out she was meeting a man she fell in love with at an Alcoholics Anonymous meeting! There, I just put in two sentences what it has taken him all night to tell me.

Seeing him sitting, crying like that, sobbing, just, with his chin on his chest, not even trying to hide, does something to me. This is a man crying, and not my fault, for once! I go over, and pull his head to my chest, and lean my cheek on his hair, and he puts his arms round my waist, and soon I am sitting on his knee, and he lifts his face to me, and I kiss his mouth and I think: this is kissing a man who has never seen me.

I think of Denny and I jump up, apologising, and the poet apologises, too, and says he understands if I don't want to come back. I look around the room, my piles of papers, the stacks of wallet files, the plants on the mantelpiece, clean floors. The sun has just set, and the garden is black with a green sky. The poet stands, sheepish, not knowing where to look, his hands hanging by his sides, clenching and unclenching fists. I couldn't leave all this. I walk over to the poet, rest my hand on his shoulder, and tell him I will see him at the usual time tomorrow. I say I will see myself out, and for once I don't even notice my tactlessness.

When I get home to Denny I can see that he is angry at me for being out so late, but he sees my eye, splendidly bruised, shining flesh, and I breezily say something about overtime, and he shuts up. We go to bed and have sex, and I try to stop myself from thinking about the poet, imagining his hands on me, his warmth, his sweat dripping onto me. Afterwards, Denny tells me he loves me, and I say I love you too, which is only the truth.

My time with the poet is even more precious, these days. Sometimes when he wants to sit and think, or read through his notes, I wander off, exploring the house, looking through drawers and at photographs, reading his bills, lying down on his bed. I have taken to cooking for us, recipes from the shiny books which the wife still has not collected. I make sure not to do anything where the page is already covered with cooking splatters. I want to give him new tastes, I don't want to bring up the past.

He has asked me to move in with him. He pretends it is simply a business arrangement, but we both know that it would lead to more than that. We take every opportunity to touch one another: when I pass the chair he is sitting on I put one hand on the back of his neck, when he kisses me, briefly and on the cheek when I arrive or leave, his palm presses a little harder into the small of my back.

I take these moments home with me, they are coloured so vividly, and life with Denny seems increasingly grey.

Denny knows something is up: he is like a dog who sees you packing and knows that you are going on holiday without him. He is trying so hard to be nice to me, it makes me feel bad that I am falling in love with another man, but I just feel I am moving further and further away from Denny and his mess and his tantrums.

I've handed in my notice at Standard Life, there is enough for me to do for the poet, without other people's insurance claims to process. I feel invigorated as I walk out of the office on my last day, as though my arms and legs are lighter, and the air is easier to breathe. I get home early, and find Denny in bed with a seventeen-year-old who sometimes comes up to the flat to score, and I am in such a good mood anyway, I have to work hard at acting angry. I throw things around the flat, gleefully smashing our horrible plates, then I pack theatrically, leaving half the things I actually need behind, and just chucking whatever comes to hand into a case. I stagger out of the house yelling that I will be back later, for the rest of my things, but when I do return a week later Denny has moved out, the flat is bare. I suppose he has sold all my stuff.

I lie in bed, next to the poet, mapping his body, staring at him without the fear of being caught. Asleep, he does not look like more than a slightly paunchy, middle-aged man, but he needs me, and I find myself loving him more and more.

Relax

J. C. Robertson

Read her note again with composure:

> *Can't wait to see your new flat. Let's not fight this time. Love and kisses. Your big sister.*

She will arrive soon. Prepare yourself. Sit in the armchair and think peaceful thoughts. Savour the tranquillity. Look out the window and appreciate the start of spring. The blue sky, the birds flying by, the way the leaves of the trees flutter in the breeze. Relax. Breathe.

Be calm. Imagine a pleasant afternoon in the company of your sister. Visualise you and her together – talking, laughing and sharing. This is possible. You are no longer the insecure girl she used to know. You have changed. You are a mature and successful woman with a terrific life.

Be prepared. Go to the bathroom. Brush your hair. Touch up your make-up. Check the contents of the bathroom cabinet (she will). Look at yourself in the mirror. Appreciate your good physical features. Think of the current great reality of your life. Smile at yourself confidently.

Return to your armchair. Consider putting on some mood music, but reject this as too contrived. (You are a natural person.) Pour a cup of tea. Sip peacefully. Look around your beautiful flat: your plants, your books, your paintings. Be happy that you have these beautiful objects in your life. Allow yourself some deserved satisfaction. This is the flat of a woman who has got her life together. Congratulate yourself.

The doorbell has started to ring. It is ringing. It has started. Relax. Breathe. You will handle this. You are mature. You are strong. (She is going to discover that you are now a completely different person.) Be positive. This is an opportunity to develop a loving relationship with your sister. Be generous. You have so much in your life.

Walk calmly to the front door and open it smiling welcomingly. Show her into the flat in a relaxed good-to-see-you way. (The last time is forgotten.) Display your loving nature by hugging and kissing her. Demonstrate your generous spirit by complimenting her on her new outfit. Take her coat. Invite her to sit down.

Pour her some tea in an easy, self-possessed way. Let it show how you have moved on. (You are no longer the person she used to know). Hand her the cup with a warm, open, confident expression.

Listen as she comments on how well you have done for yourself. Accept the compliment with grace. (Ignore the tone of surprise.) Watch her look around your room. Feel comfortable with what the room says about you. Enter into an interesting discussion about one of your *objets d'art*. Show your sophistication by commenting on its aesthetics. Suggest she too starts collecting art.

She has now noticed the computer. Listen to her joke about you probably not being able to use it. Just smile and explain that you have been on a training course. (You are self-assured and self-confident.) Discuss the advantages of information technology. Give an example of how practical you find your mobile phone. Mention in passing that you have the latest model. Impress her with some technical knowledge of future developments.

Move to the window with her so that she may admire the view. Open the window to let her see properly. (Ignore her remark about traffic noise.) Point out local landmarks and impress her with your knowledge. Inform her when the sunlight is best.

Be pleased as she introduces the topic of your new job. Be proud. You deserve this moment. Answer her questions happily but without any sign of triumphing. (Let her see that's not your style.) Say how much you love the challenge of the job. Talk authoritatively. Mention difficulties with young female employees. Admit that they think you're a dragon. Let her know that doesn't bother you.

Stop talking about work and switch to something feminine. Say something about her hairstyle. Toss your hair back with a smile. Make a suggestion about her look. Take her over to the mirror to show her what you mean. Return to your seats laughing together at some jokey aside.

Let the conversation move on. Catch up on each other's news in an easygoing girls-together style. Share feelings about friends and family. Be genuinely interested as she updates you on her life. Show your caring side with thoughtful questions. (Let her see how mature and level-headed you are.)

Discover with surprise that you can talk openly to her. Give her your thoughts on life. Listen to her ideas. Ask her opinion about something. Make it clear that you value her input. Listen attentively. Thank her.

Reflect that things are going well. Reflect that maybe this is the start of a whole new phase in your relationship with your sister. Consider that she may be genuine this time. Acknowledge that after all this time she might have changed. Smile at her with love. Breathe. Pour more tea.

* * *

Now. Do it now. Casually but with assurance, give her your news.

She is just looking. She is giving no reaction. Don't be fazed. Explain your motivation for choosing to get back with him. Admit that it was a surprise for you, too, but tell her why you nevertheless feel comfortable with your decision.

She is still saying nothing. She is just sitting there in her quiet, superior, utterly judgemental way. In a logical and unruffled manner tell her exactly why the relationship is right for you this time. List the various ways in which it is completely different. Give concrete examples of how he has changed. Make it clear that you are not asking for permission but just sharing with her. Suggest she try being pleased for you. Breathe. Leave her to think about that. Excuse yourself. Go to the bathroom. Wash your hands thoroughly. Look at yourself in the mirror. Smile at your self-possession.

Re-enter with confidence.

She wants you to listen now. Okay, listen. Take a deep breath. Keep listening. Feel sad that she can't be pleased for you. Feel compassion for her display of jealousy. Ignore her question about money. Don't listen. This is not relevant. Okay. Calmly admit that, yes, he does need money. Make it clear you are happy to help him. Give her the reasons why he needs the money. Remind her that you have never been a materialistic person and that money is simply not an issue for you. Tell her that if she needed financial assistance, you would give it to her with an open heart. Emphasis your sincerity. Smile. Suggest more tea.

Simply ignore the references to your past relationships. (She just wants to put you down.) Wonder aloud if it is a crime to make mistakes. Wonder aloud if that is not the way one learns. Give up expecting her to be pleased for you. Stop trying to explain. (She has not changed.) Don't be naive. Don't waste your breath. She will never understand because she doesn't want to understand. Recognise the sad fact that your very own sister would gladly see you alone and unhappy for the rest of your life.

Breathe.

Now she is apologising. Implying, of course, that you can't take criticism. Still the big sister. Laugh at her idea that she has got you crying. Don't even bother to reply to this. It's just too ridiculous. You are above this. Breathe. Notice that a painting on the wall isn't hanging properly. Calmly adjust it.

Pause.

Thank her for her opinion. Ask her to listen to you now. Start giving her some honest opinions. Try not to go too far. (Don't feel guilty, though. Remember she always does you down when she can.) Go through the things you want to say to her. Just make your point. Just make her see. Just enough. Mention the incident at your thirteenth birthday party. Let her know that you've not forgotten. Catch your breath. Suggest it's time she grew up.

Perhaps you have gone too far. Apologise for bringing the incident up. Explain that you have been working very hard recently and been a bit stressed. Don't let her think she is special. Let her know everyone in the office is getting it. Let her know that your life is no bed of roses. List some of the things you have to endure. Breathe. Stop talking about your problems. Smile. Say how happy and positive you are about your life.

Ignore the sympathetic concern on her face. Laugh when she says she worries about you. Tell her not to bother. Don't let her patronise you. Don't take any of that from her. Smile sweetly and suggest you just might be old enough now to make your own decisions. Walk to the window to get some air. Breathe.

(Look at her . . . Look at her sitting there . . . Imagine. You could walk right out your flat now and just leave her sitting there. Imagine that. No. Stay. Don't give her the satisfaction. Don't go down to her level.)

Now she wants to say something. Okay listen to her. Don't listen. Listen. Wonder who exactly she thinks she is. (She obviously thinks she is perfect). She is suggesting he gets a job if he needs money. Be rational. Be calm. Explain why this is not practical. Explain in such a clear and lucid way that even a child could understand. Realise that logic will not work with her. Face the facts. Your sister wants you to be unhappy. She actually wants your relationship to fail. Go ahead – ask if in her heart she wants this relationship to fail. Throw your teacup at the wall to show your frustration.

Laugh at her suggestion that you need help. Calmly explain that the current state of your life is excellent. Smile. Let her know that you have never been happier. You have a great life. Don't let her get to you. Don't let her make you feel stupid, unhappy, uptight. This is not the reality.

Take control. Breathe. Suggest a drink.

Calmly move towards the drinks cabinet. Let it show that you are completely at ease. Pour a generous measure in both glasses. (Ignore the spilt tonic water.) Add the ice and lemon with authority.

Sip the gin and tonic. Feel the benefit. Relax. Change the subject in a let's-just-chat sort of way. Smile. Choose something general to show your intelligence and culture. Talk about politics. Mention the environment. Emphasise your profound dislike of materialist society and the strength of your moral beliefs. Ask if she still eats meat.

Pause.

Calmly remind her that her life is hardly perfect. Ask about her ex. Enquire if she ever sees him or his new wife. Observe how quiet she has gone. Let her know that you feel she was lucky that relationship ended. Give her a few home truths on that subject. Don't hold back. Be honest with her. Let her know that he was no angel. Tell her about the time after the party. Tell her; she needs to know. Give details.

Pause.

Watch her collect her things and leave. Be very calm. She is uptight. She has trouble coping with the problems in her life. Suggest she needs help. Explain that you worry about her.

Close the door behind her and re-enter the room with calm. Look out the window and appreciate the start of spring. The blue sky, the way the leaves of the trees are fluttering in the breeze. Think of the current great reality of your life. Breathe.

Woman with Biro

Simon Smith

In. In through the big glass door, and here we are. Wooden floors, of course, with big matt white walls. A shiny espresso machine. And a wee lassie behind the counter, let off her homework for the night. White shirt, short black hair and a nice smile. She's eager to get on. And no one else here yet. Just the two of us.

> – Aye, grand. Yourself? A cappuccino, thanks. OK, I'll be through that door there, thanks.

Click, click, click. Don't you love wooden floors? Walk tall, and make a noise. Open space. Soft lights and a choice of chairs to sit in. Look this way and study the paintings, or look that way and study the people? The paintings. Could always move to another chair later. Lime green, or burnt orange? Both with comfy cushions. Lime green. Goes with the jacket.

And a table with brochures. My name, very fancy, down the left-hand side. Retrospective. By which they mean 'catch him before he cops it'. Including works previously unexhibited. By which they mean 'he's broke'. Reaching to the backs of cupboards, into boxes, dredging, scavenging, and pulling out anything, everything. Hoping for a good opening write-up in the papers, and some big sales, to keep him going for a while. No shame.

And here she comes with the coffee. Should have asked for decaff. But just one won't kill me. Not straight away. What a lovely smile. All in the eyes. She's one to watch. Could just watch her right now. But she'll be busy.

– Thanks. Aye, just there. Thanks.

Off she goes. Holds her head a bit like Barbara. Now, is Barbara here? How have they arranged these things? Not chronologically, anyway, otherwise she'd be right at the start, by the door there. Woman with Dog. Barbara with her daft wee dug. Whatever happened to Barbara? Older than me. Maybe gone. Or sagging, and on her umpteenth daft wee dug by now. Three days out of, God, seventy-five years. What chance of her remembering that? Running to jump on a tram, and into the last seat, next to me, out of breath but smiling at having made it, and then looking to see who she's sat down next to. Looking with those eyes. And that mouth, quick breaths in and out.

Hi, Barbara, I'd say. Remember me? Have a seat here – they've got lime green and burnt orange. Now, Barbara, what happened after I left? Did you ever tell your husband? Told him about the painting, of course. How else to explain it? But let's not dwell on the past. Have you got a coffee? They do all sorts here.

And she'd say, Oh, tea please, tea would be lovely. Am I here, hung on a wall? How grand! Do you think people will recognise me? Perhaps not without Sammy. But they don't allow dogs here, do they? I can't imagine why not. Oh, I know what you think about dogs. But really, he's no trouble at all, and such a good companion, and when you think of all . . .

Stop, I'd say. Stop. And she would stop, and her smile would start to come, and she'd tilt her head, and . . .

> – No, no. There's no one sitting there. Aye, sure, sit down. Emily? John. Yes, that's me. Guest of honour, and all. Are you here for the pictures? Daft question. Or maybe just the coffee. Cappuccino? Here's the lady with the knack for the coffee machine. Would you mind getting us some cappuccinos? I know, I let mine go cold. Always do. Listen, when you get to my age, just remembering where you put the cup down is not bad going. Here, let me pass it up to you. Thanks.

I should go and help her with the coffee – she's run off her feet. And we could chat. Lovely smile. A find.

But now, Emily. You're awfully quiet. Looking round at the pictures. Wondering what to say. Maybe, who are these women? What made you want to paint? To paint them? Do you still paint? Maybe if I lean forward a bit, you'll ask the question that's on your mind. If I lean forward, and look into your eyes. Catch your eye. Look this way.

> – Aye, they are. Big. All really quite big. Aye. Big paintings.

Christ. What do you say after that? But she's right. They are big. Just a bit bigger than life-size. That's they way it comes out. Now, if I were to paint you, Emily, I would start with your chin, because that's where you are. Chin forward. That's you. And work it out from there. And before you know it, you've got a big painting on your hands. And if I could just catch the wee wrinkle in your chin, as it is now – there's another question in there, I'm sure. If only you could ask your question, Emily, and get an answer, then that wrinkle would go. Now, to catch the wrinkle as it eases away, that would be something. We could work on that. So ask. Ask, Emily. Ask.

– Bye, then. Aye, maybe catch you later. Enjoy the paintings.

Bugger. There she goes, all wrinkly.

Maybe I should go and mingle. I could see Barbara, for old times' sake. Though it's a comfy seat. Maybe someone could push me along. The ultimate wheelchair. Now, if that wee table could come with it, running alongside, with my coffee on. And that lassie alongside the table, filling up my cup. God, the fantasies of a seventy-year-old. A well-padded wheelchair, and a woman with a coffee pot. No, it's not going to happen. Up. Up and on to the mingling. Deep breath, and . . . up.

Click, click, click. Point those feet. A smart wee gallery. And full of smart people. Wee groups of black and grey and brown, splodges in front of white walls. And all round the walls, behind them, aye, bigger than them, we have . . .

. . . Abby at the sink in her kitchen, hand-washing that wine-stained tablecloth . . .
. . . Bill and Rhona sat at a table in a restaurant, with the big plate of shattered lobster in between them, their duty served . . .
. . . and Christine, on the edge of her favourite armchair. Looking out over the heads of the people, above it all, looking straight at me. Head back a little as she blows the smoke from her cigarette up and away to the side, little wrinkles appearing in her red lips, the red bleeding over, just a little, into the pale white around her mouth. But it's her eyes you look at. Her eyes that look into you. Then she laughs, and says she's had enough sitting around for one afternoon, and gets up and walks over, onto the sheet I've put onto the carpet, to catch the paint. Come on, John. Put your brushes away for today.

Christine would love it here. Which dress, John? Which dress will I wear? What will people be wearing, John? Do you think this is too formal? How about the black? Or is it too short? Too daring? No, Christine, the black is fine. You'll be great in the black.

A wee sign next to Christine, with the label. Raised perspex, floating over the wall, saying

Woman with Cigarette (1962)

That's Christine. Woman with cigarette. Always with a cigarette.

And these two chaps, underneath Christine, they're not smiling. God, they're writing notes in their brochures. Too smart to be students. Must be critics. Looking at me. Talking to me. *The Herald.*

How does it feel to see this work brought together? A safe answer, that's all we need. And remember, maybe a wee bit of selling.

> – Great. Great to be able to give people the opportunity to see some of the rawer work, with many pieces never previously available for sale.

And who would I cite as major influences?

> – Too many to mention, from the past. But these days it's the students from the college – they're the main influence now on how I see my painting evolving.

And here is Emily at their side, taking out a biro and writing it all down. Looking at me, pointing her biro at me, and asking a question.

How would I respond to the challenge that these paintings are from an old school of exploitation of the female form and have no role to play in a society striving for equality?

Aw, bugger. Not just a wrinkle on her chin now. A full-formed frown and spitting eyes, chin forward. Weight all on one foot, and I bet the toes of the other are curling up.

Charm, John, summon your charm. Look her in the eye and talk. Deep breath, and go with it.

– Whenever a student asks me, what should I paint?, I always say, paint what you know. It's all you can do. To see into something, to understand it, embrace it, and to paint your understanding of it – that, for me, is what painting is. And once you start doing that, I say, you won't be able to help yourself. You'll look around you, and listen, breathe in the smells, feel the contours, the texture, and you'll feel you understand some things, and not others. So paint the things you understand. Maybe it's an apple on a table, placed and waiting to be picked up, or the left-overs of lobster claw heaped on a plate. Or maybe it's a woman in an armchair. As long as you have some connection, you have a basis for painting.

All scribbling now. What the hell have I said? Her foot is slowly tapping on the ground. But she's looking at up at Christine. And here's the response. Biro pointing.

Am I equating a woman with a lobster?

Aw, for goodness sake. That's not what I meant.

> – As you stand in front of a canvas, and you choose colours, you're not really looking for the right shade to represent something. You're looking for the best way to commit the moment, the moment that you are part of, that's living now between you and something, or someone, else. If you're painting, say, a lobster, then the moment has more to do

> with you as a painter than it has to do with the lobster. But if it's someone else, then they have as much control over what ends up on the canvas as you do.

Now, that's better. Biro just touching the corner of her mouth. If only she could relax and smile, that would be a terrific painting. No, John, be realistic – a drawing. This is too good to miss. A good thick pencil from the left-hand pocket. Must be one in there. Find some paper? Och, what the hell, over to the wall. Big white space beside Christine. Start with the chin. And keep talking.

> – Although, what I've just said assumes that you didn't know the lobster personally. If you did, then you might paint the scene of its demise a bit differently.

She's looking up at Christine again, and then across to her own face, slowly forming on the wall. A big drawing. Her lips moving, a slight tremble, and she's looking for a word to say. God, now, a wee knife to sharpen this bloody thing.

> – For me, painting is all about the moment – about what happens when two people come into contact. Now, I've got the brush – or the pencil – so of course, I'm in control, but really, it's all about us. About what has happened, about what is happening. What could happen. Now, even though we've hardly met, Emily, we have some history, and we're doing some things together right now, and anything could happen next. So, tell me, Emily, what do we do now?

And there it is, the start of a smile. Even if you're still pointing that biro at me. And . . . caught. Done. A frown just easing away. Aw, go on, smile. It's nice to see a picture of yourself. And, it's a very nice picture. There it is, next to Christine. *Woman with Biro.*

There. A wee smile, though you're not convinced. He's side-tracked you, tricked you. But, we had a nice moment there, didn't we? And now you're all lost for words.

> – Well, perhaps what we do now is have a coffee, and look at some of the other paintings. Let me get the coffees. Cappuccinos?

And escape, before another question gets asked.

Click, click, click. Head for the espresso machine, through the crowds. Hard to walk tall when your back is killing you. And there's the wee lassie behind the counter, with her back to me, milk jug held into the machine with one hand, the other reaching up to work the steam, and the nape of her neck appearing above the creasing of her white shirt, beneath the perfect little bob. And she turns, pours the milk into a cup on the counter, and smiles at the woman waiting for her coffee. Beams at her. What has she done to deserve that? It's her mother. It has to be her mother. There's a resemblance, sure, but it's that look. Not everyone gets that kind of look.

> – Excuse me, I know you're busy, but . . . Perhaps I could introduce myself? John. John . . . oh, you know? Of course. Anne, and, ah, I see, your mother. Delighted to meet you . . . ? Laura. Nice to meet you, Laura. I wonder, Anne, could you make three cappuccinos for the critics through in that room over there. They're beside the big picture

> of the woman in the armchair. Very important to keep them happy!

And would you mind, Anne and Laura, if I fixed this moment in my mind and kept it? The look between a mother and daughter. A classic theme, of course. Emily could not disapprove. Maybe a sketch, and bring it to show Anne. Maybe an old man's fantasy, of a young woman with a coffee pot. Then, maybe we could see about a painting.

But not tonight. Tonight, just enough energy left for a last walk across this floor, to the door, and out. Walking tall, through the crowd. Here we go. Click, click, click. And . . . out.

Three Candles

Richard Louden

Gran was in the toilet when I arrived, so I read the ward notices. Tuesday: quality perms by Kylie from Curl Up And Dye, £16.50 (over-eighties, £15). Thursday: speech therapy at 11, happy hour bingo at 3. Friday: lift up your hearts with the Rev. Joshua F. McGeachie BD BVMS, taped hymns, no collection.

She emerged ten minutes later in tweed skirt and droopy cardigan, achingly slow, her Zimmer scraping along the carpet. She peered opaquely up at me.

What nurse are you, then?

It's me, Gran. Fiona.

I kissed her on the cheek and guided her towards the day room.

Happy birthday.

Sssh, lass. They'll hear.

She was convinced they were forever listening, straining to pick up any morsel about her. You couldn't tell her it wasn't so. Most, sprawled listlessly, had long since lost touch with reality. Others sagged in uneasy slumber, but to her their ears were wide awake.

None of their business. They don't tell me theirs.

I steadied her arm. She was in this long-stay ward in Glasgow after ten falls in her flat. Squeezing the alarm button hung round her neck, she had to lie on the floor each time till community service staff came and picked her up.

I'm not going into hospital, and that's that. I can manage.

But she couldn't. Not any more. Six stone six, bent in half, fingers arthritic, eyesight going, hearing distorted if there was more than one voice at a time. Worst of all – alone. Not a regular visitor. Dad was dead. So were her all old friends. I was teaching in Aberdeen to be with Martin.

At the door to the day room, she grimaced as she saw how busy it was.

We'll go to my own room. We'll get peace there.

It wasn't hers. It had six beds and a waiting list. She had only a small storage cabinet. She stuffed it full of clothes, loath to have them locked in the communal closet along the corridor and let nurses pick her next day's wear. She had to look half decent, she said, because the others had different colours on every day.

I looked in there, Gran. The lady in the bed next to yours has visitors.

She banged the base of her Zimmer on the floor in vexation.

There's no privacy in this place. It's not fair.

Muttering, she edged into the day room, searching for an empty table. No luck. Some in wheelchairs, others hunched over inert elbows; they stared at us. It was a ritual rather than a mark of curiosity, but she tensed again.

See. Their noses are bothering them.

Alone at a window table was a puffy man in a wheelchair, early eighties, the pocket of his lumberjack shirt stained by tomato soup. I tried to steer her over.

Not there. That's him that told me to shut my trap. Bad old scoundrel.

The other tables are crowded, Gran. He's playing dominoes on his own. He won't give us any trouble.

She grunted, but let me settle her, eyes darting furiously

across at him. I took out a wrapped gift and slid it along. She thrust it back at me, under the table.

Get that out of sight. The old devil's watching. They're all watching.

I undid it discreetly on my lap. It was a box of white hankies. Hers always got lost in the wash, even with name tabs sewn on.

Oh, you shouldn't have bothered, Moira.

I'm Fiona, Gran. Moira's my aunt. Your daughter. She lives in America.

A fat lot of good she is to me there. Look at them all. Visitors every day, bringing changes of clothes, you name it. I'm the only one that's like orphan Annie. I've never been so ashamed . . . Watch out. It's you he's after.

She pushed the hankies into my bag, baring her teeth at him as he leaned across.

I'm Gabe, pet. Stands for Gabriel, but that's cissy. Who would you be, then?

Fiona.

Fiona? Nice one. Got a man?

Gran thumped a scrawny fist on the table.

Shut your trap, you. Get back to playing with yourself.

He shrivelled, sulky and resentful, but returned meekly to his dominoes.

Nasty old toad. Makes eyes at the sister, and her long expecting. You should see the belly on her. While we're on bellies . . .

Her neck looked even scraggier as she twisted it to see who was listening. Her voice fell to a hoarse whisper.

The nurses have all got stomachs on them. It's the job that does it. They're never done chewing. Some of them aren't even nice. A few are okay, the rest don't give a fig. They're at it with my drawers. They mess about in them. They think I don't know, but I can tell if things are moved. You'd hardly credit it, but they even take out stuff I haven't worn and chuck it in the wash.

* * *

When the washing machine arrived, she told the men to take it away, she hadn't ordered it. Dad had bought it as a surprise from his first pay because she had sweated all her life over washboard and mangle. Salt of the earth, he called her.

She was solid, nearly ten stone, well set up. She never stopped. When the snows came and the winds whipped up five-foot drifts in front of the house, she was first out there with brush and shovel. The ironing board was rarely put away. Every vest, every stocking had its last crease smoothed out. When Dad had mumps and couldn't sleep, she stayed up all night with him.

I made the cake myself – small, knowing that she'd want to hide it from greedy eyes. I laid it on my knee, where only she could see, and stuck three candles in it.

Happy birthday again, Gran.

Sssh.

She glanced fretfully across at Gabe, but he was wriggling in his chair, other things on his mind.

Nurse!

Listen to him. Nurse! You'd think it was an emergency, and it'll just be his leaky bladder again . . . Three candles? What's that about?

Well, there's no space for ninety-three, Gran.

Don't remind me. I hope to God this'll be the last one. I pray to Him every night to come and take me.

A lifetime of selfless love had brought her so little, yet childhood faith clung to her like a drenched T-shirt. I had the impression that, as she spoke, those dull eyes briefly glinted.

Nurse! Nurse! For Christ's sake!

She glared over at him, twitching with rage.

Watch your tongue, you heathen!

Still writhing, he growled back at her. A nurse bustled in, cheery and chubby.

See that backside, Moira. Didn't I tell you?

So, Gabe. What's it this time?

Are you blind, or what? I'm dying for a big one.

Are you sure, now? You're always saying that and nothing happens.

It's half out, for God's sake.

As the nurse wheeled him away, he pointed a vindictive finger back at Gran.

I'll think of you, Mrs Methuselah. That'll help it out.

She knew he must be having a go at her, but the TV was turned up high, though nobody was watching the *Baywatch* repeat.

What's that monster saying?

Nothing much, Gran. So, do you like your cake?

Her tongue moistened wasted lips. The sight of food was as much of an uplift as her faith. I recalled a holiday with Dad at a hotel in Jersey where the oldest guests queued outside the dining room by half eleven for lunch at twelve.

It looks tasty. You shouldn't have bothered. Put it in the bag.

Don't you want a slice?

No. I'll eat it in my own room, so nobody can see . . . It's murder in there in the mornings. They shove me out for breakfast before I'm half dressed, just so they can get the beds made. Still, I eat all I get, though you could bounce the porridge off the table and the cabbage is like seaweed. I was up to six stone nine last time they weighed me. I'd better watch or I'll end up flabby like them.

Halfway across the room, two old women jostled angrily, using their Zimmers as weapons to dispute right of way.

See that pair. You'd think they were in a hurry. One would pick a fight with a saint, the other one's always acting the Queen Mother, dishing out orders like a proper madam. No wonder the nurses get snotty. Silly old bitches.

That was the nearest to foul language she came. She leaned towards me, voice hushed as if to share an embarrassing secret.

I prefer men nurses. Easier to get along with. If my bum needs wiped, they do it better. Mind you, big Harry – him that's built like a gable end – he's not speaking to me. He made me a cup and forgot the teabag. I told him and he went all huffy. Don't let it get up your nose, I said. Life's too short.

A young female doctor had come in and was kneeling to check the pulse of a thin woman with close-cropped hair.

See her in the blouse that shows all she's got? That's my doctor, so help me. What's her name, again? Cynthia, or something stupid like that.

You call her by her first name?

She calls me by mine. Not even Janet, mark you, but Jan this and Jan that. No respect for age . . . There's a lad comes in as well. Just kids. Junior doctors, that's all we're worth. What can they know about old skin and bones?

A black male nurse handed a pill and water to the cropped woman.

Nicest of the lot, him. Gentleman. But see that half-baldy creature. She gets pills, I get nothing. If I ask to see the doctor, they say – no need, I'm doing just fine.

Pills. All her life she had craved them, placed her hope in them. She kept a precise note of every one she tried, so that she could tell her doctor she had been on that one and it was a waste of time.

She had felt let down so often. Efcortelan? It did nothing for the eczema. Diclofenac sodium? The rheumatism got even worse. E45? Allergic to it. But still she wanted more medicines, new ones not in her notebook, because somewhere out there were tablets and creams that would reverse the ravages of time.

It's not fair. At last I get that Cynthia to prescribe a new ointment for my itchy back. That's a week ago and it's never appeared. I'm in agony. The nurses won't even tell me its name. They say I don't need to know that. But what if it's one I've had before? It's like that Dr Benzie. I could tell him till I was blue in the face I'd had this or that and it was useless. All I got was, Ah, but you've changed since then, my dear, it's worth another try. My dear! And him not half my age.

It was Dr Benzie's mild manner that upset her most. Too easygoing, no oomph, she lamented. Never offered new medicines unless she asked for them. Even then, he only gave her enough for a week or two. She had to phone the surgery for a repeat prescription and couldn't make out a blessed word they were saying.

Tony, her social worker, was okay, but so busy she hardly set eyes on him. Maggie, the home help, was passable, but choosy about the jobs she did. She only came in six hours a week, not much help when the falls occurred at night. Still, she peeled enough potatoes to last for days on end and opened soup and vegetable cans, so Gran managed to feed herself.

She got by till a fall in the bathroom did for her. She had distractedly taken off her alarm button to wash her neck and, lying on the floor, hadn't the strength to lever herself up and reach it.

She lay there all night till Maggie arrived for her shift and let herself in. The ambulance soon appeared, but Dr Benzie never came to see her in hospital.

Just one more present, Gran.

I brought out a magnifying glass.

Oh, the very dab, lass. How did you know?

She hated her specs – the bifocals were half the size of the last ones, she moaned, and the frame slipped off her nose. The optician should have had more sense than to fit her when she didn't have her hearing aid in . . . She trained the glass laboriously on the print of my shopping bag.

Lizars. Is that it? No 'd'? What a silly name. See, I can read now. What a relief.

She turned her focus on Gabe, who had shrewdly settled at another table, was no longer writhing and had taken to chanting 'Where Have All The Flowers Gone?' in a drab monotone.

Now I can keep an eye on that bad old rascal. He's forever fumbling with his flies. If it's what I think, I'll report him.

Martin says happy birthday, Gran. He sends his love.

She stiffened as it sank in that she still hadn't asked about me. She turned, as if fully aware of me for the first time.

Look at that apology for a skirt. Halfway up your thighs. In my day, they'd have arrested you for that. What if there's frost again tonight?

She felt my cheek, her rough skin chafing mine.

You're too pale, Fiona. Are you starving yourself?

No, I'm fine.

That's a nice jacket. You're lucky. I haven't got a single thing that fits. I shudder when I look in a mirror. These two skirts you bought me – I just can't wear them. If only I could get into a draper's myself.

They don't make things for you, Gran. You're not a standard size any more.

She shook her head stubbornly.

I am. Back home, they kept sending me these mail-order books. I saw things in there that were right for me.

No. You were always trying that, then having to send them back.

She peered furtively round, cupped a hand to her mouth and mumbled.

I need knickers. The mail order's got them – thick, with elastic at the knees. These modern pants are too skimpy, what with me wearing pads for when I wet myself. Talk about dignity. Not much of that left nowadays.

She lifted up her hem, revealing stockings that barely reached above her knees.

See. Ruined. Everything gets shoved in the wash at one go. My stockings just shrivel up. It's not fair.

Why not try tights, Gran?

Tights? At my age? . . . I'd wear my corset and hook stockings to it, but I can't get it on over the pads. Will you look out for knickers and stockings? And if you happen to run into any white cotton vests . . .

As tea and digestives arrived, her attention shot away. Time to go. I hugged her – delicately, in case her bones cracked. She trembled.

There, now. I'll be back in no time. Two weeks – three at the outside.

I miss your dad.

I know you do, Gran.

Hide that bag in my drawer on your way out. And see if his picture . . . and yours . . . and your auntie's are standing properly. That lot twist the legs to smithereens when they dust, if you can call it dusting.

I cuddled her again, not letting her see the tears. As I walked away, an old man picked his nose and stared in awe at the product. The cheery nurse switched off *Bob the Builder* and put on a frayed tape of 'Crocodile Rock'.

Gran's voice croaked out behind me.

Look after yourself, lass. I'll pray for you.

Clear Thunder

Alan Bissett

Shona drifted from room to room, brushing the walls, hushing across the laminated floors like a ghost. Sometimes she stopped and sat on the bed, her knees close, her hands folded demurely on her lap as if someone were telling her off about her table-manners. And while listening to the thunder from outside, and the churning of empty spaces in her belly, she looked round the room at the things they had.

The Herresta shoe cabinet, the Lenda tab curtains, the Agen natural cotton armchair (cushions sold separately), the Tappa 1.41 jug in blue-glazed stoneware, the Klippen three-seat sofa in Alme natural fabric, the Vimma mirror with anodised aluminium frame (can be fixed vertically or horizontally), the Logga wine rack in lacquered steel, a cacophony of tubular metal, noisy gatecrashers at a party at which she was funless, unnoticed. In a quiet corner.

Then, after staring at these things half-stupidly, half in wonder, she stood and roamed the rooms again, searching out something to tidy, her hands jittering like trapped birds. But finding nothing out of place, nothing needing straightened or ironed, she resumed her perch on the duvet, sighing. Overawed by surfaces and health.

Shona spoke.

Shona said her name aloud as if it were new to her. As if it were an idea she was trying out on someone. And what she found was that the name slipped out of her mouth, papery, fluttering away to be lost between the nine-drawer mini-chest and the Gondol pendant lamp, between the Gamborg Wilton chair throw and the Blaklint tableware (let it get you a cup of tea).

Shona, she whispered.

Shona! she said aloud.

No echo. No returning call. Her own voice gone to join the gatecrashers.

She wandered downstairs to find Martin still bathing in the blue glow of the computer. His eyebrows were furrowed, businesslike. His left hand cradled an earthenware mug of coffee while his right tapped intermittently at the keyboard. In the clean glass of the kitchen table, she saw a second Martin the same as the first. She knew the glass was clean because she had stood over it for an hour earlier. Wiping. Wiping.

Hiya, Martin said, not looking up.

Shona turned on the tap and let it run, watching the clear rope of water kink and splash. Their kitchen had been fitted in chromium and blue. It gleamed. The floor was blond wood. All of the floors were blond wood. In the mornings, it was cold on Shona's feet, and she'd thought of draping some rugs around the place to warm it up. Martin had said no. What if they had someone's baby round? Accidental slips. Accidental slips would not do. So with the money, she'd gone with Margo to have her hair done, and even though she hadn't liked her hair afterwards, she'd told the hairdresser she did.

Besides, they didn't have anyone's babies round. People didn't show their babies to Shona anymore.

You okay? Martin said tunelessly.

Shona murmured a reply, but it meshed with the noise of gushing water and she barely heard it herself.

Did you go the doctor?

She drank. The water was cold and pure.

Yes.

Outside, a squirrel played on their enormous, trimmed lawn. Beyond the high barricade of the fence: suburban roofs and satellite dishes. It was raining, and thunder was crashing delicately in the distance.

I love you, Martin said, a foreign octave in his voice.

I know, she replied, and kept sipping at the glass of water.

On the blond wood shelves were Martin's CDs, alphabetically lined. She'd heard that if you froze your CDs overnight, it improved the sound. But why had someone frozen one in the first place? Martin sat gazing up at her through the wash of blue light. Shona stood by the chromium sink, sipping water, thinking about the CDs. Mirrored slices. Notes of ice. Martin sat gazing through the silence and she stood sipping, until he bent and resumed his tapping at the keys and Shona saw the crown of scalp that had spread on top of his head.

Then she went upstairs and brushed her teeth. Then she brushed them again. Then she sat on the bed, amazed, listening to the thunder of her stomach. Clear. Percussive.

Shona? she said, her mouth scrubbed clean and minty-fresh. Are you there?

The room did not answer.

After they'd moved in, she'd organised things as efficiently as a Field Marshall. The best wives were efficient, her mother had once told her, a note of regret in her voice. *A woman will work at love and a man will love at work*, she'd sighed distantly. And Martin had worked. And Shona had sorted out the wedding. And Martin had worked. And she'd organised the wedding. And renovated the house. And shopped and bought stuff and had her hair done and renovated the house. And sent out invitations to the wedding and hired the cars and, oh, chose the cake and drove round looking for venues, Martin's frozen CDs playing and changing on the stereo, their sound sharp enough to cut, and she hummed along numbly, and called the man from Junckers to fit the blond wood floors. And Martin worked. And at night they met up in the bed, him jammed into a book, her flicking through wedding magazines, *New Bride*, *Dream Wedding*, *The Big Day*, the sheen of the pages and the pretty models and all of the choices stupefying her, and then Martin would kiss the back of her neck and ask, When do you think you'll be ready? When can we try for another one? and she'd shirk away, cold, cold. Maybe next year, she'd say, and stare at the glass of water beside her bed – its still, blank nothingness, its invisibility of soul – while listening to the rain gurgle and hiss outside and the muffled roar of her body's thunder.

The funny thing was Shona could barely remember the wedding. The whole day had shot past like air from a balloon. Energetic and useless. There had been a storm, she remembered that. For of all of her meticulous preparation, it had poured down. Martin had beamed and greeted, making light of it, the professional groom. She'd woken in the morning, seen the tiny transparent souls sliding down the window, and inexplicably a giant crack had opened inside her, like a fork along ice.

She'd touched the glass and felt her reflection and her fingers had come away dry and it had taken a moment – a stationary moment in which the world seem distilled, slow-dripping – to work out why. The thunder was on the other side of the window. The thunder was on the other side of the window.

Everyone had laughed at Martin's speech.

And they had so many presents when they returned from

Mauritius, so many wonderful presents, so many wonderful presents that she spent her days bussing herself between appliances, bussing herself between appliances, so often that it seemed the kitchen was alive, not her, as if she was something the kitchen had bought so the dishwasher could be filled, the fridge stocked, the oven switched on and off, the floor cleaned, each appliance fighting to use her first, pulling her like a doll across the glinting floor . . .

Shona had read an argument that went 'possession is theft'. It had been in a newspaper, on a train somewhere (when she used to read newspapers and take trains). It came back to her as she cooked Martin's dinner, came back to her with the feel of the train sliding through huge green hills, and she stood there thinking about it until she realised she had a strange smile on her face and a plastic spoon dripping mushroom sauce onto the tiles. In the hiss of steam and the creak of the fridge-door lining, it seemed a radical thought, otherworldly, something she might have said in sixth form a long time ago when she'd been captain of the debating team. It hadn't really made sense to her until now, though – the theft which had occurred in that gleaming chrome room, where wedding gifts shouted spin-dryer and blender sounds, and her soul bumped against right angles.

Half an hour later, over wine and tagliatelle, she asked Martin if he thought possession was theft. He'd been talking to her about work since they sat down and she wanted to talk about something else.

Martin almost spat a half-chewed mushroom. Yeah *right*, he seethed. Some hippie in a commune 'owns' a car I worked a year to buy. And I 'own' his wigwam.

He shook his head and went back to talking about work. Shona shivered in a draught and played with her fork. She turned its prongs in her tagliatelle, watched the strands wrap and tighten on its head, imagined the fork suffocating, gasping for breath. The points made a high keening sound on the plate. A British Home Stores plate.

She pushed it away.

Darling, she said, interrupting him. I'm not going to try for another baby.

He stopped and looked over the rim of his glass at her.

Shona, it hasn't been long since . . . his eyes dropped. Look, why don't you give it some more time?

I, I don't think I'm well enough yet. I still don't feel I'm . . . coping with things.

A smile snickered across his lips. She could tell he was trying to fight it. She thanked him for that at least. It's not as if there's anything for you to cope *with*, he enunciated. You haven't worked since you came out from hospital. I've bought you everything you've asked for. You don't even have to look after any . . .

His eyes flickered back to his BHS plate.

There's something missing, she said eventually.

What? he said, a curt edge to his voice.

I don't know.

She turned her fork absently, staring into the mass of tangles.

The pause felt vast.

I think we should split up.

Martin kept eating, trying less hard to fight the smile this time.

Every two months, Shona went with Margo to the hairdresser. Margo would yell over the noise of the dryer about the Texan who was taking her to Honolulu, the student who was taking her to meet his mum, the headmaster who was taking her over his desk. There had been a time when Shona had loved these stories. Now they seemed fake and unnecessary. A bit like Margo's hair, really.

At one point, her hairdresser left to fetch the dye and Shona sighed and revolved on her seat, catching glimpses of herself in the many mirrors. She speeded up. A million of her, spinning into infinity. She was an astronaut. She was floating in space, upside down, round and round. Her space-suit reflected cold light from the sun, glinting an SOS to the Earth.

When she stopped spinning she felt sick and Margo was still talking.

Later, they went for a salad – Shona's stomach rumbling disconsolately, though she barely touched a lettuce leaf – and she found it spilling out to Margo in a rush, like water from a dam, the noise of it clear-coloured, roaring: how she and Martin had grown apart, how she felt that she was his partner, yes, but his *business* partner, how she was there, just there to help him collect the set of wife, job, house, car . . .

Kids.

Margo assumed it was the sex. Shona knew that she would. The sex, as it happened, hadn't existed since she'd come out of hospital, Shona feeling too hollow to be touched by another living thing.

Have you got a fella? Margo cooed. Is it the guy from Starbucks?

There's no one else, Shona said. I just need to leave.

Shona enjoyed Margo's deflating excitement.

But where would you go? Margo said. What would you do for money?

I don't know, Shona shrugged. I could get a job. I did used to work.

Margo looked at her, appalled, and Shona saw nothing in her friend's eyes to connect them, nothing that would make her want to tell her she was lost in a cave of mornings, days, months, years, her life so empty it had swallowed her, its belly so huge that she couldn't hear her own echo in it.

Shona, Margo began, hesitantly. Maybe it isn't *Martin*'s fault. You haven't been well since the . . .

Margo dropped her eyes, just as Martin had, afraid that the word would break her into pieces.

Shona didn't reply.

Margo sat back, sighing.

For no particular reason, Shona found herself thinking, I can't feel anything in here.

You're far too thin, Margo tutted eventually, calling the waiter to take away Shona's uneaten lettuce. Men won't find it attractive.

Later, Shona bought a book called *Getting Better Bit(e) by Bit(e)*. The man behind the counter looked at her tenderly, sympathetically, the way a teacher might look at a struggling child. What a strange way to look at another adult. And when she outstretched her hand to receive the change, she could see how close her skin skated to the bone, how pale and brittle her wrist seemed, how the coins – the second before they dropped – seemed as though they might pass right through her palm and make a crashing-plate noise at her feet. She tried to say 'Oh!'

But had no voice.

She ran from the bookshop into the shopping centre. Her veins felt thin as salad and her stomach empty. She ran into pools of artificial light, bathing her face. She ran between the people, who seemed not to see her, smell her, sense her, because she was not there, it wasn't happening. She touched the glass of shop windows. Things owned. Things unowned. The spirits of vacuum cleaners and mobile phones and wedding dresses and health foods passing through her like weak, translucent love. She went to the fountain at the intersection of escalators which gurgled window-cleaner-blue fluid. Her hand drew through the shallows, brushing coins from their places. She stepped in. She stamped. Muzak soundtracked her screaming and splashing, her churning of the fountain into a thunderous foam.

When she woke

she was searching

radio stations.

A snatch of pop song. A violin screech. A newsreader.

The *Woman's Hour*, on which an American gospel singer called Mahalia Jackson was being interviewed, her voice booming and singing with sass.

Such a voice.

Shona popped the lid from her box of pills, and swallowed one. Cylindrical. It tasted of a dry kind of happiness.

She hung pictures round the tiny room while listening to the singer. *It's easy to be independent when you've got money*, Mahalia Jackson was saying. *But to be independent when you haven't a thing? Honey, that's the Lord's test.*

She took a piece of paper from her bag and scrawled on it in biro. The handwriting (when had she last seen her own handwriting?) reminded her of things she used to write in a notebook when she was a girl: random thoughts, descriptions, poems, song lyrics, professions of love which she could never dare to say. On the paper she'd written

> You may be disappointed if you fail, but you're doomed if you don't try.

and stuck it to the wall with Blu-tac. She sat looking at the scrap of paper. It flapped in a slight breeze. She pulled the top back off the pen, jammed it between her teeth, and underlined:

doomed if you don't try

Shona's heels echoed on the bare floorboards. She'd hung the pictures unevenly, but decided to leave them that way. A doctor's prescription and a bank statement lay on the unmade bed. When they'd arrived, she'd giggled at the strange address slotted beneath her name. She'd stopped giggling when she'd opened them.

Shona crossed the furniture-less room to the window, to the rhythm of the world on an unfamiliar street. Notes of it. Unfrozen. Moving. Traffic and young mothers, pensioners and shitting dogs, skateboarders, shift workers, adulterers, couples unsuited to each other, pigeons, charity collectors, chronic worriers, door-to-door salesmen, kids going to their first day at school, their packed lunches swinging by their side, everything painted in vivid technicolour as if she'd woken from a blanket-white dream.

And when she spoke, the room replied.

Shona! she said.

ona! her voice mouthed back.

It's me! she shouted.

me! her echo said, the echo of herself.

And there she stood, making noises, gleefully, like a child throwing rubber balls against a wall.

And it was a life.

The Rules of Perspective

Ross Wilson

Ye need tae git yir priorities right, Steven said as they stepped out the pub. His dad said the same thing to him some hours earlier.

Linda tightroped the kerb, arms like wings, listening to the different sounds the soles of their shoes tapped on the pavement.

– Jist ignore uh'm, she advised, but Steven couldn't shake it. Criticism like that niggled, nibbled his head like lice.

– How kin Ah when the man is determined tae run and ruin ma life?

– Oh stop overreacting. Linda prodded his ribs. He snatched her gloved hand in his so they swayed freely between their bodies.

– So what's this surprise, then? She asked him, squeezing his hand, tugging his arm.

Steven grinned. It widnae be a surprise if Ah told ye, would it?

He could be leading her into anything. It was exciting, the not knowing, the wondering.

He'd picked her up at the station. Literally. Lifting her body into his, burying his nose into her hat, breathing in the perfumy soapy shampoo scent of her. He'd lift her up like that every weekend as if they'd been apart for years. And the being apart was good in that sense. Like how people claimed arguing was good for relationships: to break up, to make up. Linda would find it funny, though, at how cuddly he'd become. It was as if he'd learned a whole new way of touching her that wasn't strictly sexual and was spontaneous, despite it now being a bit of a ritual every weekend. Somehow he could make it seem new each time and she liked that, it was nice.

He'd driven her home from the station in his dad's car. And this was before his dad or their future or anything came into it. This was their catch-up hour when they'd recount their week and speak in too much of a hurry to tell it; they'd forget bits and interrupt each other and laugh at their own effusiveness. They'd know most of what they'd tell each other anyway through mid-week emails and phone calls, but that didn't matter; such communications were only calculators adding up the miles between them and the time until they'd see each other again. They never bothered with letters. Linda sent pictures. Self-portraits to begin with; later, portraits of her new friends, sketches of her room, the halls, the city; postcards from her new world. Steven would post her crude clumsy cartoons with heart-shaped speech bubbles burst with jokes that weren't so much romantic or funny as cute. Linda kept them on her fridge door.

– Ah'm sorry fir gaun oan aboot it, he apologised, squeezing her hand softly – It's jist *he* keeps oan aboot mae settlin intae somehin. Ih says ma job as jist dead end as if *it* wis ma life, as if Ah'm nivir gaun ih go anywhere or dae anythin. Ah mean, why wid Ah want tae settle intae anythin, anywiy? Ah'm *eighteen* fir Christ sake n he's talkin aboot *pensions* n careers!

– Ye should move oot then, Linda said. Move in wi me.

Steven smiled, though knew she was only half joking. She cuddled into him as they walked and he put his arm around her, drawing her into him. Aware of the heat they could summon by the closeness of their bodies, they stuck together, keeping the cold at bay as if it were wary of attacking two people at once.

– So ye been drawin any naked men this week? He asked her and she smiled.

– Oh loads.

– That's what Ah should dae: be a role model.

– *Life* model.

– Imagine what ma dad wid say!

Linda laughed.

– Nah, bit imagine it! Jist sittin aroond in the buff bein drawn bae sexy young lassies.

– You'd be embarrassed, she said, nudging him with her shoulder.

– What ye sayin like?

– Nuthin.

– Ah'm a stallion! He shouted and thumped a fist off his chest. An old woman happened to be passing them at the time. That's why he'd done it.

Linda nudged him again – *Shut up!* Her words were smothered in a giggle.

– Ah ahm! Steven insisted – It said in the Chinky horoscope, mind.

– Yir sign wis the year ih the horse, Steven.

– Same thing, ih. Nah, bit Ah'd be like yir man, whastihsname? Big Dave, Davie the Italion, Big Dave the Italion Stallion thit decked yir man fae the Bible.

Linda was laughing – What ye oan aboot?

– Ken him ooty yir book? Mike's statue.

– Michelangelo's David? That's a sculpture, Steven. David wisnae aw that well endowed, anwiy.

– Wis ih no? Ah thought ih wis a giant. No a bad career though, ih?

– Bein a sculpture?

– Bein a model. It's a bit like bein a prostitute, though.

– It *is* not.

– It is, though. Your ey oan aboot catchin the models soul n aw that, ihs inner bein, ihs essense n aw that crap, n how yir no jist drawin thir body like. That's worse thin bein a prostitute, least they jist sell thir body.

– You dinnae half talk some rubbish.

– Naw, bit think aboot it. Your drawin men in the scud bit ye git oan it me lookin it scuddies!

Linda nipped his bum.

– Ah!

– That's hardly the same thing, she said.

Steven sniffed – It's art tae me.

Linda stopped walking and tugged him by the elbow so he stopped too, jolting him back sharply into her lips. Her kiss was a brief tease. She pushed him away, running laughing up the street, Steven chasing her with a smile. Like a weapon, it had her backing away from him, but slowly, wanting to be caught. She turned as he closed in on her but it was too late and he had her up and in his arms, squealing laughter, wriggling to escape. He spun her around almost falling over onto her, their feet entangled, their arms flailing for balance, concentration shattered by laughter. Their kiss was slower this time, with tongues, their embrace broken by an old man shouting: *Here there, steady oan, son, yil huv the lassie up the duff!* Linda pulled away with a snotty snorting laugh and they resumed their walk, Steven's arm draping her shoulder like a scarf, Linda's a tight belt around his waist.

– Fancy some chips? he asked, observing the golden glow of a fish bar window up ahead.

She laughed – That yir surprise, is it? A bag ih chips, how romantic, Steven.

– Tch. Ye want some or no?

Linda cuddled into him, mumbling aye into his shoulder, eyeing teenage boys ahead, drinking, smoking against a graffiti-covered wall, their faces as unreadable in the dim light as their scrawls.

– Awright, Stevie man?

– What's happnin, Deek?

– Nuthin's happnin, man. Wir jist like waitin oan somehin tae happen, ken what Ah'm sayn? Deek blurted drunkenly, ambiguously, stepping forward. His friends didn't say anything, kind of eyed Steven and Linda a bit. They were all a year or two younger. Steven recognised most of them by face, a couple by name.

– Ah'l go order, ih? Linda suggested – Fish supper?

– Aye.

She went inside, Deek's eyes following her, blatantly rolling up her body from heel to head, cigarette a miniature torch an inch from his lips, hat pulled down over eyebrows. He swallowed a few mouthfuls from a bottle, ran his sleeve across his mouth, offered Steven the bottle. Steven took a slug.

Linda glanced at the news on a wee portable on a shelf across the counter then turned to the shop window, a bigger telly, with Steven and Deek turned down, their mouths moving, voices wrapped in a mist. A car pulled up behind them like a magnet drawing the teenagers in around it like pups round their mother, smoke swirling about their heads in the dark. Linda could make out the top of a red baseball cap from inside, nothing else.

Deek was shouting something, swearing, loud, aggressive. Heads turned from inside the shop as Steven entered, but he was only having a laugh, Deek was, and they soon enough turned back to whatever he'd snapped their attention from.

– Ye dinnae go aboot wi *thaym*, dae ye? Linda asked.

– No. Why?

Eyebrows raised, Linda turned back to the telly.

– Deek's awright.

Linda said nothing.

The old woman made a noise, a kind of groan or sigh. Steven looked at her. She was watching the news. So were the men behind the counter. Steven looked up. The picture of a wee boy was on the telly. A voice told them he'd been abducted and murdered. The word torture came up twice. The wee boy came from a nearby town. He was only seven.

– Oan yir doorstep, the old woman mumbled, shaking her head – Oan yir doorstep.

Steven frowned at her. Outside the car revved, voices were raised, and then music, a pounding drone. They left soon after the car had moved from the kerb in a skid amid the whoops and whistles of Deek and his crew, now further down the street, in the middle of the road, one or two shouting, the rest talking, kicking some can or cone or something down the road.

– What *ir* 'priorities' anyway? Steven asked her as they walked, and Linda told him they were like an order you put things in according to importance and he said well then having a laugh, having a good time was his number-one priority and why shouldn't it be? At his age anyway. Even his dad was always saying life was too short. But Linda wasn't really listening. She was gazing up the road into a starless black sky. She'd read somewhere something about light pollution and that in years to come future generations might never see the stars, lampposts like needles injecting poison into space.

Steven was still talking – Least Ah huv a job, ken? So what if it's menial, s'no is if Ah'l be dayin it aw ma days or anything, ih? Thirs plenty time.

– Ye kin dae better fir yir sel though, ih.

– Ah'm no sayin that.

– That's aw yir dad's tellin ye.

– No, he's tellin mae what Ah *should* dae rather than what Ah could dae.

They were silent for a minute or so, eating. Steven's fish

supper was wrapped in a greasy red-sauce-stained war in the Middle East, Linda's chips in the African Aids epidemic.

– Tch, ye tryin tae pit mae aff or somehin? He asked her when she informed him of this.

– Ah read it as the man wis wrappin thum up, she explained.

– Christ. What's rang wi ye oanywi? Yeh'v gaun aw quiet.

– Ah'm eatin, you wir talkin.

They eat as they walked, drifting from each other, looking at the sky and the houses they past along the way, what they could see of things in the dark. He half expected her to talk about the light and tone and shade and all that kind of crap but she didn't. She didn't say anything.

– Ye awright? He asked.

– Aye.

– What's the maytir?

– Nuthin.

They didn't say anything for a bit, their walk slowing as they ate, a cold wind rising, blowing out the sound of their shoes and the faint rustle of newspaper. Linda shivered – It's gittin cauld.

– Supposed tae snow er the weekend, he said.

Linda looked up and sniffed.

– Wil jist huv tae stay indoors, he said.

– Oh aye.

– Keep warm, he said – Hibernate.

Their lips were twisted with the thought, struggling to contain their food in their mouths.

– Ye should take the week aff.

– Ah cannae jist take a week aff when Ah feel like it, Steven.

– Ye kin so. And anyway it's part ih the plan.

– What plan?

– That's a surprise.

– You ir foo ih surprises! So this surprise demands Ah take a week aff, does it?

– No really, bit it wid last longer if ye did.

They were smiling again and silent, walking and eating, and looking down at their moving feet, not paying too much attention to where they were leading them.

– It's weird, the weeness o things, she said after awhile. She'd been looking at the bungalows they had passed along the way and thinking about the labyrinth of city buildings she'd been lost within all week.

– What dae ye mean?

– This place.

– What aboot it?

– Jist . . . it's sae wee.

– It's a village.

– Ah know its a village, Ah'm jist meanin when ye git used tae livin in the city n that, ken? Comin back . . .

Steven looked around him as they walked – When Ah'm visitin you Ah git claustrapherbia . . .

Linda smiled, corrected him – *Claustrophobia.*

– It's too closed in, ye ken, too cramp.

– Ah dinnae mind it, thirs ey somehin happnin.

– Bit that's cause you're used tae it. Ah'm jist a hillbilly.

– Yir hardly a hillbilly, Steven. It's too sleepy. Nuthin ivir changes.

– *You*'ve changed.

– How?

– Ah dunno. Ye talk funny er the phone, like yeh'v adopted the accents ih yir new pals or somehin.

– That's jist cause Ah'm roond thum a loat, that's aw.

– Nah bit it's what ye say an aw.

– What dae ye mean?

– Ah dunno, he said, frustrated. A few seconds later he said – Ma mum thinks will split up.

– Dinnae say that.

– Ah'm no sayin wi will, jist . . .

– Jist dinnae say it, Steven, okay?

– Aye.

He stopped walking and turned to face her, but Linda stared to the side at nothing in particular. Steven opened his mouth to say something, but there was nothing he could think to say. She looked down into her chips – Ah'm no even hungry, she said and she smiled and he did too – It's jist a waste, she said.

– Ye kin pit thum in the microwave fir later.

– Aye.

And they were walking again.

– So what wis Deek dayin tae it? The way she asked was obvious she didn't care but Steven told her anyway.

– Ye ken Wullie crashed ihs car?

– Aye.

– A lassie wis killed.

– Who?

– Dunno. She wisnae local. She wis sixteen.

They were silent again for a bit. Then Linda said – Ma tutor says Ah lack perspective away fae the canvas.

– What's that supposed tae mean?

– Ah'm no sure. Ah think ih meant mibbe Ah dinnae stand back tae grasp the foo picture or somehin, ken? No seein the world it large, like Ah'm too wrapped up in ma ayn heid or somehin, or mibbe Ah intellectualise too much, think rethir thin feel, Ah dunno, Ah'm no sure, it's like . . . it's like Ah git too entangled in ma ayn ideas n stuff; like Ah cannae step back n see clearly.

– Awbdys like that, though.

– What dae ye mean?

Steven shrugged – Jist awbdy's heids bound tae be a bit preoccupied ih, he mumbled, mouthful of chips – Wi thir ayn stuff, things in thir life n that, problems. Probably maist folk cannae see through thir ayn eyes in a sense at the world or where thir gaun cause thir ayn world's too cluttered up tae see past. He smiled – Like tryin tae see ooty ma bedroom windae.

They stopped walking again. Linda could see his bedroom window from where they stood as well as in her mind: a clutter of discarded clothes and junk. The analogy made her smile. Steven was dipping a chip in sauce. She looked at him, smile broadening, surprised a bit that he hadn't laughed at what her tutor had said, but just a wee bit surprised. He could do that Steven, he could . . .

– What? He asked, frowning.

– Ye could dae well though, she said.

– It what?

– Ah dunno. Somethin. Anythin.

Steven looked over her shoulder – Ah'v no a clue what Ah'l dae or where Ah'm gaun, where *we* ir gaun.

She threw what was left of her supper away to embrace him and the wind almost took her hat with it. She yelped, clasping it to her head. Steven stapled it with his lips. And their arms were like wands extracting that magical heat from the cold, enfolding each other.

– That's you back hame then, he said. He was grinning.

– *Your* home.

– Same thing, ih.

– Yir ma n da's home, she said and Steven smiled.

– Ah, bit *they* ir oan hoaliday, he said, pulling back to look down at her, to catch her expression in his eyes. He was dangling his keyring before her own between forefinger and thumb, key glinting like a hook.

– They are? Linda smiled, eyebrows raised coquettishly. She grabbed the bait.

He chased her to the door and she yelped, helpless against it, struggling to open it as his fingers played her ribs like an accordion, squeezing this distinctive laughter from her, this music he loved so much. Her body doubled up, knees buckling, ribs aching with laughter. She somehow managed to wriggle free and run inside, screaming to get away. She stopped in the middle of the lobby and turned, out of breath, hands on knees, wee hat on head, wee smile on lips; Steven, closing the distance between them, was smiling; stained newspaper wrapping flapping in the doorway, sucked out into the wind at his heels.

Round-trip Spaceship

Michael Russell

They drove round the town all afternoon looking for the boy.

'Remember,' said Phil, 'he's got blond hair and blue eyes and he's about ten. Watch out for him.'

It was late in the year and the nights were drawing in, so the streetlights were glowing a faint sodium yellow before Tony saw the boy. He was circling round and round on his skate-board under the streetlights in a large area of pavement in front of some shops. His multiple shadows circled and en-twined with each other as the plastic wheels slowly rumbled over them. He had blond hair and blue eyes and was about ten.

'Hey, there he is,' said Tony. From the back seat, he raised his arm over Phil's shoulder and pointed. 'Is that him?'

Phil slowed the car and craned his neck round as they passed the boy. 'Yeah, he'll do,' he said.

He pulled the car up to the kerb just past the boy and put the handbrake on. He switched the engine off, grabbed a folded map out of the glove compartment, and opened the door. 'Stay in the car,' he said and got out. Tony twisted round in his seat, leaned back against the side door and watched Phil walk back to the boy, who was still flexing his knees and balancing himself with outstretched arms as he circled under the luminous streetlights. The blue haze of twilight had begun to deepen, and in the yellow artificial light Tony couldn't make out the true colour of the boy's skateboard or clothing. The car gave off quiet irregular ticking noises as the engine cooled. Phil was standing in front of the boy, who had stepped one foot off his skateboard and was watching him unfold the map. The boy said something to Phil which Tony couldn't hear, and Phil must have told a joke in reply because the boy laughed. Tony wished he knew what the joke had been, and wished he could hear the boy's laughter.

After a couple of minutes, Tony saw Phil start to fold up the map; as usual, he did it the wrong way and ended up folding it against the creases and crumpling it into one of his jacket pockets. The boy pressed his foot down on the raised lip of his skateboard so that it tipped up and then scooped it up into his arms. He walked with Phil towards the car. They were still laughing.

Phil walked round the car and opened the driver's door and the light came on in the front of the car, turning the windows dark and glossy. Tony heard him say across the roof of the car, 'Get in, it's open,' and the boy opened the front passenger door and got in, laying his skateboard wheels-up on his lap. Phil sat in the driver's seat and they both closed their doors at almost the same instant, like the double beat of a heart, and the light went out.

'Mark, meet Tony,' said Phil. 'Tony, meet Mark.' He started the engine.

In the gloom, Tony could barely make out the boy's face as he half-turned and nodded to him. 'Wotcha, Tony,' he said and Tony caught the faint gleam of his teeth as he grinned before turning away.

The car pulled out into the traffic and Phil switched the headlights on. 'Getting dark early these days,' he said. 'Soon be winter.'

'You looking forward to Crimbo?' asked Tony. The boy turned his head again.

'Yeah. I got this as a present last Crimbo.' He half-lifted the skateboard off his lap then let it flop back down. He gave a hesitant smile.

Tony smiled back. 'I used to have one of those when I was a kid, when I was your age. While ago it was, back in the seventies.'

'Have you still got it?' asked Mark.

Tony shook his head. 'My mum gave it away to a jumble sale years ago. Said I was too old for it.'

Phil laughed. 'You're never too old for it, are you, Mark?'

Mark laughed with him. Then the conversation went quiet, and Tony watched Mark from the back seat of the car as it eased its way through the late-evening traffic. He felt the pushing and tugging of invisible hands as the car turned corners or accelerated away from traffic lights. The interior was too dark to make out the boy's face, but an approaching car's headlights would periodically shine through the dirt-mottled windscreen like the probing beam of a lighthouse and illumine everything in a cold white light before flicking away and past them. Tony leaned his right arm on the headrest of Phil's seat and watched the boy's face as it strobed in and out of view, assembling itself out of the fragments which would surface like tiny silver fish hooked by the passing headlights. First his blond hair, silver-grey in the cold light, then the tapering curve of his jawline, then the smooth bulge of his forehead and the snub of his nose. After a while, the boy kept glancing round at Tony out of the corner of his eye. He looked nervous.

'So, Mark, you were telling me about the competition you won for skateboarding,' said Phil.

'Yeah,' said Mark. 'It was a few weeks ago.' He paused. 'The trophy is made of silver; it's in a glass cabinet in the lounge. I get to keep it for a year.' He paused. 'Are you sure it's okay for me to hitch a lift? You are going my way, aren't you?' he asked.

'Course we are,' said Phil. 'It's getting dark early this time of year; we were worried about you out on the streets on your own.' Phil turned and grinned at the boy. 'Thanks for the directions, by the way. We'd be lost without you.'

Tony watched the boy stare out of the side window at the radiant shop fronts spilling their brash light onto the pavement as they flicked past the car. He heard the boy idly spinning one of the plastic wheels of his skateboard, round and round, and he leaned forward again and said, 'Anyway, Mark, what TV programmes do kids watch nowadays? When I was your age, *The Clangers* were still on, and *Bill and Ben the Flowerpot Men*, and *Doctor Who*. I used to love *Doctor Who*. Course, the bastards cancelled it. You can bet your life those bastards will always cancel anything good, like *Play School*. Or *Andy Pandy*.'

Tony saw Mark and Phil exchange glances, and Phil said incredulously, '*Andy* fucking *Pandy*?! You're still upset they cancelled *Andy* fucking *Pandy*?! You talk as though you're fucking mentally retarded. Sometimes I just don't know about you, Tony, I really don't.' Phil shook his head sadly, glancing up at Tony in the rearview mirror. Tony couldn't tell whether he was joking or not. Mark started sniggering.

Tony sat back in the rear seat and folded his arms.

A few minutes later, the car began to accelerate slowly, bending along the curve of a slip road and sliding into the stream of traffic on a dual carriageway. Only the small red lights and the illuminated yellow number plates of the cars in front of them were visible, and the cat's eyes silently stuttering beneath them like tracer bullets in a night sky.

The boy stirred in his seat, trying to peer out of the glossy black windows, a faint ghost image of his own face staring anxiously back at him. 'This isn't the way home. Where are we going?'

'It's a short cut,', said Phil. 'Don't worry about it.'

Tony unfolded his arms and gazed out of the windscreen, past Phil's shoulder. The sky looked as though deep-blue ink had been spilled over it, and the constant muffled roar of the air hitting the car was soothing and hypnotic. The lights of the dual carriageway curved into the distance, and beyond the dark hunched shapes of bushes and stunted trees which lined the verge he could see the lights of a town nestling in a shallow valley. The lights were warm orange and yellow and white and they seemed to Tony to be unconnected to anything on Earth.

'Hey, Mark,' he said. 'Do you ever read any books? I mean kids' books. I used to read lots of books when I was a kid. Funny that, 'cause I never read any books now. I've heard the opposite is supposed to happen: most people read more as they get older. Anyway, I suppose the only thing that matters is how well you remember the books you've read. What they mean to you.'

He paused. Mark said nothing. In the dark, Tony couldn't see his face.

'Anyway, I read this book when I was a kid, about your age I think I was. Anyway, it was about this spaceship that lands in some kid's back garden and the alien that gets out is just a kid itself, and this kid whose back garden the spaceship lands in befriends the alien kid, and the alien says, Do you want to go back with me to my home planet? So the kid says, do I? Just you try and stop me; and so they both go back in the spaceship to the alien kid's home planet and they have various adventures there. I can't remember them all, 'cause it's been so long since I read it when I was a kid, but I remember they were having a meal once and it was just thin wafers so the kid, I mean the human kid, he goes to take a huge bite out of the wafer because he's hungry but the alien kid stops him just in time and tells him to take only a small nibble because it expands in your mouth. So the kid does as the alien says and sure enough as soon as the tiny bit of wafer is in his mouth it expands to fill his mouth, and it tastes like roast chicken. Anyway, they have other adventures and then they come back to Earth in the alien kid's spaceship and the kid, the human kid, goes back to his everyday life as an ordinary kid and he has to pretend like nothing happened, that he's just an ordinary kid and he never left Earth. It's a great book, I loved it as a kid but I can't remember who wrote it. I do remember it's called *Round-trip Spaceship*, that's because it's about a spaceship journey to an alien planet and then back again to Earth, like a round-trip, yeah? I loved that book when I was a kid. I used to wish I could get whisked away in a spaceship, leave everything behind me, and maybe never come back. Not ever come back.'

Tony leaned back in his seat and sighed. He looked out of the window beside him at the car lights drifting slowly past, the cars themselves just dark shadows against the night road.

The boy started to cry, quietly, almost inaudible above the noise of the car's motion. Phil turned his head to the boy and snapped, 'Shut the fuck up! You're crying like a little girl. Anyone would think you were a fucking puff. Just shut up!' He turned his head back to the road, his neck stiff with anger.

Tony touched his finger to the glass and drew a line through the condensation that had misted the lower half of his window. The orange lamps along the grassy central strip of the dual carriageway stretched in a curved, looping line into the distance. They seemed to float in space, detached from any physical substance, like warm stars on a cosmic string that stretched across the universe.

He imagined he was drifting through the interstellar womb of space, dark and enveloping and warm (not cold, space was not cold), and the muffled roar of the air sliding over the car was really the hiss of the solar winds streaming out from the stars and caressing the metal skin of the spaceship. And the lights of the town, street lamps and shop windows and bedside lamps, were really the suns of some distant galaxy, condensed out of the interstellar dust. And they were on their way to a new life on a new world circling one of those stars.

They would be there soon.

Closing Time

Alastair Chisholm

George was first in, for a change. He usually came in a little later when the place was busier, but it was just after seven when he arrived tonight and it was still quiet. He took his usual seat at the counter, hanging his thick black coat and beaten-up hat off one of the brass hooks underneath the bar.

'Evening, Lewis,' he said. Lewis nodded.

'Evening, George. What can I get you?'

'Eighty, please.'

Lewis took a long straight pint glass from under the counter and flicked the nozzle on. In the empty room the silence stretched a little.

'So how's things with you then?' he asked absently, watching the pint form.

George laughed, slightly. 'Oh, you know. Business is down.'

Lewis smiled. 'Aye. Same here. But there might be one or two folk in tonight. There you go . . .'

George handed over a fiver and took the change.

'Cheers,' he said.

'Aye, cheers.'

George pulled a long sup of the beer. 'I saw Tam headin' off this afternoon, just past five.'

'Oh aye?'

'He said he'd been trying since two. Got as far as the bypass and just couldn't move. Had to turn around to try again.'

'Where's he going?'

'Oh, I dunno. He said somethin' about a sister in Inverness. I think he was just trying to get away. Won't do him any good.'

There was a slight pause. Lewis coughed.

'Aye, well, Tam's a nice guy, but he's only half-full o' brains.'

George looked around. 'Who do you reckon'll be in?'

'Eh . . . I dunno. Willy, probably. A few others. We'll see.'

'Aye.'

They lapsed into silence. It wasn't uncomfortable. Lewis stood in the classic landlord's stance; neither in the circle nor out of it, distant enough to not be part of the conversation, close enough to smile when a joke headed his way, always on hand. And George slowly drank, staring unseeing at the counter in front of him.

After a while a few others started to appear. Not too many, not tonight. But some of them. All regulars, hailed by George as they came in, taking up their usual places at the stools next to the bar, or at one of the few small tables in the room. It was a small pub. A long mirror against the back wall made it seem larger, but not much. There was just about space for three or four tables, a dartboard and a puggy, besides the bar.

The punters were mostly of a certain age. It wasn't a young man's pub. Normally the only young folk there were the ones joining their dads for a pint. It was an old, straightforward, ordinary place where folk came to have a beer and a bit of craic. Tonight the craic was quiet, and tended to come in clumps, fits and starts. Lewis didn't worry; he knew that as things went on folk would relax, and so they did. After a while the dozen or so people there started to calm down, talk about little things.

It was still quiet though; quiet enough to hear what was happening outside. For the most part people seemed to not hear it; not hearing it in that peculiar way though, like folk trying not to see a beggar. Noises from outside, shouting and calling, were drowned out by new, slightly strained conversation. At one point there was a sound like a car backfiring, close to the building. Everybody stopped dead, frozen. Then there was slight nervous laughter. When the car drove away, everyone blew out breaths and grinned, oddly.

Lewis busied himself behind the bar. Barwork is tremendous; a keen barman can spend the entire evening in a clean pub on his own with no customers and still manage not to get a break. A pub is just a collection of things to do with punters getting in the way. Lewis cleaned and dried glasses, emptied ashtrays, fetched bottles from the store, topped up optics. Occasionally he looked up at the bar lights, which were dimming and returning ever so slightly. Eventually he said to George, 'Mind the bar for a second will you, George?'

'Eh? Oh aye, yeah. No problem.' Lewis nodded and headed off for a bit, making a few trips to the cellar and getting stuff ready. He started pouring beer into large jugs, which he kept on the back of the bar.

About twenty minutes later the lights dropped from white to brown. There was a sudden silence in the pub, then a noise that people make, something like, 'Oh, aye?', when they don't really know what to say. As soon as the lights dimmed it felt colder.

Lewis picked up one of the three lamps he'd brought up. 'No problem, folks,' he said. 'We're all prepared here, don't worry.' He lit the lamps carefully and they glowed white, not as bright as the electric lights but enough. He put one on each end of the bar and one on one of the tables. They kept burning bright as the electrics dipped further and further. In the end they were the only source of light in the room; people instinctively orbited around them. They drew together.

'How-do, Norman?' said George to a short, neatly dressed man beside him.

'Oh . . . fine, fine. Yourself?'

George grinned. 'Getting on.' He looked at the man's suit and trousers. 'Hey, you were never at the office today, were you?'

Norman looked uncomfortable and reddened slightly. 'No, no. It was just . . .' He stopped. 'It just seemed, well. I don't know . . .' He lapsed into silence. There was an awkward pause.

Willy, further down the bar, laughed. 'So you dressed up just for us then, Norman? Why, I'm touched, I really am.' He smiled. 'But you're still no gettin' a shag, like.' The others laughed and the tension dropped a little. George grinned at Willy and drained his glass.

'Same again, Lewis,' he said. 'And whatever Norman and Willy here want.'

The noise outside had dropped a little when the power dimmed. Now it was coming back, with a different edge to it. People were shouting. There were noises just out of range, on the edge of hearing. Lewis finished pouring the pints and looked up.

'I reckon that's everyone who's coming, don't you?'

George looked around the pub and nodded. 'Aye. Bill won't be in tonight. He'll be with the wife.'

Lewis nodded. 'Then I think we'll have a bit of an early lock-in.' He went to the outside front door and locked it, then the inside door too. Then he closed the thick wooden window shutters as well. The punters tried not to notice.

The conversation picked up again, once the noise from outside was quieter. The folk at the back tables moved nearer the bar and brought the third lamp with them. Lewis poured pints and chatted to the older ones; the rest talked among themselves. Someone even tried to play darts, but it was almost pitch black in the corner of the room and they gave up after a bit.

Around ten there was banging on the outside door. The folk at the bar looked up at Lewis, who was talking to Dave McCauley about Landrovers. Lewis didn't seem to hear it.

It came again, louder. Then something started crashing against the door. The punters stopped talking. They stared slightly into space, or left trails of conversation. A low feeling of tension spun from one to the next.

' 'Scuse me for a minute, Dave,' said Lewis. He went to the far corner of the bar and reached underneath. The others could hear the people outside now, shouting to get in. The crashing had become methodical, like a battering ram. George could feel the tension turning to something darker.

'Steady,' he murmured. Then louder, 'Hey Willy, you were in the Army, weren't you?'

'Aye.'

'You must've learned to bust a few heads, eh?'

Willy grinned. 'Self-defence, George, you know me. Ah'm no one to cause trouble.'

There was the sound of a gun being fired, and then a massive splintering. Screams and shouting were suddenly much louder, through the first door, at the second. The punters stood up quietly. The first door was only thin wood, it didn't last beyond a bit of a kicking, and then they were through.

George thought he recognised one of them, though he couldn't be sure. Perhaps the son of someone he knew. The other three he'd never seen before. They came bursting through the door, laughing and screaming, wearing knives and covered in blood and black dirt, knees torn in manky jeans, short cropped hair. The leader had a gun that he was waving in the air.

Yahoos. The word flicked through George's mind. He wondered where he'd heard it before.

The four stopped short when they saw the punters. The leader stared at them all, grinning.

'GIMME THE FUCKING BOOZE!' he screamed.

The punters said nothing. They stood silently and looked at him. He waved the gun in the air again, then pointed it towards them all, vaguely.

'What's the fuckin' *problem* here?' he asked. He tried to make it sound menacing, but they still didn't react. It was unsettling. He could feel the others behind him, wondering what to do. They were losing the initiative.

One of the old bastards at the bar took a sup of his beer and cleared his throat.

'Lads,' he said, softly. 'Why don't you just head off, eh?'

The leader pointed his gun straight at the old bastard's head.

'Give us the fucking booze or I'll blow yer *FUCKING HEAD OFF!*' he shouted.

The old bastard looked at the gun, then straight back into his eyes like he didn't give a shit. *None* of them seemed to give a shit. It was starting to freak the yahoo out. He felt like shooting the old bastard just to make the rest of them stop it.

'Evening, boys,' said another voice. The leader looked to the back corner of the bar to see the landlord there, carefully holding a shotgun. It was pointed right at him. The leader swung his arm round to point at the landlord.

'*Fuckin' put that down*!' he shouted. The landlord didn't move. Why wasn't anyone *moving*?

'Johnny, this is shite, man,' said Andy behind him.

'*Shuttup!*'

The others with him were wavering too, he could feel them. It was just too strange, he couldn't get his head around these people. They were looking through him like he didn't even exist, like the gun was irrelevant. The whole pub was one big stack of fucking weirdos. The landlord was still pointing the shotgun at him, steady as a rock. He wasn't even shaking.

Johnny was shaking. He could see the tip of his gun tracing little circles, moving around the landlord. The more he noticed the worse it seemed to get. His arm was tired. He could feel new sweat on his face.

The old bastard said, 'C'mon, lads. Just fuck off, eh?'

'Aye, c'moan, Johnny,' said Andy. 'C'moan, this is fuckin' weird like.'

Johnny said nothing, but he could feel empty space behind him. The others were retreating. He moved back with them, trying to point the gun at the landlord and the old bastard at the same time. And the others at the bar. And the ones at the table. Because they were all still *looking* at him.

He lasted four more seconds, then ran out, past even Andy. Andy watched him go, then turned to the punters, his face full of baffled anger.

'What's the fuckin' matter wi' you people?' he shouted. The old bloke looked at him.

'We just want to have a drink is all,' he said.

'It's the end 'o the fucking *world* out there! You're all fucking mental!' His voice cracked. He didn't sound vicious or dangerous anymore, just bewildered. He stared at them for a couple of seconds longer and then turned and ran after the others.

There was a pause, then the noise of a dozen people breathing out after a long wait. A certain amount of nervous laughter, theatrical wiping of foreheads. George turned to Willy.

'I thowt you said you were in the Army, Willy?'

'Aye, ah was.'

'Then why the hell was I doin' all the dangerous work?'

'Ah, dinnae worry, George. If he'd shot you, ah widda had 'im.'

'Well, what fucking use would that have been?'

'Well,' said Willy, slowly. 'Ah been waitin' twenty years for that seat there.' He grinned.

George laughed. 'Bastard.'

Lewis, in the corner, carefully put down the shotgun under the bar.

'Now then,' he said briskly. 'Anyone waiting on being served?'

'Aye, in a minute,' said George. 'I'll just try an' close the door.'

Five to midnight. The noise outside had changed again, quietened down slightly, or more likely just headed to another part of the city. Inside, things had got quieter too. The tables had moved still closer to the bar, sharing the little pool of light. George wasn't sure but he thought a couple of folk had headed off.

The dark seemed darker now the lamps were all together. There was a little circle of shrinking . . . what? Hope? Civilisation? Just a little circle of light. It made the shadows around them seem higher. They reached over everyone. Conversation was drooping. The punters now supped their beer with a different feeling, a grim determination to see the pint through.

'Mum's in Australia,' said Norman, out of nowhere. His voice was surprisingly loud and he blushed.

'Oh, aye?' asked someone.

'Yeah. I tried to get through to her today. I think I heard her, for a second, but then we got cut off.'

He paused.

'I – it's so silly,' he said, and laughed, oddly. 'I was on the phone to her, and I thought I heard her and then she was gone, and I started shouting for her. And then I was shouting and shouting and I, ha, I couldn't *stop*. It was so funny.' He stopped again, took a quick nervous drink. 'I don't know what happened to me,' he said softly, looking down.

There was an embarrassed silence. George reached out and awkwardly clapped him on the shoulder.

'She'll be fine,' he said. 'I mind your mother, she could scour paint wi' her tongue, no bugger'll give her grief. She'll be just fine.' Other punters murmured the same, even ones who'd never met her.

Jean said, 'I was phoning my sister Angela and we got a crossed line. This old lady was screaming at me, over and over. She was asking for someone called Kenny. I tried to tell her it was a crossed line, but she just kept going. "Where's Kenny?" she was screaming. "What have you done with him?" ' Jean shivered. 'I had to put the phone down, in the end. I didn't want to. But she just kept screaming. When I tried to get back to Angela the line was dead.'

One of the lamps gave a tiny soft flicker, sending a ribbon of darkness round. The punters looked at it. Then Lewis's voice came out of the edge of the circle.

'Last orders, folks,' he said.

A couple of the punters looked at their watches. One said, 'C'mon, Lewis, just a bit longer, eh?'

Lewis shook his head. 'Sorry, you know the rules. Last orders, ten minutes to finish up.'

'But it hardly matters tonight, does it?'

Lewis hesitated for a second.

'Yes,' said George firmly. 'It does. It matters tonight.' He handed his empty glass to Lewis.

'Same again, Lewis. And one for yourself.'

'Thanks very much, there.' Lewis poured two pints, and then served the rest. They sat or stood, drinking. Trying too hard to enjoy the taste, sucking the beer for comfort. Finishing too soon, and the dregs bitter like ashes.

Then in dribs and drabs they headed out.

'Evening, Lewis.'

'Goodnight, gents.'

'See you later, Willy,'

'Aye, g'night.'

In the end there was just Lewis and George. One of the lamps had faded to brown and Lewis moved the other two closer together. He poured a measure of Lagavulin and handed it to George, taking a Highland Park for himself.

'On the house,' he said. George looked at him and nodded. He slopped the whisky round in the glass, watching it fall away slowly. When he spoke, his voice was very tired.

'I miss Anna,' he said. Lewis said nothing.

'It's been twelve years, and I miss her all the time and it never stops. Sometimes I think I've forgotten her, but I never have, not really. Twelve years.' He looked up at Lewis. 'I'd give anything to have her back. But now, where we are . . . I wouldn't want her to see this.'

He took a small sip. 'Where's Lorna, Lewis?'

Lewis coughed. 'She went to her mother's with the bairns, a couple of days ago.'

'She wanted you to go with her.'

'Aye . . .' Lewis looked embarrassed. 'We had a bit of a fight about it.'

George laughed. 'You're a stupid bastard, Lewis. You should have gone with her, not stuck around with a bunch of lonely drunks.'

Lewis smiled sadly.

'Then who would open the bar?'

George smiled. He threw back the dregs of the whisky, feeling the salty smoky sweet liquid on his tongue like it was the first he'd ever drunk. Then he got his coat and hat out from the hook under the counter and stood up.

'Aye, well,' he said. 'Time to go.'

He put the coat on and straightened his hat. For a second he allowed himself to look around the pub, almost completely dark now. His shoulders stooped.

Then he straightened them.

'That's me away then, Lewis.'

Lewis nodded. 'Right you are, George. See you around.'

'Aye. Goodnight, Lewis.'

'Goodnight, George.'

George headed away. Lewis watched him go. In the brown glimmer of the remaining lamp he started cleaning the last of the glasses.

Hell-bent

Anne Bree

It is Saturday morning and my father is staring out through the sooty window. The new Forth Road Bridge flashes in and out of sight. The man sitting next to my father has been up all night drinking.

'Lookin good, eh, Rev.? Bet oor wee Queen never seen nuthin like thon this side o the Atlantic.'

He takes a slug of his screw-top, rasps the back of his hand across his mouth, and regales us all with '*I left my heart (oo-hoo-hoo) in San Francis-co-ooo.*' Even my father knows the tune of that one. He glances round at the man – the stains on his dun-coloured macintosh, the blue-black etching of his fingernails – then turns back to the window. Everyone else smiles with sardonic tenderness as the drunk man coories in against my father's thin black back and falls asleep. I wish I could do that.

To my left stars glisten in the Firth like fools' gold in a slate. To my right an elderly woman peels a spitting orange. The boy in the corner sniffs and trails his eyes across *The Dandy*. The train hurtles into a cutting and toots at a woman hanging towels on a line. On the luggage rack above my father's head is a brown cardboard grocery box tied with string. It contains the remains of his grandchild.

It was my twenty-first birthday yesterday. Sad but true. Julie

Browne had her twenty-first in a marquee, in the garden of a big house in the Borders. She's the one that turned up in First Year with a bouffant hairdo and said she had been out on a date with Jim Clarke. Her father hired a coach and the whole Junior Honours Maths class met up in the Men's Union and went down together. Julie's party lasted till dawn, with as much champagne as you could drink. Then we all had bacon rolls and went back to Edinburgh. Seven people were sick on the bus. It took me two days to get over it. I had never drunk that much in my life before. That was also the night of my first and only. He seemed really nice at first. A lot older than me. But now all I can remember is his rancid tongue, and my suspender belt digging into my hip-bone, and the stickiness of the rhododendrons.

Of course I would never have expected a birthday party like Julie's. My mother would have put on some kind of family get-together. Probably. To be honest it's hard to visualise life before God Called My Mother To His Side, as the Very Rev. Dr Herbert Milne insisted upon calling it at the service. Anyway, even if my father had thought of organising something – spurred on by the incomparable Mrs McLeish of course – I couldn't have gone home yesterday the way things turned out.

At least I got all the money together. Great Aunt Jean was first to stump up. She took me out to tea in Jenner's and gave me ten quid. It was last Monday – the day before my appointment with the man. The struck-off Ceylonese doctor.

'Gosh, thanks very much, Great Aunt Jean,' I said. 'A tenner in Jenner's.'

Great Aunt Jean thought that was hilarious. She wanted me to go straight to the lingerie department and blow the whole lot on something frivolous. Her words, not mine. 'Let's go and spoil you. If you can't indulge yourself on your twenty-first when can you? At least you've managed to put on a little weight. You were away to nothing after your poor mother. A girl your age ought to have a bit of shape to her.'

I managed to head her off. I told her I'd asked everyone for money to buy one big thing – like a portable wireless or an electric sewing machine.

On Thursday two postal orders arrived by the same post – one for £20 from Uncle David in New Zealand (he's my godfather) and one from my father for £25. I must say I never expected that much from my father. But it was a real godsend in the circumstances. (Sorry, God.) Even Mrs McLeish sent a card with a ten bob note inside, wrapped in lavender-scented toilet paper – presumably to bamboozle sharp-nosed Edinburgh card-thieves. Who but Mrs McLeish could hunt down a section marked 'birthday cards for the recently bereaved':

'*This time is sad for everyone, but rainbows come before the sun.*'

Aye, that'll be right.

I can still see the struck-off doctor's eyes staring at me like eggs, then the top of his black head disappearing between my legs.

'Very nice. No problem. Try to relax. Pretend I am your boyfriend. Just a little sharp prick now. You may find you want to cough.'

I did not want to cough. I wanted to roll up like a hedgehog and cry 'Mummy come'. But I pinned the pad in place, gave the struck-off doctor Marion's £50, and thanked him politely for his help.

'A day or two and it'll all seem like a bad dream,' he said, washing his hands behind a grubby cotton screen. 'Keep active. Scrub a floor or two – that's what I tell all my girls.'

A gelatinous tear snailed its way down the inside of my thigh as I straightened my shoulders and walked to the bus stop. By the time I reached the Common-room Ladies' Room there was nothing whatsoever to see. I remember thinking that must be it. Easy come, easy go. How daft can you get. I was even in time for my tutorial.

I'm sure Marion would have waited for the money, but £50 is a lot to owe. And to be honest, Marion wasn't comfortable about any of it. That's a real friend. Someone who'll help you to do something that's against her own principles. I said as much to Marion, and she raised one eyebrow.

'I wonder,' she said.

My father has always had a soft spot for Marion. He used to lend her books from his study.

'The sort of books in which my own daughter has never demonstrated the slightest interest,' he used to say. I think he was more shocked that the saintly Marion was caught up in my little misadventure than he was at what was happening to me.

The North Sea appears suddenly, magical as ever, the other side of the glass. If only you could jump out and wade into it. Lie down and let the waves wash all the mess away.

We'll be getting out soon. I uncross my legs. My father eases his shoulder away from the drunk. He tries to stand up without wakening him, but the man is on his feet, swaying in all directions, pretending he was never asleep.

'This'll be yours, Rev.?' he says, making helpfully for the brown cardboard box.

My father wrests it from him. For a hysterical moment I imagine it bursting out of its string and cowping its unspeakable contents across the British Railways upholstery. And then we are juddering to a halt and I am concentrating on the effort of walking in an upright position. My father strides across the platform, carrying his box as though it were crystal. I creep after him, keeping my knees close together to contain the pain in my back. My father sits waiting for me in the back of the taxi. The box sits on his knee, with his black felt hat on top.

'Been away shopping, Mr Wilson?' the taxi driver asks.

My father smiles and nods vaguely.

'Princes Street, eh?' twinkles the driver in the mirror. 'Some place. Can't get the wife away from it. You'll know all about that, young Janet. And the traffic. Nobody crosses Princes Street but the quick and the dead. That's a good one, eh? The quick or the dead.'

My father was carrying the same brown cardboard grocery box under one arm when he arrived on the doorstep of our flat yesterday afternoon. Out of the blue. Marion nearly fainted when she saw him standing there.

'Oh – Mr Wilson. How nice to see you. I'll just away and tell Jan you're here. She's not feeling too good today.'

'What? Not well on her birthday? We can't have that!' I heard my father exclaim with self-conscious jocularity. Marion has always had that effect on him.

'What are we going to do?' she hissed at me from the door. 'Can you get up?'

'I suppose so.'

'Well, hurry up before he comes through. Did you know he was going to come today?'

'Of course not. What do you take me for? Anyway, it was supposed to be all over by now.'

I pulled my dressing gown tight across my chest and shuffled into the kitchen. The brown cardboard box was lying open on the floor, spewing scrumpled newspaper, tissue paper, grease-proof paper and string across the speckled lino. My father was bending over our red formica table, his cheek-bones melting in the light of a blazing birthday cake. I never had time to count the candles before the ground cracked in front of me and I fell down into a dark gully of pain.

The taxi-driver is round to my father's door before you can say knife. Opening it, wanting to carry the box for him. My father is having none of it. He places the box carefully on the ground, gripping it between his heels while he digs into his trouser pocket and straightens a crumpled pound note between his long bony fingers. The driver takes the money apologetically, gives him his change, then shakes his head helplessly as my father plants a couple of coins ceremoniously in his palm.

'There's no need . . .' he begins.

'Now now, Archie. You need every penny while the children are wee.' I walk up the path and stand waiting at the door.

'See you later, alligator,' the driver shouts to me. 'You're sure you'll manage that box, Mr Wilson?'

My father unlocks the door and walks into the house. The hall smells of Mrs McLeish now. Lavender and Jeyes Fluid. My mother's piano is covered with a linen shroud. I follow my father down into the kitchen. Its bareness stings my eyes. The incomparable Mrs McLeish has managed to tidy away every trace of human life before knocking off for the weekend. All except for a plate of curly sandwiches lurking under a diaphanous nylon tray-cloth with satin-stitch fuschias, which I have never seen before. My father must have expected to be home in time for supper last night. A flying visit to Edinburgh to deliver Mrs McLeish's birthday cake: 'Go on, Mr Wilson', she must have said. 'Give Janet a nice surprise. You can always leave the box with a neighbour if the girls aren't in. You could do with a wee day out.'

He must have looked forward to getting home, putting on his leather slippers and lighting the fire in the study. Laid by Mrs McLeish, of course. Matches at the ready by the well-swept hearth. Settling down with a small glass of Glenlivet to listen to Malcolm Muggeridge on the Home Service. What more could any man want? He certainly picked a queer moment for his first visit to Marchmont.

I remember at one point last night opening my eyes and seeing him floating above me, his dog-collar off and his sleeves rolled up. He seemed to be praying. Marion was crying. I remember that. Someone she knew died of a haemorrhage last year after being at that doctor. She wanted to phone for an ambulance but my father said that I was in God's hands now.

'Haven't enough people died in the name of your bloody God?' Marion shouted. I had never heard her swear before.

My father became deadly calm.

'You are distraught, Marion,' he said. 'I suppose it is little wonder, considering your own involvement in this terrible business.'

Marion went out the door and I heard her running down the steps to the street. She often went out walking late at night. Wrestling with her devils, she called it.

While she was out, the waves of pain reached their climax. I whirled and kicked to stay abreast. It was only when I finally surrendered and began to sink downwards into oblivion that I felt something slipping away between my legs as softly as a fish gliding through seaweed.

My father went to run a bath, and by the time Marion had returned with a hot loaf from the all-night bakery I was shivering in a clean blanket and my father was back at the kitchen table lashing his cardboard box with string. The birthday cake stood beside him like a tomb, encrusted with alabaster candle wax. Outside the birds were singing and the milkman's van purred against the kerb.

My father makes a pot of tea. Mrs McLeish has transformed my mother's old tea-cosy from tannin beige to sugar pink and baby blue. My father puts three spoonfuls of sugar in my cup.

'What are you going to do with that box?' I ask him.

'I'll deal with it,' he replies. 'Drink your tea. You had better get some sleep.'

'I haven't taken sugar since I was eleven,' I say.

'It'll do you good,' he replies.

I trudge up the sixteen stairs to my own room with its

lumpy bed and its carefully dusted ghosts. From the window-seat I can see my father below in the garden, a spade over his shoulder, walking through the apple trees to my mother's rose-garden. He digs awhile, then returns for the box. I lie down on the bed and stare at the poppies on the curtains until darkness falls.

When I go downstairs, he is in his study writing tomorrow's sermon.

'Will I make something for the tea?' I ask.

'I have little appetite,' he replies without lifting his eyes.

In the kitchen I put cornflakes into a bowl, pour milk into it, and go back up to my room. My bookshelves are unchanged: *Heidi*, *Little Women*, *What Katy Did*, the Beatrix Potters my mother collected when she was a girl. Sitting on the shelf above is my first-ever doll, made from pink and white lint during the war. Its features are all worn away, just like my mother's are beginning to do. Already. I climb into bed, curl myself around the doll and put my thumb in my mouth.

In the night my eyes are shaken open by a terrible sound. My father is weeping – great retching sobs that shred my guts. I clutch the door handle, my heart hammering in my throat, snot running into my mouth. But my father turns away angrily, waving at me to leave. I feel my way downstairs to his study and close the door. Sitting on the edge of his leather chair I pull his neatly-written sermon across the mahogany desk:

> Today's text is taken from the Gospel according to Luke, Chapter 15. *What man of you, having a hundred sheep, if he has lost one of them, does not leave the ninety-nine in the wilderness, and go after the one which is lost, until he finds it? And when he has found it, he lays it on his shoulders, rejoicing. And*

> *when he comes home, he calls together his friends and his neighbours, saying unto them, 'Rejoice with me, for I have found my sheep which was lost.'*

I can see tomorrow's congregation smiling their Steradent smiles and nodding their black angora berets. I can see the groupies sighing up at the pulpit with humility and sublimated lust. I can see my father looking straight at me across the sharp-clawed eagle of righteousness:

> *Just so, I tell you, there will be more joy in heaven over one sinner who repents than over ninety-nine righteous persons who need no repentance.*

Working methodically page by page, I tear my father's sermon to confetti and throw the whole lot high into the air. Repentance rains down upon the desk and flutters from my hair. Then I take a clean page and write:

> Gospel according to Lennon and McCartney, 1964. *I call your name but you're not there.*

From my bedroom window the garden shines with autumn frost. I hunt feverishly for warm clothes – the bobble hat I had when I was twelve, Willie Mackie's Dunfermline scarf, a pair of red wellingtons that my cousin Flora left behind when she went back to New Zealand, my mother's furry mitts . . . Carrying my old doll under my arm I go out the back door and crunch over the grass to my mother's rose-garden. It is easy to make out where my father's box lies buried. I pat the cold earth into a cairn and lay the doll on top. Then I hurry on – through the rhubarb, past the compost-heap, and over the wall. My old short-cut. The freezing stone catches on my skirt and scrapes the backs of my legs. Sliding down the bank, buttocks roasting, I am on the pavement and away, off down Merkland Terrace towards the Edinburgh road.

I am standing under a light, thumb extended, throwing flames of breath across the sky, when a motorbike roars round the corner and loops around me in a deathwall pirouette.

'Hiya,' says the black helmet.

'Hiya,' says I, winding a frond of hair round one finger like a corkscrew.

'Where you off to this time of night?'

'Edinburgh. Where else?'

'Fancy doing a ton over the new bridge?'

'How can you . . . ?'

'Dunno. Just I thought I'd give it a whirl.'

'OK.'

I climb up behind him, settling my pad carefully on the throbbing saddle, wrapping my arms tightly around the strange spider body. My breath is knocked out of me and the freezing wind whips a streak of hair into my mouth as we thunder away.

ABOUT THE AUTHORS

George Anderson was born in Twechar. He works in conservation, sings the blues with The Arhoolies and performs regularly at The Stand Comedy Club's 'Rhymes & Misdemeanours' show.

Alan Bissett was born in Falkirk in 1975. Editor of the collection *Damage Land: New Scottish Gothic Fiction* (Polygon), he has also had stories published in *Shorts* 2, *Shorts* 3 and most Scottish literary magazines. His first novel, *boyracers*, is published in September 2001 by Polygon.

Anne Bree lives in Ayrshire. Her work includes children's books, newspaper articles, film scripts and an autobiography. She has three grown-up children.

Anne Callaly is originally from East Kilbride. She spent a number of years working in London and Germany before settling in Dublin. Her short drama, 'A Routine Awakening', is currently being produced by UCC Radio. 'Wee Fishes' is her first published story.

Alastair Chisholm lives in Edinburgh and claims he actually doesn't mind the tourists, really. His attempts to master the dark art of transmuting base metal into whisky have been unsuccessful to date.

Barbara Clarke lives and works in Edinburgh. She has a film short and a novel in progress and is working on an anthology of short stories.

Sophie Cooke was runner-up in the 2000 Macallan/*Scotland on Sunday* Competition. Since then she has written several short stories, including 'At The Time' – published in *Damage Land: New Scottish Gothic Fiction* (Polygon) – and a screenplay. She is currently working on her first novel. Aged 25 and living in Stirlingshire, she commits the occasional act of journalism.

Morven Crumlish was born in Edinburgh in 1975. She studied at the University of Edinburgh, spent a year in Seattle and now lives back in Edinburgh with her two-year-old daughter.

Jonathan Falla, born in Jamaica, has worked with aid agencies in many countries. A musician and nurse, he has won awards for film, plays and stories. His novel *Blue Poppies* is published by 11:9 in October 2001.

David R. Fernandes was born in 1975. He is currently studying English at Stirling University. 'Brick' is his first published work.

Ella Henderson, born in South Africa, read English at Rhodes before pursuing postgraduate studies at Edinburgh. Currently an English teacher, her interests include literature, theatre, music, film and wildlife.

About the Authors

George Kobilnyk was born and currently resides in Dunfermline. He works in an electronics factory and enjoys writing in his spare time. 'Tragic Kingdom' is his first published work.

Richard Louden lives in Glasgow. A former teacher and lecturer, he retired early from the post of Depute Director of Education for Strathclyde Region and now engages in freelance journalism.

Esther McLeod currently lives in Edinburgh. Previously published on-line, this is her first story to appear in print. She also exhibits visual pieces of work using her words.

Janette Munneke, a New Zealander, lives and works in Edinburgh where she facilitates the Fountainbridge Writers' Group. Her contribution to *Shorts* 4 emerged from a moment of nostalgia for 'home'.

Douglas Noble comes from a village in the Borders, but has recently completed a six-year tour of duty in Dundee. He is currently writing a comic and a novel.

Vale Nordmann has had short stories and poems published under the pseudonym A. M. Galbraith, but has now decided to drop the mask. She is presently working on her second novel.

Kate Percival is a Mancunian living in Aberdeenshire, where she tutors English and raises boys, plants and cats. She writes ideas for stories between the items on shop receipts carefully stored in a capacious handbag.

Lydia Robb had a short story in the first volume of *Shorts*. Her first book of poetry, *Last Tango with Magritte*, has just been published by Chapman.

J. C. Robertson, who previously worked as a journalist in Glasgow, now lives in Paris. He was shortlisted for the 1997 Macallan/*Scotland on Sunday* Competition.

Sue Rullière lives in the East Lothian seaside town of North Berwick. 'Drying the Man Out' is her first publication in *Shorts*.

Michael Russell was born in Edinburgh in 1965, and brought up in England. He has written several short stories and is currently writing a screenplay, to be filmed in 2002.

Jas Sherry lives in Glasgow with his wife and daughter. He is currently working on a collection of short stories as well as various poetry projects.

Simon Smith grew up in Edinburgh and studied in Glasgow. He writes when he can – mainly short stories – but could be persuaded to concentrate on writing film scripts somewhere sunny.

Simon Stephenson was born in 1978. He studied at the University of Glasgow and now works in that city as a doctor. 'Jackson's Hotel' is his first published story.

Fiona J. Thackeray has worked as turtle conservationist in Greece and horticultural therapist for disabled and blind people in Bristol and in Brazil, her current base. She writes on days off and journeys.

Isabel Walter, born in Nottingham in 1972, is a graduate of Oxford and South Bank Universities. She now lives in Fife. This is her first work of fiction since her schooldays.

Ross Wilson, 22, has been published in *New Writing Scotland* and *Fife Fringe*. He is at work on his second novel and a screenplay for CAT productions.

While every effort has been made to compile accurate information about the authors, *Shorts* is produced to a very tight schedule. The Publisher will endeavour to rectify any inaccuracies in any future edition.